DARK HARMONY

Michele Scott

DARK HARMONY

FAIRMONT RIDING ACADEMY:

A Vivienne Taylor Horse Lover's Mystery

• BOOK 2 •

SKYSCAPE

SKYSCAPE

Published by Skyscape, New York

www.apub.com

Amazon, the Amazon logo, and Skyscape are trademarks of Amazon.com, Inc., or its affiliates.

ISBN-13: 9781477847268
ISBN-10: 147784726X

Book design by: Ryan Michaels

Library of Congress Cataloging-in-Publication Data available upon request.

Printed in the United States of America

To the girls of Summer 2013 Camp GME.
I loved being your camp mom, and I can't wait until next summer
to see your beautiful faces and awesome horses again!

PART I

the return

CHAPTER *one*

I sigh heavily as the plane lifts off the Portland runway, rain hitting the window, the weather in some ways mimicking my feelings, which are somewhat dark and melancholy. I pull the shade closed to avoid the dismal view and shut my eyes, thinking about Christmas break and everything that happened. I wish that going back to Fairmont felt easier.

It's true that I can't wait to see my mare, Harmony, and my friends at school, but it's hard leaving home again. Even the thought of seeing Tristan when I land in LA doesn't take away the sadness of saying good-bye to my family and my friends in Oregon, not to mention my big Thoroughbred, Dean, who I first started riding when I was only eight. Maybe it's also hard to return to Fairmont because I'm worried the second semester will be as crazy as the first one. But . . . how could it be? Between the start of school and Christmas break, I'd tangled with some of the school's elite students and—oh yeah—solved a murder. Then, there was that part where I'd almost been killed. Needless to say, leaving all that behind and coming home for the holidays was a break I really needed.

As the plane reaches cruising altitude, I recline my seat and close my eyes and let the memories of the past few weeks rush through my head. For sure, it was a high point to be reunited with the horses I grew up with both at home and at Gail's barn. Riding Dean felt so good—I'd missed him so much. During vacation, I'd finally made good on the promise I'd made him before leaving for Fairmont at the end of last summer: that we'd trail ride through the parts of the Cascades that are close to my mom's small ranch in the tiny town of Sodaville, Oregon. During our time on the trail, I'd told Dean all about the drama I'd lived through at school. Some people might think it sounds weird to confide in a horse, but my relationship with horses, especially Dean, is extra special.

The truth is, though, that I can communicate with all horses, not just Dean. I guess I could be called a horse psychic or equine telepath—that is, if anyone knew that I have this "special gift" and tried to give it a label. Only my mom knows that I can sense horses' feelings, translate their emotions, and have an actual dialogue with them. It might sound crazy, but it is true. But, of all the horses I have communicated with, Dean is probably the one I understand the best, and I am sure that is because he was my first horse and we have an unbreakable bond.

I told him about meeting my beautiful gray mare, Harmony, at school and how together we figured out who had murdered Dr. Miller, a vet who worked at Fairmont and Harmony's former owner. I told him about my friendships with Riley, his horse Santos, and my roommate, Martina, and about the host of mean girls that

I'd termed the DZ—the Drama Zone. And of course, I couldn't leave out Tristan, who I was officially now calling my boyfriend.

Trail riding with Dean had helped me feel like life was getting back to normal. So did seeing my oldest friends, Kait and Mia, who still go to my former high school. We'd spent what seemed like half my vacation hanging out at our former trainer Gail's place and being our typical goofball selves. We'd stayed up until all hours talking horses and guys, and gossiping about my old schoolmates. It all felt charmingly boring and normal compared to being around the glossy queen bees at Fairmont. When I was there, I'd missed boring and normal, in some ways. However, the drama at Fairmont was worth dealing with, considering all the opportunities that came with going to such a prestigious school.

Besides playing catch-up, Mia, Kait, and I pigged out on pizza, chips, and pretty much any food item that could be qualified as junk while listening to Carrie Underwood, Miranda Lambert, and Taylor Swift.

And then, there was Austen.

Given the kiss we'd shared at the end of the summer, right before he'd left for UC Davis and I left for Fairmont, the thought of seeing him over the holidays had made me just a little nervous. Austen Giles and I had been friends for almost eight years—and that kiss had changed everything. Because before we'd locked lips, I'd had no clue that Austen had any interest in me. Or even that I might have feelings for him—feelings I'd pushed aside when I'd gotten to Fairmont. No point in pining away for a guy leaving for college. At least, that's what I'd tried hard to make myself believe during my first months at school. It got easier after I met Tristan and fell so hard for him, though—especially when it finally became clear that he had fallen for me. With his short golden-blond hair, light-green eyes, and amazing talent for riding, it was almost hard to believe he was real. But he was, and I found him impossible to resist. I think it must have been sometime around the first time Tristan and I kissed that Austen got shoved far back into the recesses of my mind.

Until this last Christmas break.

Because the memory of that kiss Austen and I had shared the September before came rushing back the first time I saw him walk into Gail's barn. Even from yards away, the sight of his tall, muscular body made my stomach lurch. A few months of college looked good on him. Let's just say, he'd obviously been working out. I had always noticed his dimples, but not so much the chiseled definition of his face. This time, I noticed. My buddy Austen Giles was no longer the boy I remembered growing up with. He'd kind of graduated into that man territory in a way that seemed impossible to ignore.

"Hey, V," he said, lifting me off my feet and twirling me around. He set me down. He put on a terrible English accent, running a hand through his dark brown hair that held just the right amount of wave and fell kind of sexily into his intense blue eyes. "How's the *Fairmont Academy* treating you?"

I couldn't help but laugh. "Well, first off, it's not in the UK, so the English accent isn't working."

"Huh. It's not? Seems to work on the sorority girls on campus, at least." He smiled widely and winked at me.

I punched him lightly in the shoulder. "Those poor innocent girls! You never change."

Austen's ability to charm girls with jokes and accents has been a running joke between us for years—now that he was charming me, too, I didn't quite know how to act.

Clutching his shoulder dramatically like I'd somehow managed to injure his rock-hard muscle, he smiled. "Easy there, slugger. You might knock me over with that right hook."

"You should see the left jab."

He smiled in a way that made me feel we were back to our normal routines, almost like the kiss that I remembered so well had never happened. And after that, as Christmas break continued on, our occasional meetings at the barn seemed totally normal.

But my sense of relief only lasted until Gail's Christmas party, when I found myself alone with Austen in the barn. He plopped down next to me in the tack room on one of the old trunks. I'd come outside to say good night to the horses before leaving the party.

"So, how is school?" he asked. This time, his tone of voice was serious.

"It's good. It's a little crazy."

"I heard all about what happened." He shook his head. "I didn't like hearing you got hurt. How's the ankle, by the way?"

"It's fine. I haven't had any real issues with it, outside of worrying that the metal rods they put in there might set off alarms at airport security," I said, smiling.

"You got my card and e-mails, didn't you?" he asked.

"Yes. I did."

"You didn't reply and I thought . . . I thought maybe you were mad at me or something."

My stomach sank. "I wasn't mad at you at all. Why would I be mad at you?"

"You know," he replied.

"No. I don't know."

"The kiss. When we said good-bye last summer."

I felt heat rise in my cheeks. I shook my head. "No. No, I wasn't mad at you for that at all." I knew why I hadn't responded to his e-mails, and avoiding the subject any longer seemed unfair to him. "I have a boyfriend now."

He nodded. "Oh. Yeah. I know. Mia and Kait mentioned it. I was just waiting to hear it from you."

I leaned back against the wood-paneled wall. "I mean, I'm sure you have a girlfriend."

He shook his head. "No."

"What about all of those sorority girls who like your English accent?" I laughed.

He looked at me and gently pushed the loose strands of hair that had come out of my ponytail back behind my ear. "No, Vivvie. I was joking about that. I'm not into sorority girls." He paused. "I'm into you. I meant it last summer when I told you not to forget about me."

I didn't know what to say. We had been friends for years, and the kiss was nice. I mean, it was great, but really? C'mon, the guy had been heading off to college. I figured that he would be living up his freshman year with as many girls as possible. With those eyes, those dimples, the great hair, and that disarming sense of humor? Girls had to be all over him, and here he was saying this to me?

"I guess you forgot about me, though." He broke the silence, but not the tension between us.

"No. Of course not. I just thought . . ."

He put his arm around me. I caught a look in his eye that made me turn away for a second. There was hurt there, and I didn't want to ever be the source of any pain for him. I didn't know what to say.

He pulled me in close. "It's okay, Vivvie. No matter what, we are always going to be friends."

I know it was wrong, but in that moment, I didn't just want to be *friends* with Austen. I wanted to kiss him again. I leaned my head on his shoulder and we stayed there for a few minutes like that.

Then my phone rang.

I glanced at the screen and saw it was Tristan. I smiled meekly at Austen, but I didn't answer the call and shut off the ringer instead.

"Boyfriend?" he asked.

I nodded.

He stood. "I guess I'd better get home. My parents have been complaining that I haven't spent enough time with them this break."

"Yeah. I'm getting some of that from my mom, too."

"I'm taking off tomorrow for Hawaii. Family vacation."

"Sounds nice," I replied.

"Yeah." He shoved his hands into his pockets as he stood. "I guess I'll see you this summer."

I looked down at my feet. "Maybe."

"Maybe?"

"I, um, I . . . well, I've been offered . . . I mean, it's only a possibility, but I may be going back to Virginia to train—out at Liberty Farms. That is, if I qualify."

"Oh. That's great. I mean that would be so good for you, Viv. I hope that happens. I know what that will mean for you." He reached his hand out and I took it. He pulled me up and into him. We hugged for longer than just friends would. Then he whispered in my ear, "Someday, Vivienne Taylor. Someday," and he walked away.

I stood there a moment, confused. The realization that he possibly meant that someday the two of us would be together came over me slowly, and brought with it a sense of bewilderment and also desire. I couldn't ignore that piece of it—I'll admit it was a pretty big piece.

When the flight attendant leans over and asks me to return my seat to the upright position, I almost jump in surprise. I lift the shade on the window and see the city of Los Angeles spread out below me, shimmering in the glaring sun. Oregon—and the good time I had at home—is hours behind me now. *Get it together, Viv,* I tell myself. *Time to get back in the game, which includes dealing with school, enduring the drama that I am sure awaits with the mean-girl crowd— why does every school have one?—and, also, being with Tristan.* I know the easiest part of coming back will be seeing my horse Harmony, who I adore as much as I love Dean. Yes, it's time to wrap my head around being back in LA, and at Fairmont.

In what seems like minutes, I've got my baggage in hand, and I'm walking through the automatic doors. Blue sky and sunshine are overhead—I am back in Southern California, which I have learned is truly the land of golden gods and goddesses. It has to be due to all the sunny days—it can't be a result of fresh air because, let's face it, that isn't as prevalent in Los Angeles as the sunshine is. But what I do know is that despite the way things look on the surface in LA, nothing here is perfect. Especially for me. There is always a good and a bad side to everything . . . isn't there? The good is that I have made friends—some really great friends—despite coming from a different world than the rich kids around me. My grades are good, my riding is better than it's ever been, and, like I've mentioned, I adore my horse. And I have Tristan. But then there's the bad, which at Fairmont is dealing with psycho rich girls like Lydia Gallagher and her crew. Not to mention always sensing that I don't completely fit in . . . and part of that feeling comes because of my gift. I keep it to myself, but the fact that I have a higher level of communication with horses makes me very aware that I may go through life never truly fitting in anywhere.

I only wait for about two minutes before Tristan pulls up in his black Jeep Cherokee. He gets out and is all smiles, which melts my insides. He looks tired to me, even though his green eyes shine and his smile is sincere and sweet. The minute I throw my arms around him, I leave Christmas break behind.

"I missed you," I murmur into his ear.

He pulls away for a second and gives me a quiet look, reaches out to touch my face, and sends a surge of electricity through me. Then he kisses me, which turns that electrical surge into an instant reaction of crazy butterflies and stars in my head and my stomach—all over. I wish I could find a less stereotypical way to say it, but the truth is that Tristan's kiss and touch puts me in such a dazed state of happiness that I have to lean on stereotypes to even put my feelings into words.

A minute later, we pull apart with smiles, and he walks to the passenger side and opens my door.

I sink into the leather seat and close my eyes, happy to be back, and wondering what challenges I'll face this semester at Fairmont. God knows it couldn't be nearly as—how should I put this?—*exciting* as last semester. And, frankly, I'm looking forward to some calm and having the chance to put all of my efforts into schoolwork and moving up in my riding abilities with Harmony, so that we can hopefully ride at my first one star instead of wasting my energies on unexpected drama.

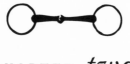

CHAPTER *two*

H ow was Christmas?" Tristan asks.

"It was good. My mom was busy as always. My little brother was a pain as always. My grandma drove me bananas as always."

He laughs. "Yeah. Family. I get it."

The edge in his voice as he says the word *family* tips me off that his time at home left something to be desired, but before I can ask how his break was, he says, "And how was your other favorite guy?"

With a sinking sensation in my stomach, I stare at him for a few seconds. How is it possible for him to know about Austen?

Then he glances over. "Dean. How was Dean?"

"Oh," I reply, hoping I don't sound too relieved. "He was amazing. He's such a great horse. I wish he could be here, too, but you know, he's an old guy and my little cousin Ren adores him. They seem to have really connected. It's pretty cool that he's bonding with a new kid."

"That's good. I wish I had a horse to be with at home. I hate saying good-bye to Sebastian every time I leave school for break."

"I'm sure he missed you, too," I say. Sebastian is Tristan's gelding. "So, how was your Christmas?"

He shrugs. "Formal. Our holidays are always formal, which is another reason why I can't stand them. Like I said, I get the family thing."

I look over at him and there is something in his eyes that makes me realize that he has never talked much about what his life is like at home.

"Are you okay?" I reach for his hand and give it what I hope is a reassuring squeeze.

"Oh, totally," he says, a little too quickly. "Fine. I'm just happy to be back, and more than happy to see you. I'm sorry we didn't get to talk much over break." He sighs. "My dad has this lame rule that when I'm home I need to be with the family. Like I told you, he puts limits on my cell phone and computer use." He shakes his head. "It's stupid."

"I understand. My mom likes for me to tone it down, too," I say. It's not totally the truth. I mean, sure, she would get on me if I started spending all my time on the computer or phone, but I don't, so it's not really an issue. Besides, it's not her style to be all over my case about anything. I do think that Tristan's dad sounds a little bit over the top.

"Here we are. Good to be back." He slows the car and turns into the front gates of Fairmont.

"Agreed," I say. "It was great to see my family, and my friends back home, but this feels like my life now."

I look out the window and the familiarity of the campus envelops me. The green pastures that overlook the expansive Pacific, the horses grazing—some taking naps as the sun's rays beat down on them. In this moment, I'm glad that at Fairmont they allow students to return and work on riding lessons for a few days before kicking off the academic part of the school year. I especially am excited to get back to my riding lessons with Holden Fairmont. Holden and his wife, Kayla, run Fairmont Academy, and Holden teaches the dressage lessons, which I think Harmony needs to work on. I have to say, I have total confidence in Holden's teaching abilities. All of my instructors are pretty great, and I realize that I am a very lucky girl.

Yep. I'm actually telling the truth. I am happy to be back.

"Should we unload our stuff first?" Tristan asks. "Or should we . . ."

"Horses first," I say, finishing his thought for him.

He parks the Jeep and reaches for my hand as we make our way down to the barns.

"It is really good to see you," I say.

"You have no idea how good it is to see you, Viv. I really, really missed you. I missed being around you, talking to you . . . I even missed the way you smell." He pulls me in and smells my neck, sending a shiver down my spine—a good kind of shiver. "God, did I miss you."

We pass some new landscaping going on around the pond and say hello to a few workers planting rosebushes. Our pace quickens as we get closer to the barn that houses both of our horses. It's kind of perfect luck that Harmony lives in the stall next to Sebastian. I mean, it doesn't get better. Right? I love that my boyfriend's horse is always right next to mine. I've even wondered if the two horses might have some kind of equine love connection. That would be kind of cool. I'd never seen either of them get after each other through the corrals, but I had also never seen them groom each other, which is common for horses that live side by side to do. Did they dislike each other? Or like each other so much they avoided contact? Humans do that, but I don't know about horses. They are herd animals and typically make strong bonds when they live side by side. I made a mental note to ask Harmony what her story with Sebastian might be.

Tristan lets out a low whistle as we enter the breezeway, and immediately Sebastian's head appears at the stall window. "There he is," he says.

"And, there she is," I say as Harmony sticks her nose out, too. I take a horse treat from the pocket of my jeans and hand Tristan one, saying with a smile, "Always come prepared."

He kisses me on the cheek and unlatches the door to Sebastian's stall while I let myself in to see Harmony. She looks great, as would be expected, given the good life she has. The horses at Fairmont live as cushily as the students. They all have twelve-by-twelve-foot stalls that open up into twenty-four-by-twenty-four-foot piped corrals. Their stalls are bedded with several bags of shavings a day. Yep— Fairmont is pretty much the Ritz as far as horses are concerned.

A few minutes later, I hear Tristan say, "Hey, Vivvie, looks like there's a newcomer." I walk out of the stall and into Harmony's pen that runs alongside Sebastian's. I can see just on the other side of Sebastian's corral is a well-built chestnut with a stripe down his nose. He looks to be about seventeen hands, and most likely a warmblood. Harmony follows directly behind me. "Huh. Yeah. New student?"

Tristan shrugs. "I guess."

Just then, the latch on the chestnut's stall door clicks open. The slim, sandy-blond-haired guy who walks out into the pen looks vaguely familiar.

"Oh, hello, Vivienne," the guy says. I get a sinking feeling in my stomach as I make the connection and realize who he is.

Tristan glances at me, raising his eyebrows.

"Joel," says the slim guy. "We've met before, remember?"

"Right," I say. "You're Riley's, uh, um . . ."

"Friend," he answers.

I twist my face into a smile, although I can't say I'm happy to see him. When I'd met Joel at Parents' Day last semester with Riley and Riley's parents, he hadn't made a good impression. He'd dropped the word *splendid* like a normal seventeen-year-old might drop the word *cool*. He'd worn clothes that probably cost more than my entire wardrobe. Worst of all, he'd looked at Riley with cold eyes that spoke volumes about how Joel felt about Riley ending their relationship. And Riley hadn't trusted Joel's motives for coming to visit on Parents' Day—given that Riley is one of my best friends, this made me instantly skeptical about Joel.

"I loved that visit last semester with Riley's parents so much that I talked my own parents into letting me transfer here for the second half of my junior year."

"Oh," I reply. "That is truly *splendid.*"

Tristan looks completely baffled. First off, I am sure that he is curious as to who the guy is and how I know him. Not to mention the fact that the word *splendid* isn't one I use in everyday context.

I shoot Tristan a look of reassurance, but inside I'm consumed with worry about Riley. Does he know his ex has transferred here? I'd spoken or texted with him almost every day over break, and he hadn't breathed a word about Joel attending Fairmont. And considering that Riley's big fear is his secret coming out, well, he must not have known Joel had plans to come in as a new student after break. If he'd known, he would definitely have brought it up to me.

Riley isn't going to like this news—especially since nobody at school knows he's gay except for Tristan and I. When he hears that his ex will be living here with the rest of us, I can only imagine his feelings. Ri is scared to death of his parents, or anyone else for that matter, learning the truth. I've met his parents, so I get why he is afraid. They're not what I'd call open-minded and accepting. Another reason I know he wants to stay in the closet is to fit in at Fairmont. I know firsthand what it feels like to be an outsider at Fairmont, and it's not pretty. I'm sure that staying under the radar and fitting in is a big part of why Ri doesn't want to be outed.

All these thoughts zip through my head until I land on one: I have to find Riley and tell him Joel is here before he runs into him and finds out the hard way.

CHAPTER *three*

armony gives a little shove into my backside. "Hey, silly!" I turn around and kiss her nose, burying myself in her neck for a second to collect my thoughts. Her earthy, salty smell is familiar and comforting.

"Looks like you were missed," Joel says.

Tristan is still giving me an odd look, so I figure I'd better make the introductions. "Yeah." I try and laugh, but it doesn't lighten the tension I'm feeling. All I can think about is how seriously I need to get to Riley so that this isn't just sprung on him. "I'm so sorry, Joel," I say. "I was so busy saying hello to Harmony that I didn't introduce you. Um, this is Tristan."

Joel brings his hand up and waves once. "Hey. Joel Parker."

"So you know Riley?" Tristan asks.

"Oh yeah, since we were kids."

My brain is scrambling to find a reason to escape the barn. I blurt out, "I hate to run off, Joel, but I am actually starving. Just realized I haven't had lunch. I didn't even eat the snack on the plane." I turn to look at Harmony, hoping to make her understand that I'm only leaving so quickly because I have to find Riley.

"Tristan?"

"Yeah. Okay." He gives Sebastian another pat on the neck and says, "Nice to meet you, Joel. I'm sure we'll be seeing you around."

"Splendid," I mutter under my breath. I shut Harmony's stall and meet Tristan back in the breezeway.

He's looking at me with his arms crossed and a suspicious frown darkening his green eyes. "What's the story?"

"Come on." I grab his hand. "We have to find Riley," I hiss.

Outside the barn, Tristan places a hand on my shoulder. "Stop, Viv. What's going on? You got really weird back there with that Joel guy."

I sigh. I'm not sure just how much Riley confided in Tristan, and I don't want to betray my friend's trust. Of course I also want to be honest with Tristan. The irony of this thought isn't lost on me—and I roll my eyes at my own hypocrisy as Austen's face flashes through my mind.

"We just really need to find Riley," I say.

"Vivienne?"

"Okay," I say, heaving a sigh. "Riley and that guy Joel were—" I search for the right words—"I'm not sure, exactly." I stop there, since I feel like anything else is Riley's story to tell.

Understanding dawns on Tristan's face despite my curt explanation. "So you're worried that Riley doesn't know Joel is here and that he's going to lose it when he does find out. You want to deliver the bad news to Riley before he, say, sees Joel in line at the dining hall and chokes to death in shock."

I stand on my tiptoes and kiss his cheek. "And that is why I am totally crazy over you. You're a genius."

He kisses me back smack-dab on the lips. A familiar floaty, light-as-air feeling bubbles up inside my stomach.

"Oh, please." A girl's sarcastic voice jolts me out of the kiss. "What obnoxious PDA."

We stop kissing and turn to see Lydia Gallagher and a couple of her friends—Alicia Vincenzia and Shannon Burton, charter members of the DZ, to be specific—coming toward us on the path to the barns.

"Happy New Year, Tristan," says Lydia, batting her lashes.

I resist the urge to roll my eyes. The DZ enjoyed making my life as uncomfortable as they possibly could the first semester, and I am sure this semester will be no different, considering that I am now dating Lydia's ex. Plus, I helped to put her brother behind bars, which surely didn't endear me to her. Lydia shoots me a cold look. "Hey, Scholarship. I'd wish you a Happy New Year, too, but I'm not totally sure you'll have one."

Tristan puts an arm around me. "Call her Vivienne like everyone else," he says.

"Oh, now you're going to be like that? It didn't seem to bother you when I made up that nickname for her just a few short months ago. In fact, if I recall, you even laughed the first time you heard it. Besides, she *is* here on scholarship, and that's obvious from her clothes, so it's not like I'm making up insults. I'm just calling it like I see it."

He shakes his head.

We walk past them and, as we do, Lydia pipes up again. "By the way, T, how's the fam? Your mom still hidden away? Your dad still playing the ponies?"

I feel his arm tense around my shoulder. We keep walking. "Once a bitch, always a bitch," he says to me.

I know Lydia was just trying to get under Tristan's skin, but I can't help wondering what her comments mean, exactly. Why would Tristan's mom be hidden away? And so what if his dad is into horse racing? I don't get it, but then again, I don't understand much about Lydia Gallagher. All I do know is that blonde, beautiful, and bitchy is never a good combination.

CHAPTER *four*

I drag Tristan to his dorm suite in search of Riley, and when I open the door, there he is, sitting on the couch with his head in his hands. His posture says that he already knows about Joel, but then when he looks up, a huge smile spreads across his face.

"Thank God you're here!" He jumps up and throws his arms around me.

"Hey, what about me?" Tristan asks.

Riley pulls away from me and high-fives Tristan. "Good to see you, too, man."

Tristan then pulls him into one of those quick guy hugs, which endears him to me even more.

Suddenly, I realize that I'm not sure if Riley knows about Joel or not.

"So, did you hear?" he asks.

"What?" I say.

"Christian Albright is our new jump coach."

I feel my jaw drop open. See, Christian had been engaged to the vet who owned Harmony, Dr. Serena Miller—the woman who was murdered last semester. Her killer, Newman Becker, was a retired champion rider who had once been an instructor at Fairmont, and had also been one of my childhood idols. Yeah—not so much once I learned he was a criminal.

Anyway, after Dr. Miller's murder, I'd noticed Christian getting close with Kayla Fairmont—close as in definitely more than just friends. I'd witnessed the way they'd hugged each other when Kayla's husband, Holden, wasn't around, and while I am no expert by any means when it comes to relationships, I am also no idiot. What made it all worse was the fact that Holden Fairmont and Dr. Miller were cousins. I didn't want to care, but I couldn't seem to push away my feelings about it. I can guess why, I suppose. First off, I really like Holden and Kayla, and I like the idea of people sticking it out and being together. That is what people who get married are supposed to do, isn't it? Maybe my strong feelings over the whole thing stem from my dad leaving my family when I was little, but I don't like to think too deeply about it. There's another reason why the thought of Kayla possibly cheating on Holden really bothers me, and it's selfish. As the married co-owners of Fairmont, what might happen to the school if Holden and Kayla have issues and break up? Furthermore, what will it mean for me? For my scholarship? I have opportunities and advantages here at Fairmont that I would never have anywhere else. Don't get me wrong . . . I love home, and my old trainer, and my friends. But Fairmont represents the promise of really going somewhere, not only as an equestrian who has

Olympic-size dreams, but also academically. It's not just me who truly values the education that I am receiving at the academy—it's colleges around the country from the Ivy League on down.

Most important, though, is Harmony. I don't own her. The Fairmonts do. So, I have to wonder: If their marriage fell apart, what would that all mean for me and for my horse? Could I ... would I lose everything?

The affair I'm suspecting seems even more likely now that Christian Albright has moved from Virginia to the West Coast to teach here at Fairmont. I am so going to put those kinds of thoughts out of my mind. I try and cover up my deer-in-the-headlights look that I am certain is reflected on my face.

"Then who is going to teach the summer riding program?"

"You mean the one back east?" says Riley.

"Yeah, the one at Liberty Farms in Virginia. Everything Kayla has told me so far about the summer program there involved Christian Albright heading it up. It seems weird he'd give up that job to come to Fairmont and teach jump lessons."

Riley and Tristan don't appear to share my curiosity. It's probably less important to them than it is to me to win a spot in the summer program. They have rich families who can probably pay for them to get lessons with the country's best coaches. For me, winning a spot in the summer program—which Kayla promised my scholarship will pay for—is probably one of the only chances I'll ever have to ride with the premiere coaches on the East Coast for the summer.

Riley shrugs. "Who knows? Maybe he'll go back there in the summer and do it again. Maybe his stay here is temporary. I'm sure we'll get the lowdown."

"I guess so," I say, hoping that my suspicions about the affair aren't valid. I've worked too hard to get here to have something as stupid as cheating adults change my life.

Now that Ri has sprung this info on us, I am considering how to drop ours on him, because I am beginning to think he has no clue that Joel is on campus.

I try to look casual as I ask Riley, "Any other news around campus?"

He looks at me, then at Tristan, and finally down at his feet, nodding his head. "I already know, you guys." He shrugs. "I know Joel is here. What have you told Tristan, Vivienne?"

Tristan glances at me. "Hello. I'm right here. See, it's me in the flesh? No need to talk as if I am a third party. All Vivienne said to me is that you guys have known each other since you were kids."

Riley nods. "Yeah. It was more than that. Joel and me, um . . ."

"It's okay, Ri. I get it," Tristan says. "I'm cool with it. It's no one's business."

"You're right," Riley replies. "It isn't, but I am afraid that Joel will make it everyone's business. Let's just say that when I ended it between us before coming to Fairmont last fall, he didn't take it well, and he's done everything he can to infiltrate my life since then, even though he was back home in Virginia. I got constant e-mails and texts, and tons of messages on my phone. He stopped short of telling my parents, but he got his point across. Maybe he still thinks . . . crap. I don't know what he thinks. That I am just going to out myself to everyone and that we can be together. The truth is, even if I do come out here at school, I don't want to be with him. I don't know what to do."

"Have you talked to him?" Tristan goes over to the fridge where he grabs us each a bottle of water.

"No. Nah, man. I don't want to talk to him."

"You can't avoid him, Ri," I say. "Fairmont isn't that big, and he's obviously here because of you. At least that would be my first guess."

"You're brilliant, Viv. Any suggestions? I'll take pretty much any idea you have right now. Unless it involves talking to him."

Silence fills the room. After several long, tension-filled seconds, I say, "I'll talk to him. See if I can feel him out and find out if he has ulterior motives for being here, or if he is here just to go to school."

Riley frowns. "You don't know this guy, Vivvie. I am sure he has ulterior motives. He's a master manipulator. I mean *master*. His dad is a well-known defense attorney back home who has a knack for making a killer look like Little Red Riding Hood. What's the saying? Oh yeah—the apple doesn't fall far from the tree. You'll probably leave the conversation convinced that Joel is only here to become a better rider. Not here to get even with me for . . ." He sighs.

"For what?" I ask.

"For dumping him."

I can't help wondering if Riley is being entirely honest with me. It kind of seems to me like there is something missing from this story. "That doesn't sound right, Ri. I mean it sounds like a lot of trouble for someone to go through just to get even over a breakup."

"Like I said, you don't know this guy. And, you are way too trusting of people."

I cross my arms and give him a look that says *Really?* I raise my eyebrows, cock my head, and smirk. "Riley Reed, do you not know me all that well yet? I am far from trusting. I am not easily manipulated, much less charmed."

"She is right about that. I am still trying to charm her," Tristan chimes in.

"Oh no, now *you* have me charmed completely," I say.

Tristan walks over and puts his arm my shoulders. "Good. And trust me, I am not finished charming you."

I lean my head on his shoulder. "I think I like the sound of that."

"Hey, lovebirds . . . um, I have a dilemma here. Can you hold off on the sexy talk until I'm not around?" Riley says.

"Sorry." I lift my head off Tristan's shoulder and smile up at him. "He's just so irresistible."

Tristan kisses my nose.

"Hey! Come on, you two."

"Fine. It sounds like it's about time for me to have a chat with our pal Joel Parker, anyway," I say.

"You're a good friend, Vivvie." Riley looks relieved.

"I know." I smile. "The best. I've got your back, Ri."

I don't say it out loud, but the truth is that I'm not exactly eager to go and speak with Mr. Splendid. But I've always been loyal and protective of my friends—and Riley definitely falls into that category, so I'm willing to do anything to help him. I understand his fears about being outed, and if I can help him avoid the anxiety that talking with Joel will cause, it's worth dealing with my own feelings of trepidation.

"All right, boys," I say, making my voice sound more confident than I feel inside. "You hang out and relax. I am going back to the barn to find the newcomer and do some fishing. Find out if his reasons for being here are legit, or if he has a nasty agenda in mind."

Tristan hugs me and gives me a kiss.

"You two really are so cute," Riley says, teasing. "But kind of obnoxious."

"We are, aren't we? Cute, I mean. We aren't obnoxious. It's just that she's my girlfriend and I want her to know at all times how I feel," Tristan says.

Riley puts a finger in his mouth and mimics gagging.

How much sweeter could Tristan be, though? I don't think all that much. "I could stay all day listening to compliments, but I'd better get out of here," I say, completely thrilled that Tristan just said what he did.

"Be careful, Vivienne," Tristan says.

"Oh, trust me, I will watch my step." I reply. "Although around here, who knows what good it will do me." I've learned the hard way that getting into people's business at Fairmont can have unexpected results.

CHAPTER *five*

My first thought is to look for Joel at the barn, and, sure enough, he's just walking out of his horse's stall when I arrive. A look of surprise crosses his face.

"I thought you went to get something to eat," he says.

"Change in plans, actually. I wanted to come back here to talk to you."

"Oh. All right, what's up?"

I push through the awkwardness I feel. "It's about Riley."

Joel crosses his arms in front of him. "Oh."

This time the way he says *oh* sounds 100 percent more irritated than the first time.

"Look, I know about you two."

Joel's eyes widen. "Really? What exactly do you think you know?"

I lower my voice. This is so not easy, and I shift my weight back and forth on my feet, crossing my arms, too. "That you guys were at one time more than friends."

He nods. "Wow. He told you that?"

"Yeah."

"I'm shocked. Riley has made it pretty clear to me that he doesn't want anyone to know he's gay, and he's made it even clearer that he wants nothing to do with me." He runs a hand through his sandy-blond hair and looks at me intently, as if he doubts what I'm saying.

"He did?" Playing stupid is going to be my number-one tactic— but looking at his skeptical face, I don't get the feeling that Joel is going to trust me.

"Yes. Before he left for Fairmont at the end of last summer, he totally blew me off, but I wasn't quite ready to say good-bye. I wanted to explain to him that I understood we were over, and I thought I'd have the chance when I visited Fairmont with his parents last semester. It was never my plan to make him uncomfortable, or tell anyone about him, or us. Plus, I, uh . . . well, I needed to get away from the barn I'd been working at." He waves a hand in front of his face. "That's another story."

I detect a sadness in his eyes with that last comment, and something inside me churns at how stricken he looks. I don't know if I'm being manipulated or not, but I suddenly feel sorry for Joel. I'd judged him pretty harshly when he'd visited with Riley's parents. Too harshly, maybe.

He continues with, "More than anything I just want to be Riley's friend again. I mean, did he tell you that we've known each other since kindergarten? We had a lot of good times before anything happened between us. I miss the chance just to talk and hang out with him."

As I'm studying Joel, I notice the guy even has tears in his eyes. He seems totally unlike the cold person I met on Parents' Day, who, honestly, came off like a jerk. Now my intuition says he's sincere. Could my bad first impression of Joel have been wrong? The comment Riley made about him earlier suddenly runs through my head: *He's a master manipulator*. I also remind myself about the stalker factor—and the way that Joel had tormented Riley with e-mails, texts, and voice mails for months.

"I can understand that." I smile gently, hoping that it doesn't seem totally obvious that I'm trying to use psychology to get him to confide in me. "But, can you see Riley's point? I mean, you obviously know his parents and how they would react if they knew. I'm sure you can imagine that he feels terrified of what might happen if they find out. Do your parents know?"

"I do know Riley's parents and, yeah, their attitudes are straight out of the Dark Ages. My mom, though, is cool—she knows that I'm gay. She's the only one. But I never told her anything about me and Riley. I definitely haven't told my dad. We haven't spoken much lately, other than to deal with paying my tuition and getting my horse out here to Fairmont. My parents are going through a divorce at the moment. My dad decided to leave my mom three months ago. I haven't seen him since. I deal with my dad on a business level these days. He's busy working on a new family."

I am speechless, which is rare, but yeah . . . I am speechless, because I can relate. My dad left us when I was ten, and I know what kind of scar it leaves. I doubt that it's much different whether it happens when you're the age I was or when, like Joel, you're seventeen. When your dad abandons your family, it just is what it is—not cool. Beyond not cool. More like damaging in a way that feels impossible to recover from.

"You okay?" he asks.

"Yeah. Sure. Uh, my dad left my family, too."

"Sucks."

"It does," I agree.

"Please let Riley know that I am not going to tell anyone. I'm not here to make his life miserable. I am here for the education, and to become a better rider, and to get away from a complicated situation at home. That's it. I swear. I don't want anything from him. I wish we could get beyond our past, and just be friends, but if not, well, there isn't much that I can do about it."

I hide a smile as I remember Riley's words earlier. *You'll probably leave the conversation convinced that Joel is only here to become a better rider.* The thought again makes me question whether or not Joel is for real. His words sound perfect. Are they practiced? They really do sound good. Sure, my heart goes out to him because I can relate to what he's been through with his parents. But, Riley knows him better than I do, and insists his character is not good, so I have to question the guy's sincerity. Plus, it's weird how the Joel I'm with today seems like the polar opposite of the awful, snobby guy I met on Parents' Day weekend. Then again, it's possible that Joel has had some sort of change, some epiphany that has caused him to really take Riley's feelings into account. I mean, people do change, don't they? I know I have. After all, I'd promised myself that I'd avoid getting involved in a relationship when I came to Fairmont. I didn't exactly stick to my guns on that issue. Within a few months of my arrival, I was with Tristan.

"Okay, Joel. I'll tell him." I don't know what else to say. I figure I sort of have to take him at face value.

"I mean it, Vivienne. I'm not out to embarrass Riley, or make him broadcast who he is to the world. I'm still bummed out that he hurt me, and continues to by refusing to talk to me, but I'm not some callous jerk who wants to force his hand."

I nod. "Well, thanks. That's good to hear, and I'm sure Riley will be happy, too."

Joel starts toward the door of the barn. "You walking back to the dorms?"

"Not yet. I'm going to spend a few minutes with my horse. I kind of hurried out of here before."

"To find Riley, I suppose?"

"Yes."

"Okay. I'll see you around."

"You will." I smile and leave it at that, then head into Harmony's stall. She gives me a low little nicker. It's very faint, but I know she's saying hello. At the same time, she sends me images that pose the question: *why did you leave me so quickly earlier?*

She's communicating in her way—the way I became so familiar with last semester when I finally got to the point where I could understand Harmony's thoughts, thanks to the images she shares with me. For example, right now: to let me know that she missed me, first she shows me an image of her looking up and down the empty barn aisle, and then she shows me an image of me.

I feel a jolt of happiness over the fact that this horse and I can finally communicate easily. Last semester was tough initially because when I first started riding Harmony, she didn't communicate with me at all. That bothered me because it had never happened before. Now, being in sync with her feels great.

"I told you, big girl, that I was going home for Christmas and that I'd be back." The only problem with having my ability is that you tend to talk out loud to horses a lot—which is exactly what I'm doing. Luckily, the barn is empty. "And here I am. I know you got exercised and turned out in the pasture, so it couldn't have been all that bad."

She takes a step toward me and gives me a nudge. "Yes, I have another cookie, and tomorrow I will take you out. But first I have to have a discussion with Riley that I don't want to have." Harmony now pictures Joel and shows me his image. "You're right. You were listening, weren't you? Smart girl." Then, I almost gasp in surprise. She shows Joel again, but this time there's a noticeably troubled look on his face. It's an expression only Harmony could have seen, maybe in the moment right before Tristan and I first arrived at the barn, and I can't say that it's a look I like at all. If I am not mistaken, the look on Joel's face is one of hatred, or at the very least anger. He's frowning and his hazel eyes are dark. His nose crinkles as if he tastes something bitter or dank.

I put a hand on the side of Harmony's elegant head. "Are you sure?"

I show her an image of Joel smiling, but immediately she returns the image she showed me initially of him looking angry or disgusted—or something along those lines. As the image fades from my head, I wonder if I am misreading it altogether. Maybe what I'm seeing on Joel's face is a look of fear.

I try something that works sometimes with Dean back home when he gives me confusing images.

I place my hands where her heart is, and start by expressing my feelings toward her—pure emotions of love and friendship. Within seconds I begin to receive from her a sense of gratitude, love, and respect. I can't really explain how I know that this is what the emotions are, just as I can't explain how I received this gift in the first place. I just know how the emotions *feel* and that the good feelings flowing between us seem to somehow open the channel of easy communication. I wish I could understand it better, but I don't.

Next, I picture Joel again, and direct all of my intention toward communicating with Harmony. There is a huge difference between someone feeling hate or anger and someone feeling fear. What I need is to decipher what Joel's troubled expression meant in that moment. If Harmony can help me nail that down, I am hopeful I'll be able to determine if the guy is for real or completely full of crap and filled with bad intentions that might ruin Riley's life.

Nothing becomes clear right away, so I keep trying. I go back to my personal feelings for Harmony and place my hand on her heart. Then I picture Joel again and express that I'm confused.

What I get back from her is a similar type of confusion. I perceive feelings that come across as a mix of fear, spite, anger, and sadness . . . yet slowly, as the seconds tick by, I understand that fear is the overriding emotion. In a way, that is a relief to me.

I now go back to sending her waves of good feelings, because I know doing these types of investigations with Harmony can drain both of us. This is the first time we've really been together since I got back from Christmas break, and I don't want to ruin our good connection. I have to be very careful in communicating negative feelings to Harmony in this way. She's not used to it like Dean is, and it could backfire on me.

Seconds later, I finally receive back that wave of love, gratitude, and respect I'm hoping for. I put my arms up around her neck and lean into her shoulder. "You are a very special girl," I say. I kiss her on the nose to say good-bye and start to make my way back to the dorm, wondering about the complex emotions Joel is dealing with, and also what he is afraid of.

CHAPTER *six*

After walking back up the hill from the barn, I head straight for my own dorm suite. As much as I love my roommate, Martina—other than Riley, she's my best friend at Fairmont—I'm glad that she's not supposed to get back to school until tomorrow. I need some time alone. I'm not quite ready to go back and see Tristan and Riley because I'm not sure what to say. Honestly, between the talk I had with Joel and the insight Harmony provided, I have no idea what to even think.

When I open the door, though, I realize my moments alone are not going to happen. Through the open door from our small living room to our shared bedroom, I see Martina sitting on her mattress with her knees hugged to her chest. Her suitcase and a few boxes of new things are scattered on the floor.

"Hey, I thought you weren't coming back until tomorrow," I say. When she looks up, I notice right away that she's been crying. I perch next to her on the bed and wrap an arm around her. "You okay?"

She nods and says, "I'm happy to see you," before the tears start.

"Funny way of showing it," I reply, trying to lighten things up. "What's going on?"

She wipes her eyes. "It's my parents. The stalker thing, you remember?"

"Yeah." Last semester I'd learned that Martina's mom, Erika Martín, who is a famous actress, was being stalked by some freak, which put the entire family on edge.

"Well, the guy is back again, and this time it seems like he's following my mom around with a camera. He took some picture of her with an old friend from acting school named Lee Ocean. I guess he's a producer now, but they met in acting school—and back then I'm guessing they were *more* than friends. Not that she ever said anything to *me* about it. But why else would my dad have told her that she was not allowed to see this guy? Anyway, now there's this photo of her kissing Mr. Out-of-bounds and my dad is furious."

"How do you know all these details?"

"Vivvie, I listen. I am good at finding things out. I'm good at watching people and putting two and two together. It's how I've made it through dealing with Lydia and her crew."

"Understood. But will this give any proof about who the stalker is? Maybe this will help break the whole case open."

Martina is shaking her head. "I don't think so. The thing is that when the photos were delivered to our house, they came with a note from the stalker explaining that the same ones had also gone to a tabloid. I don't think that typed note will provide any clue about the stalker's identity. Worse, my mom's illicit kiss is going to be on the cover of *The Hollywood Scene* for everyone to see."

"Oh." I sit down. "I hate to ask, but what kind of kiss was it?"

"My mom says it's innocent, and that she just took a meeting with the guy because he wanted her to play a role in one of his upcoming films. I suppose that could be true, but the kiss is on the lips, and what makes it worse is that my dad had already told her not to see him again. Naturally, my mom and dad are fighting now, and sent me back to school early so they could figure some things out."

"Oh God, I am so sorry." I hate when I have nothing smart to say, but I just don't. I am feeling pretty helpless because first Riley and now Martina, are both going through hell. "Maybe chocolate will help?" I say, laughing.

"No. Well . . . actually, that's not a bad idea. I have some in my purse. It's on the couch. Want to grab it?"

"Sure."

I go out to the living room and get her purse. In my clumsiness, I trip over the rug and all of the contents of her purse spill out. Just as I start to shove everything back inside, I see something that shocks me—a condom. I'm at a loss as I return everything to its place. Martina and I talked about guys a lot fall semester, and we were both virgins then—as far as I know that hasn't changed for her. It hasn't for me.

Did she meet someone over Christmas break, or is there somebody at school she's hoping to seduce? If so, why didn't she say anything during all our long phone conversations over break? I'd even told her about Austen. It had been a relief when she'd insisted that I not feel bad about being attracted to someone besides Tristan. And an even bigger relief that we'd agreed to keep no secrets from each other—and to always share everything.

I hand her the purse, and she digs out the chocolate bar, breaking it in half and handing me a piece.

"Thanks for listening," she says. "And I'm sorry to unload like this. But you're the only person I know who I can tell everything to."

I smile. "I feel the same way about you." As I bite into the chocolate, though, I can't help but wonder if she's the open book she claims to be. Is my friendship with Martina the real thing, or has something shifted while we were on break? All I can hope is that the girl I have been calling friend is still exactly that. But if that's the case, why does she no longer trust me?

CHAPTER *seven*

ave you seen Tristan?" Martina asks.

"Yep, and he looks good, too," I say. "He picked me up from the airport."

"How did the rest of the break go with Austen?" She tosses back her dark hair and smiles at me, her brown eyes lighting up with curious interest.

I pause before answering. Now that I suspect she's not sharing her secrets with me, I almost regret that I've already shared pretty much everything with her. My connection with Austen *is* my big secret, other than my *teeny tiny* secret about the psychic communication thing I have going on with horses. That one I'm just not willing to share whatsoever.

"Nothing much more to tell," I say. "I told you everything that happened, which wasn't much. I was just feeling confused about Austen. But in hindsight I'm thinking it's just leftover kid stuff. You know? Because we grew up together and everything."

She gives me an odd look. Even I can tell that my voice sounds edgy. Fortunately, I am saved by the ringing of my cell phone.

I'm relieved to hear Tristan's voice when I pick up.

"Hey, you," he says. I'm guessing he's calling because Riley is desperate for an update on my talk with Joel.

"Hey you, yourself," I say, smiling, as I realize that the sound of his voice has made my stomach get that fluttery feeling it tends to get when he's around.

"Yeah, well, Riley has been on me for the past twenty to give you a call and see what went down with Joel."

"It was all good. Why don't we meet up in the cafeteria? I'm still hungry, and I can fill you in."

"Okay. Ten minutes?"

"Yeah." I hang up the phone and look at Martina.

"Fill him in on what?"

Boy, is she inquisitive today. Or else, I am being ultra sensitive. "Oh, nothing. We just haven't had the chance to talk about Christmas break."

Great. I feel weird being dishonest with her, but here's the thing . . . I promised Riley that I would never tell a soul about him being gay. And I keep my promises. The only problem is that lying to Martina doesn't feel right. Oh, being caught in the middle of all of these secrets feels like migraine material, or worse—precursor to a breakout.

"Guess you won't be mentioning Austen," she says.

"You guessed right. Like I said, though, there's nothing to say. It's just, you know, we've known each other forever so we'll always have this connection . . . I don't know why I was acting weird about it. It's nothing."

She raises her eyebrows and cocks her head. "Whatever you say. But don't worry; your secret is safe with me. You going to eat?" she asks.

"Yes." I have to invite her, otherwise she'll wonder. "You want to come? Might take your mind off of things."

"Sure. I'm hungry, too."

I smile but can't help thinking that I should pop some aspirin, and quickly. That migraine might be just around the corner.

Walking to the cafeteria, we pass by some of the grooms that work at Fairmont. They're sitting on a grassy knoll eating their lunches. There are only about six or seven of them because only the owners of Fairmont, Kayla and Holden, and the instructors, have personal grooms. As students, we groom our own horses, which is how it should be. I know some of the guys' faces because they help clean and bed the stalls during the week—we only do that on the weekends since it's time-consuming. I don't know how I'd get that done along with all my homework.

As we pass by the group of guys, I can't help but notice the way Martina gives one of them a bright smile. I don't recognize him. He must be new. He smiles back at her. I'm not good at guessing ages of college-age guys, but I can tell he's young, maybe twenty or so. He's good-looking—dark hair, soulful eyes, tanned skin, all muscle. I can understand why she would smile at him. When I steal a sideways glance at her, she's blushing.

"I'd say it looks like there have been some new additions around here while we were on break," I say. "Not complaining. That one is hot."

"I agree," she replies. "He's Holden's new groom."

"And you know this because . . . ?"

"I hung around here over break like I told you I was going to. I turned Harmony out for you, and rode Jetson," she replies, referring to her dark bay Thoroughbred gelding.

"I've been meaning to thank you for that," I say.

"I was glad to have extra things to do," she says. "But I think Harmony missed you."

"I missed her, too. I wish I could have taken her back home with me." I sigh. "I have to tell you that I'm scared that someday I'll lose her. I mean, after all, she isn't mine. She belongs to the Fairmonts. What will I do when I go off to college?"

"Maybe they'll lease her to you," Martina suggests. "They know you have a strong bond, and it's obvious that you two make a good team. Everyone sees that, including the Fairmonts."

I smile at her. "Maybe . . . and thanks." I appreciate her compliment. If she only knew what Harmony and I have really been through together. Without Harmony's help in solving Dr. Miller's murder last semester, it's likely that Newman Becker would still be a free man teaching students like us at Fairmont.

"It can't hurt to approach them sooner rather than later to start that conversation," she says.

"Maybe you're right," I reply as we round the path. The cafeteria is straight ahead of us.

By the time we walk inside the dining hall, Tristan and Riley are already there. I spot the DZ—Lydia, Shannon, and Alicia—and notice that they're present minus charter member Emily Davenport. I can't help wondering where she is. Emily had provided the missing link to me last semester when it came to discovering that

Newman was the murderer who'd killed Dr. Miller. Helping me seems like enough wrongdoing to make Lydia and her crew shun Emily, and worse, her information also led to Lydia's brother having to spend some time in jail. Given this, I can only assume they've kicked her to the curb.

In a way, I think it will be good for her. I believe Emily is probably a decent girl deep down and deserves better friends. If they've kicked her out of their mean-girl sessions, I hope she knows that we have an empty seat at our lunch table waiting for her. But then again, I don't want to jump to conclusions. Just because I don't see Emily does not mean that she isn't a part of the DZ any longer. If I've learned anything at Fairmont, it's that things are hard to predict.

Riley's eyes widen when I arrive at the table with Martina. I'm guessing he's annoyed, since her presence means that I can't exactly spell out the details about my discussion with Joel. But, being a good sport, he jumps up and gives Martina the obligatory embrace. She hugs him back. Ah . . . this would be bliss . . . if only my two best friends weren't both suffering and seemingly hiding things from me.

Tristan stands up and takes my hand, tugging me in the direction of the food. "Can we *finally* eat?"

"Yep." I feel rather than see the resentful looks fired at me from the DZ's side of the room as I walk up to the salad bar with Tristan. I just don't look. I can sort of understand the hard feelings, but it isn't my fault that Lydia's brother was such a heartless and greedy criminal that he made the decision to kill Lydia's horse just for the insurance money. Okay, maybe it was my fault he got caught. But it was what he deserved.

Riley gets behind us in line and nudges me as soon as Martina walks off to fill her glass at the drink dispenser. "So?" he asks.

"I think it's all good, Ri. I don't think Joel has any intentions of causing harm, or making waves, or anything. I think he's here to go to school and ride. I really do." I'm not sure that I really believe this, but the only thing I can think to do right now is try to put Riley's mind at ease.

"So he did it to you, too."

"What?"

"Worked you. That's him. I told you. That's how he does it." Riley's light-green eyes fill with an anger that I haven't seen in them before.

"No. I really don't think so."

Tristan gives us a head nod as Martina approaches, and we all grow quiet as we finish making salads. We sit back down at our table. I try and start up a conversation about our schedules for this semester to brush off the awkwardness I'm feeling about everything that is going unsaid.

"Wonder what Christian Albright will be like as a jump coach," I say. Then, I feel Riley tense up. He's seated on one side of me and Tristan is on the other. I look at him and see the issue.

Joel has just sat down at the table occupied by the DZ. He looks over at all of us and gives a wave. I hear Riley mutter under his breath, "I think I'm going to puke. I told you, Viv. This isn't good."

I don't know what to say. I'm not even sure what to think. When

I'd talked with Joel at the barn, I'd wanted to believe the possibility that he was being truthful. I'd hoped that he had nothing but good wishes for Riley. But I feel those hopes dissipating quickly as I watch Joel sit down across from Lydia.

Maybe Riley is right—maybe Joel is exactly the bad guy Riley claims he is. If the table he's decided to sit down at says anything, it's that Joel just may be a snake. After all, he's sitting down in the snake pit.

CHAPTER *eight*

iley eats in near silence. Actually, he barely eats at all. Tristan gives me a sideways glance. He's trying to be playful with me, but as much as I'd rather mindlessly flirt with him, I can't—the moment is too awkward. But I appreciate that he's trying to make things seem totally normal so Martina won't be alerted to the fact that something is obviously wrong with Riley. Tristan knows as well as I do that Riley would be mortified by having to tell anyone else what's going on with him.

Tristan pats my knee. "You know, I want to get our things and check in at the office. My dad asked me to be sure they received the board check for Sebastian. Let's meet up later. I'll text you," he says.

I know when he says this that Tristan is being his usual decent and sensitive self. He knows that Riley's suffering and that he's going to be more comfortable sharing his feelings with me than with another guy—even a guy as cool as Tristan. I get that Tristan is giving us the space to talk. We just have to get away from Martina, and I'm not sure how to do that. I don't want to leave her out of things, but I want to be super respectful of Riley.

Tristan stands and bends down to kiss me. He gives me a quick peck on the lips, but just because it's fast doesn't mean it doesn't send a warm rush through me. "I'll see you tonight," he says. "I'll drop your stuff by your room if you want. Is your door open?"

"I think so. We left it unlocked, didn't we?" I ask Martina.

"Yeah." She glances up from her cell phone where she is punching out a text. "It's open. Hey, I hate to run off, but I need to take care of something." She puts her phone into her purse and withdraws a tube of lip gloss as she stands up. "See you in a bit." She gives us a little wave, and I am kind of baffled. Martina isn't exactly one to reapply lip gloss for no reason, and her hasty departure makes me wonder what's up. But, it does give Riley and me some time to talk.

I give Tristan one more quick kiss and watch him go. He turns back on his heels as he's halfway to the door and smiles at me. I wave and find myself giggling. I glance at Lydia's table, and, sure enough, discover her eyes trained on my boyfriend like a hawk. Whatever.

"Let's get out of here," I say to Riley. "Doesn't look like you're in the mood to eat."

But even when we leave the dining hall and its massive balloon of tension behind, it's clear that poor Riley is still a ball of nerves.

Neither of us says anything until we make it over to the pathway that leads to the duck pond, which is a quiet location that's out of the way.

"It's going to be okay," I say. "It will."

Riley doesn't look at me. "You don't know that, Vivvie. There's a lot of history between Joel and me, and it isn't all good. I can't go into it. Crap! I don't like it at all. How could Joel do this? He is here to ruin my life."

"Did you ever hear him talk about wanting to come to Fairmont?" I ask.

He shrugs. "Yeah. I guess so. Who doesn't? But I didn't believe it would happen. We're going into the second semester of our junior year. How did he even get in? Who moves from the East Coast to the West, and changes everything about their life in the middle of their junior year? Why would they want to?"

I have no good answers other than "Maybe you should try to take it at face value for now. There isn't much more that you can do. I mean, maybe Joel is here for the reasons he gave me."

"I doubt it. Seriously doubt it. Look who he was already hanging with. What if he's already told the DZ about me? If so, it won't be long before the entire student body knows, and then my parents . . . Once they find out, Viv—there'll be hell to pay."

I rub his arm and say, "I'm sorry. Let's try and not think the worst." I just really have no great advice. We take a seat on a bench in front of the pond. A half-dozen ducks are on its surface creating ripples. A spray of water from the fountain in the middle sprinkles them with a light shower.

"If my dad finds out, he'll pull me out of here. He'll sell Santos, and send me to a *retreat* where some skewed psychotherapist deep within the church will use the church's beliefs to make me 'right,'" he says, his remark dripping with sarcasm.

"Are they really that close-minded? Your parents?" I ask.

He laughs, but not as if it's funny. "Like two doors slammed shut. That's how close-minded."

"Riley? What can I do?"

He shakes his head. "Nothing. You know what? You know why this sucks so bad? Because of what you just said. Asking me if my parents are that close-minded."

"I'm sorry," I reply, somewhat confused.

"No. No. It's not you. It's that they are my parents, and aren't parents supposed to love you no matter what? I mean, I'm their kid, and I'm scared to death to tell them that I'm gay." He sighs. "You know, you hear people say that it's a choice, but that's such bullshit. Sorry."

I shake my head. "Don't be."

"Really, when you think about it, does anyone in their right mind think that anyone says, *Oh, I'd rather be gay now?* No matter what, no one *chooses* to be gay. Let's face it, for as 'far' as we may have come, there are still plenty of people, my parents included, who think that being gay means I'm some heathen, something evil."

In the silence that follows this remark, tears start to stream down his face. I reach out and wipe them with my thumbs. "It is crazy," I say. "I wish I could say that I know how you feel." Ironically, I kind of do. I am sure that if people knew about my ability to communicate with horses they'd see me as an outcast of sorts—an oddball at the very least.

"No, you don't, Viv. Trust me. You don't. I just wish that I had a mom like you have. What makes me sadder is that I love my parents. They're my parents, but because of who I am, I know I'll have to leave my family behind at some point to make a life that feels true to me. I won't be one of those people who lies forever just to make others, including my parents, feel better. I just need to wait until I graduate. That's it. Then, I'll have the freedom that I need to be truthful. I can't risk telling them the truth now and losing Santos. I can't live without my horse."

"I know. I do get that. But what do you mean that you just have to wait until graduation?"

He looks at me. His eyes are red rimmed from his tears. "I've got plans. I've been saving from the poker games and from summer jobs. And, my parents have given my brothers and sister big chunks of change at graduation, so I'm thinking I'll get the same. Once I have that in hand, I plan to take Santos and go to Europe. Hopefully, find a barn where I can be a working student."

"That would be amazing." I want to tell him to stay here. I want to tell him that it's all going to work out, but I can't because even I am not sure if those words are true. Riley knows his parents better than anyone, and given the turbulent emotions he's feeling, I trust what he's saying. All I can do is be supportive. "So, what do you think you want to do about Joel?"

"I have to get Joel out of here. I can't have him change my life just because he feels I wronged him in some way. I'm scared. I really am. And, it doesn't take a brain surgeon to figure out that even if Joel is on the up-and-up, and what he told you is true, he still might create a problem for me. Especially if he's going to be all buddy-buddy with Lydia. It won't take long before the gossip starts flying. That girl can get people talking. She has a knack for it. Trust me."

"You know what, Ri . . . you know the saying, 'Keep your friends close and your enemies closer'?"

He narrows his eyes and gives me a *you have to be kidding me* look.

"I'm not kidding," I reply. "What better way to keep Joel from spreading harm around here than to get him away from the DZ and bring him into our little fold?"

I look at Riley, who has gone a bit pale. I don't think he likes my idea so much. "Riley? Do you have any other ideas? If you do, I am all ears."

He finally shakes his head. "Nope, I don't. Suppose it's time I make nice with the enemy."

"I'd say so."

"Tomorrow night, I guess. I heard some people are going down to the beach for a get-together."

"Ah." I nod. "Is this an official Fairmont get-together or a sneaking-off-campus-and-possibly-getting-into-trouble situation?"

"The latter."

"No can do, Ri. I can't risk the scholarship."

"Come on. You have to do this with me. The sooner the better, right?"

"Don't make me do this. You know as well as I do that if anyone else gets caught besides me, it will probably be a slap on the wrist and a phone call home. For me, the stakes are higher. It states clearly in my contract that if I don't mind my p's and q's I will be sent packing."

"But it's the perfect opportunity! Tell you what, you just drive my car down and wait for me."

"No. Wait for, like, two hours? It's not like you're going to show up and then just walk up to Joel and say, 'Hey, dude, we need to be cool and you can't go flapping your mouth and crap.'"

Riley rolls his eyes. "First off, I never call anyone 'dude.'"

"You have to go without me. Sorry."

"Fine. Fine. I see how it is. I'll take your boy with me."

"I don't like that idea, either," I reply.

"Vivienne, you are being selfish."

"And you are trying to guilt me."

"No, I am not. I am stating facts here, and this is my life. It's you, your boy, or both of you. I need backup."

I sigh. "Fine. If Tristan is willing to do it, then I guess so."

"You're willing to get your boys busted, but you won't take the heat yourself." He laughs.

"Riley, you are not going to guilt me into this. I cannot do it. Being at Fairmont is my shot and I won't risk it. You know that."

"I'm sorry. I just like it when you hold my hand."

"I know you do." I take his hand and squeeze it. "But this time, you have to go and be a big boy on your own. You can do this, and it will all be okay."

"Right. You know, if this whole riding thing doesn't work out for you, you could always become a cheerleader. You're awfully good at it. And you're awfully good at being a smart-ass."

"True story," I say. "True story. But this is one smart-ass you are stuck with, Riley Reed."

He gives me a noogie on top of my head and says, "Come on, smart-ass, let's figure out how to make nicey-nice with the enemy."

CHAPTER *nine*

R iley and I part ways deciding that we will deal further with the Joel issue tomorrow. Anyway, for now it kind of is in Riley's court because he insists he will handle it at tomorrow night's bonfire. I find myself feeling pretty tired. It has been a long day. This morning, I was out of bed before the sun came up to get on my 9:00 a.m. flight back to school. The drive to the Portland Airport from my mom's house is a couple of hours, so my mom had us packed and in the truck by five in the morning. No wonder I want to take a nap.

When I get to our suite, I'm surprised to see that Martina isn't back yet, but decide maybe it's a good thing. As much as I want to visit with her, I can say that lying down and closing my eyes sounds even better. So that's what I do.

The text alert on my phone wakes me up. I roll over and reach out to get my phone off the nightstand next to my bed. I see the text is from Tristan, and rub my eyes. I also notice the time. It's after five! I must have been exhausted.

I read his text. *Hi, beautiful girl. Meet me in an hour down at the barn?*

I stretch and feel happy. How can I not? *Would love to.*

Wear something casual. I have a fun night planned for us.

I text him a smiley emoticon and set down the phone. I roll out of bed and, as I do, my cell goes off again. I pick it up ready to see what else Tristan might have to say.

I swallow and my eyes open wider. It's not from Tristan. But it is from Austen.

Hey, Vivienne Taylor, what the hell is up? Thinking of you. Get to school okay?

I sit back on the edge of the bed and close my eyes for a minute. *Austen, Austen, Austen . . .*

Another text rolls in. *You there, Viv? Think of me talking to you right now in my charming British accent.*

I can't help but smile at this. I have to answer him. *Hi! Yes, I'm at school. All good. Busy. I'm late for a meeting.* I press send and regret it.

Oh. My. God. I am such a liar. Such. A. Liar. A meeting? As if I work on freaking Wall Street or something. Why am I not honest? Although honesty would mean typing in that I have to take a shower so I can go on a date with my extremely hot boyfriend. I'm clearly caught. Right? Two guys. Both hot. One has been my friend since the beginning of time. Why did he ever kiss me? Because now I have to admit that I have some kind of feelings other than friendship for him. I don't know exactly what they are, but this just sucks. I want to throw the phone at the wall.

I take a deep breath. My text goes off again. It's Austen. *Meeting? Like sorority or club, or what?*

Oh geez. Um, okay, first off, not his business. However, if we are just talking friends here then it should be no big deal that he is asking me what kind of meeting. So I have to text back. And when I do, I feel compelled to say it's a horse management meeting. Yes. That is exactly what I am doing.

I get in the shower before any more texts can distract me, and when I come out there is one more from Austen that just tells me to have fun with the meeting. I don't respond, but instead get dressed.

I hate getting dressed for dates when I don't know the destination, but I figure jeans and a sweater is casual but still cute—and I got both items from my mom for Christmas so they look new. Not that my outfit matters all that much. I'm just excited that Tristan wanted to plan something special. I wish Martina were here to weigh in on my hair. I'm curious as to where she's been all afternoon. And I'm even more curious about the condom I saw by accident in her purse. But I don't want to push her. If Martina has something she wants to share with me, then she'll share. At least that's what I'm hoping.

I can't decide if I want to pull my hair back or leave it down. I am so much more comfortable with it pulled back, but my friends from home, Kait and Mia, who have both been totally guy crazy since we were all, like, nine, insist that boys love long hair left down. I mess around with it until I finally decide to pull it off my face with a hair tie.

Hair done, some makeup on, and I leave my room to meet Tristan over by the pond in between the dorms and the barns. Walking along the paved path I feel good and happy to be back here and around my horse, my friends, and Tristan.

I look to the right of me out at the green pasture and see that Harmony is on the grass. I hadn't noticed her on the turnout schedule, but she must have been on it. One of the grooms must have taken her out. I call out to her and she lifts her head.

I stop along the rail and watch in admiration as she trots over to me—with her graceful neck and just slightly dished nose, indicative of the Trakehner breed, she's such a beautiful horse. Tristan's horse, Sebastian, is also in the turnout with her. He lifts up his head for a few seconds as if to study me and then goes back to eating.

"Hey, pretty girl," I say, scratching up behind her ears in the way she loves and twirling my fingers through her mane. I lean my head against hers and we stay like that for several long seconds. It's a good moment. The best. I feel any remaining negativity still lingering from the images she shared with me of Joel clear away in this moment. "What's the story with you and that handsome boy in there?" I laugh. I glance up and out at Sebastian, who looks up at me again, and I watch as he slowly starts to walk my way. Harmony, though, looks almost past me and snorts. She turns around and heads back out onto the grass. "Hey, big girl, we weren't done talking," I say.

"You are so interesting."

I turn quickly and see why my horse took an abrupt leave—it's Lydia Gallagher.

"I didn't get the memo that we were wearing cheap jeans instead of True Religion. But, nice sweater. I see you've been taking note of what and what not to wear. Or, you've been spying on me. Quite an improvement from last semester, Scholarship." Her hands go to her hips, and I can't help notice that she is wearing a serious diamond tennis bracelet—it must have cost a small fortune. I want to roll my eyes at her but instead keep calm, even though I am somewhat stunned to see that yes, indeed, Lydia is wearing the same sweater as I am. I want to make a response to her snooty-ass remark but I swallow it—doesn't matter what she thinks, because the truth is, my jeans were not cheap.

"Always nice to see you, Lydia," I say. "But have you ever thought that maybe it's you who has learned to dress more appropriately? I mean, you look great in that. Far better than how you look in your usual attire of short shorts with butt cleavage and T-shirts that leave nothing to anyone's imagination."

"Are you saying that I'm tacky?" she practically screeches.

I wrinkle up my nose. "No. No. But less is more, you know. You shouldn't feel so insecure. You're a very pretty girl."

"And you're a freak."

"Right," I reply.

"You know, I was actually going to try and see if we could be friends. I thought that maybe we could forget about last semester and move on. But I see that your maturity level isn't much more than a five-year-old's."

"You've been wanting to be my friend? You have a funny way of showing it. But I guess criticizing clothing options is all there really is to your friendships."

"I was complimenting you."

"Oh. I missed that. Silly me. Sure. Let's be friends," I reply sarcastically. "Maybe you could start by using my real name instead of calling me Scholarship."

"Never mind. I have all the friends that I need."

"I have to go," I say. "I have to meet Tristan."

She frowns and turns, heading in the opposite direction from me—thankfully. After a minute my horse makes her way back over and I give her a kiss. This time, Sebastian comes along closely following her. I look at my watch. I still have a few minutes to spend with the horses before I'm supposed to meet Tristan. "She is such a jerk," I say to Harmony.

I run my hand down her nose and an image arrives in my mind directly from her: oddly, it's Lydia's bracelet. I think she must simply be agreeing with me that the girl is completely obnoxious, but then another image comes into my mind that I can tell is directly from my mare. She shows me an image of myself from the morning that she colicked last semester during our first event together. We couldn't compete because of it.

"What are you trying to tell me?" I ask.

Again, in my mind, I see the diamond bracelet. Then the image of me wearing pajamas on the morning she colicked.

"Is this about Lydia?"

Sebastian nudges me with his nose. "Hey you," I say, my hand going up alongside of his neck. I lose the thread of my discussion with Harmony now that Sebastian is involved. At least so far in my life, I have never been able to communicate with two horses at the same time. I always just focus on one. I might pause to ask another horse something on the same topic, but generally I keep the communication channels all very separate, so that I don't get confused.

One thing I know is that it's obvious to me that Sebastian knows I can understand his kind. Either he has picked up on this fact himself, or in some way my lovely mare has clued him in. It's amazing to me that even though I can communicate with horses, there is so much I don't understand about how the animals talk to each other. I am positive they do. If they talk to me, I sure in the heck believe that they talk to each other.

"What is it, Sebastian?" I go through the same motions as I did with Harmony and lean my head against his face. He is as much of a gentle giant as any horse can be. Then I get a flurry of images. They move quickly, but I am sure of what I'm seeing. First, there's Tristan. Then I see his father. I also see Lydia standing in a dark corner. The giveaway is the sparkling tennis bracelet glittering in the shadows. The image is blurry, but I'm sure that it's her. But I get the feeling that Tristan has no idea about Lydia's presence. And that's when I am shocked as the images coming from Sebastian turn violent. I gasp out loud as I see Tristan's father wrapping his wide hands around his son's neck and choking him, and then letting go just long enough to shove him to the ground.

I am jolted out of the horrifying imagery by the sound of my name being called.

"Vivvie. Hey, beautiful!" I turn to see Tristan walking down the pathway. I try and smile, and for the first time in my life pray that a horse has just told me a big, fat lie.

CHAPTER *ten*

Tristan reaches me, grabs me around the waist, and twirls me around. For a second my mind jumps back to Christmas break when Austen made the same move. What is there—a school on how to win girls' hearts? If so, did they both attend? He sets me down and then kisses me on the forehead, which strikes me as the sweetest gesture ever. "You look beautiful, as always. You okay, though? You were looking a little lost when I was walking up."

"I'm fine. I was talking to those two and kind of daydreaming." That is pretty darn close to the truth. Except the communication with Sebastian was more like a nightmare than a daydream.

"And, did they tell you anything?" he asks, laughing.

I grin. If he only knew!

"They told me they love to eat." I nudge him in the ribs.

"Well, then, should we let them go back to their grass? We have plans. You ready?"

"Ready for what?"

"The surprise."

"I like surprises."

"Let's go then." He takes my hand and we walk the rest of the way down the path to the parking lot.

"So where are you taking me?"

"You'll have to wait and see."

He opens the door for me. "You are such the gentleman." I laugh.

"I try." He walks around and gets into the driver's seat of the Jeep. As we exit the gates of Fairmont, the sun is just beginning to set.

"So," he says as he presses the accelerator and moves smoothly into traffic. "What do you think about this whole thing with Joel and Riley?"

"I don't know," I say. "I think that Riley might be overreacting a little about Joel. The kid seemed sincere to me when I talked to him. I told Riley that if he is really worried, that he should go and try to make some kind of peace with Joel. You know, the whole 'keep your enemies closer than your friends' thing."

"Speaking of that, Riley asked me to go with him tomorrow night down to that beach party, and I bet Joel will also be there. Not exactly what I want to do, but . . ."

"I'd go if I could. I really would."

"No," he replies. "I understand why you can't go, and I don't want you to go. It's not your scene at all."

I am a little perplexed by this statement. "What do you mean?"

"The kids that will be there can be pretty big partyers."

"Oh." I don't want to say it out loud, but I find myself wondering if Lydia will be there. Then I realize—of course she will be.

"I just don't think you would have a very good time."

"Because I am not a big partyer?" I ask. I really am not sure how to take this entire discussion.

"Yes. No. I mean, you don't drink, and that's all these kids will be doing."

"And?" I ask. "Hooking up?"

"Probably," he replies.

It's quiet and a little tense between us for a minute or two. I don't like that he's going tomorrow night, and I also can't shake what Sebastian had shown me. I want to bring it up, but really don't know how. Tristan starts to speak at the same time as I do. Right as I say, "Will Lydia be there?" he says, "Lydia will probably be there."

"Oh," I reply. "I thought so."

"I don't care about her anymore, Vivienne."

"I know." My voice sort of gives me away. I can hear insecurity running through it, and I hate myself for it. And, I despise my father for it, because I am smart enough to recognize that so much of my distrust of other people comes from the fact that my dad left us behind. My trust issues are my problem, not Tristan's, and I feel bad that I can't keep my emotions in check. But there is more going on with me than feeling insecure about my relationship with Tristan, because truth be told, I am actually pretty confident in what we share together. I am completely into him, and I think he has the same feelings for me.

What is more troubling right now is what Tristan's horse just revealed to me. I need to go further with Sebastian and investigate. Is Tristan abused by his dad and has Lydia witnessed it? There are even deeper questions than just these two, but for now I try and shove away my spiraling thoughts. I want nothing more than to enjoy my evening with my boyfriend.

"I really don't care about her."

"I know." I take his hand. "And you are it for me, too."

"I'd better be. There better not be some secret guy hidden away at Fairmont that I don't know about."

I shift a little uneasily in the seat.

"I have to tell you, when you first introduced me to Joel, I was kind of curious as to how you knew him," he says.

"Were you jealous?" I ask teasingly.

He shrugs. "Maybe a little bit. Maybe I was."

"There is obviously no reason for that, and there is no reason for you to be jealous over anyone. Like I just told you, you are *it*, Tristan Goode."

We turn into the state beach and park. "Good. Now come on." He walks around the back of the Jeep and unloads a picnic basket. "Leave your shoes in the car."

I kick off my shoes and he takes my hand. We walk out onto the sand, and Tristan finds a perfect spot before laying down the blanket. He sets the basket down and opens it. He takes out another rose and hands it to me, and I am so charmed in this moment that I am not sure if I am still even on this earth.

"I wanted to do something special for you since we didn't get to spend Christmas together."

I get a sinking feeling as I realize that he probably has a

Christmas gift for me. I mailed his over break, never thinking that it might be more fun to exchange gifts in person. I had kind of wondered why he hadn't sent me a present, actually, but had tried not to dwell on it.

As if reading my mind, Tristan says, "Thank you for the picture of Sebastian and me. It made my entire Christmas vacation to get your package."

"You're welcome. I took it when you weren't looking and loved how it came out. You are happy when you're around him." I'd actually made a copy of the photo for myself, too. In the image, Tristan is looking back at Sebastian, whose nose is almost touching his shoulder, and Tristan is wearing the sweetest, happiest smile that I have ever seen. It's as if in that second when the photo was taken Tristan felt nothing but pure love and had no other cares in the world. Thinking about the photo now reminds me again of Sebastian, though, and I realize I have to find out if the images that Sebastian showed me are true. If so, when did Tristan's dad do that to him? Could it have really happened? I have to think it must have. I haven't known a horse to lie to me yet.

"I was going to send your gift, too," he said. "But then I thought that I would rather see your face when I give it to you."

"Oh?"

"Yes," he replies. He opens the picnic basket. "But first, we eat."

"You're going to make me suffer, aren't you?"

"Maybe a little bit. Enjoy the moment, Vivienne Taylor. Enjoy the moment."

I look at him and reply, "Are you for real, Tristan Goode?"

He leans in and kisses my lips softly and sweetly. Together, we fall back onto the blanket, laughing, and then suddenly his kiss becomes harder.

"Is that real enough for you?" he whispers in my ear.

I look up at the sky and nod slightly. "Yeah. I think so."

We both start laughing, and then we tickle each other—two kids with no cares in the world, at least for that moment. We sit up, out of breath. "Vivvie?"

"Yeah?"

He's got those intense green eyes focused on me, and I can tell that what he wants to say is important, maybe deep—just from the way he is looking at me. "Let's eat," he blurts out.

"Okay," I say, trying to keep my expression neutral. "Let's eat."

Are guys always this confusing?

I *ooh* and *ahh* as Tristan unpacks the picnic basket he filled with goodies from a local organic market in Malibu. In addition to gourmet turkey and bacon sandwiches, there are strawberries, potato chips, chocolate chip cookies, and sparkling flavored water, which he pours into champagne glasses. We stuff our faces and talk horses and also about this semester's possibilities. Then, we talk about Liberty Farms.

"What do you think?" he asks. "Will you go if you're chosen?"

I nod with a strawberry in my mouth. "Definitely. The opportunity would be incredible. I'm not totally sure how I'll afford all of it. Kayla told me that my scholarship will fund most of it, but I am not sure about the details and whether they'll need my mom to pay for things, too. I guess we'll find out if we get there."

"I bet you'll get chosen, and I bet it'll work out," he says, with a warm smile.

"What about you? Will you go if you make the cut?" I ask. He looks away and I follow his gaze out to the ocean, which is slate colored. Small waves topped with whitecaps roll in toward the beach. It's almost sunset and a tinted rose color is spreading across the sky.

"I don't know."

"Really? Why wouldn't you? It's such a great opportunity."

He sighs and turns to look at me with greenish-blue eyes that look thoughtful. "I know, but my parents usually expect me to come home for the summer. My dad gets really busy with work, and my mom likes having my help."

I take a sip of my water, not really knowing how to respond. I set the glass down. "Is everything, um, is everything okay at home for you?"

"Yeah." He nods. "Yeah. It's status quo. I just don't know how they would feel about me being gone all summer. Actually, maybe they'd be happy. Keep me out of their hair. I know I'd love to avoid being there."

I want to ask more and delve deeper. There is definitely something that Tristan isn't telling me about his home life. At the same time, I have to be careful not to cross a boundary that he may not want crossed. But, physical violence is something different. If Tristan is being hurt at home, I have to find out. I care so deeply for Tristan that it troubles me to think something bad has happened to him, or could be happening when he goes home from school each break. And, I want to know what Lydia knows about it.

He puts his hands behind his back and stretches. "You know what? I think it's time that I gave you your Christmas present." He takes out a small gift-wrapped box and puts it in my hands.

He's facing me now, cross-legged, and looking as anxious as I feel.

"Open it," he says.

I carefully take off the wrapping paper. The light-blue box is from Tiffany's, and I look at him with what I know must be wide eyes. "Oh my God. What did you do?" I ask.

"Open it." He smiles.

I do. I take out a silver chain bracelet with a heart on it. Engraved on the heart is *VT* + *TG*. I am shocked and happy and . . . yeah . . . shocked because this is seriously the sweetest and most romantic gift anyone has ever given me. I mean, it's not like I have had a slew of boyfriends giving me gifts over the years. Okay, I have not had *any* boyfriends—my time has always been dedicated to my horses—so this is pretty wonderful. I throw my arms around him. "This is so sweet. I love it."

"I'm glad." He takes it from me and unclasps it and then puts it on my wrist. "It fits perfectly."

"Yes, it does." For a brief second I think about the charm bracelet my friends back home gave me at the end of last summer before I left for Fairmont—Austen included. I don't wear it that often because it's sentimental and special. Ironically, I will probably wear this bracelet all of the time for the same reasons. It also helps that it's from my boyfriend and doesn't have a boxer underwear charm on it that requires an explanation. Of course, my friends at home would immediately know that goofball Austen gave me that particular and somewhat embarrassing charm. Austen always found it hilarious to wear all sorts of humorous boxers over his riding breeches on a regular basis, so it's an inside joke with our little group.

Tristan stands up and takes my hand. "Come on, let's take a walk down to the water."

We walk along the water's edge as the sun continues to set. Just as we get about a hundred yards away, we see two people up ahead. They are facing each other—a man and a woman. Their conversation looks pretty intense. I glance at Tristan. The woman crosses her arms. The man pulls her close and wraps his arms around her. She leans her head on his shoulder and to me it looks like she is crying. A second later, I recognize who we're looking at . . . but before I can voice it, Tristan does.

"Hey, isn't that Kayla Fairmont and Christian Albright?" he says.

"Yeah. I think it is."

"Looks serious."

"It does." My stomach sinks, and those happy feelings that had taken over me fade away. "Maybe we should go back before they see us."

"Definitely," he replies. "Otherwise things could get really awkward."

We start to walk back to the blanket in silence. He finally speaks up. "What do you think that's about?" he asks.

"They're old friends," I say. "Maybe she needs a shoulder to cry on. I don't know."

"You believe that?" he asks.

"Do you believe the alternative?" I ask.

Tristan pauses. "No. No. I don't think so."

"Right. Neither do I." I think we both respond this way because we know what's at stake. If Kayla is cheating on Holden, it could change our futures at Fairmont. I know why I don't want that. My dreams are wrapped up in the school. My guess is that Tristan also has reasons for not wanting to believe the worst of Kayla Fairmont—I just hope the reason isn't that school is the only place he feels safe.

CHAPTER *eleven*

I'm on the couch in our dorm suite fingering the bracelet that Tristan gave me last night and smiling when Martina comes through the door looking very unhappy. She tosses down a tabloid. "There it is in black and white. Says that my mom is being unfaithful to my father!"

"Oh, Martina, I am so sorry." I put my arm around her. "You know that isn't true."

"Do I?"

I take a step back. "It can't be true. I've met your parents. They seemed totally in love. Your mom told you it wasn't true."

She hangs her head. Her long dark hair falls across her face, hiding her expression. "I guess. But either way, people will believe it. Even people around here."

"I know. I get it. And, it sucks that you have to be a victim of all this."

"It does, but it comes with the price of having celebrity parents.

You would think I'd get that. But my parents have always been really good about keeping our family out of the limelight. They aren't the stereotypical Hollywood celebs. They've kept me sheltered. They keep even themselves pretty isolated, and they don't give reasons for stupid magazines like this one to air the family laundry. But ever since this stalker thing started with my mom, they've been printing all kinds of trash about my family."

"Have you told your parents you've seen this?"

"Yes." She plops down on our couch. "My mom called me a little while ago to let me know that the story was out. She didn't want someone else to tell me. I hadn't seen it in person until Shannon Burton so kindly gave me her copy, while Lydia watched and giggled like the stupid moron that she is."

"Figures. Ignore them. They're total idiots and they love crawling under people's skin."

"I know. I just wish it didn't hurt."

"Of course it hurts. You have every right to feel that way, but you have to keep in mind that you know the truth. Your parents know the truth. The people who love you know the truth, and that is what is important. This will blow over. The stupid writers for these rag magazines will find other stories. They'll claim that Angelina and Brad are breaking up, or that Justin Bieber is being sued by some skank who claims he's her baby's daddy."

She laughs at this.

"Oh, I can come up with more, if you like."

"Maybe you should write for one of the tabloids."

"Better yet, I should start one around here. The first story can be about Lydia Gallagher's nose job. . . ."

"Did she?" Martina says.

"No. I don't know." I laugh. "But see how easy it is for people to believe a rumor? And that is what this stuff about your parents is. Pure rumor."

"You're right." She looks at her watch. "You know what I'm going to do? Go home for a couple of hours. See my parents. I think I'll feel better."

"I think you're a smart girl."

"You're a good friend. When I get back, what do you say we eat junk food, watch a movie, and hang out?" she asks.

"I can't think of anything better," I reply. I don't say it out loud, but I feel relieved that Martina will be back here to take my mind off Tristan being down on the beach at the bonfire, where Lydia and the DZ will likely be flirting and fueled by plenty of alcohol.

"See you later then."

I look at my watch and realize I have a dressage lesson with Holden in a half hour. After changing into my breeches and riding boots, I race down to the barn to tack up Harmony. I bump into Riley, who is just getting off Santos. "How was it?" I ask.

"Good." He kicks his right leg over and slides down off Santos. "Kind of weird, though. I had my first lesson with Christian."

"Oh yeah?"

He nods. "He's good. He's really different from Newman, that's for sure."

"That has to be a plus. Because Newman was not easy."

"No, he wasn't. Plus, he was a murderer."

"Very true," I reply. "Sociopaths aren't so easy to work with."

"Right." Riley nods. "I think I'll like working with Christian, but he is kind of, I don't know . . . he's different. He's emotional in a way . . . I guess it's passion."

When Riley says the word *passion*, all I can think of is the embrace Christian and Kayla shared on the beach. I don't know for sure if what Tristan and I saw was passion, but it was definitely serious.

"I guess I'll see how I like him soon enough, huh?"

"Yep. What do you have right now, dressage?" Riley asks.

"I do. I'd better get moving. You know how Holden feels about being on time."

"Yeah." He puts Santos on the cross-ties.

"You worried about tonight? About talking to Joel?" I ask.

He walks into the tack room and gets a treat for his horse, who eagerly takes it from the palm of his hand, and then Riley begins untacking him. "I'm a little anxious." He pulls the saddle off and sets it on the saddle rack to be cleaned.

"It'll be okay," I reply. "I really believe that."

"I hope so."

I take Harmony out of her stall and begin grooming her. As I slide a brush along her body, I feel that mutual rush of affection that so often precedes our communication. Moments later, she shows me an image of a pony I don't recognize. I set the brush down and lean my head against hers for a minute and the picture becomes clearer: an all-white, expensive-looking hunter pony with a little girl on its back. This is quickly followed by another image, but this time the pony is on the ground. I concentrate on the emotion Harmony is giving me and pull back, alarmed. The pony she's showing me is dead. Wow! The horses are telling me all sorts of things these days that I really don't understand.

I stroke her neck and encourage her to tell me more. The next image I get is a horse I recognize—it's Joel's horse, whose name I've learned is Melody. The first time I heard it, this seemed kind of funny, considering my horse's name. Now that Harmony is trying to talk to me about Melody, I'm wondering if they have more in common than their musically themed names.

"Okay. So, you and Melody have become BFFs? And she is giving you a lot to talk about? Maybe I need to go and talk with her," I whisper. "I know I need to go have a few more words with Sebastian."

"Are you talking to your horse?" The sound of Riley's voice catches me by surprise.

I laugh. I was in the zone and he caught me off guard. "Sometimes. We talk a lot."

He raises his eyebrows. "Okay. I get it. I talk to Santos, too. He's a good listener." He laughs.

If he only knew. I put on Harmony's saddle and bridle and we walk out to the mounting block. I don't know what Riley heard or whether he thinks I'm crazy. There are moments when I really want to share this Doctor Dolittle thing I have going on, but at the same time, I really don't know how my friends would react. I have become very comfortable and happy with the friends I've made here. I'm not prepared to lose any of them because they view my ability as completely weird and freakish. No. I don't think that I am quite ready for that.

Holden is seated in the gazebo just outside the dressage court.

"Hi," I say as we enter the arena. "I'm not late, am I?" It wouldn't be the first time a conversation with Harmony made me late, but I hate to miss even a second of Holden's great dressage lessons.

"No, not at all. I was thinking. Good to see you. Say we get started?"

"Yes. We're ready." I do a warm-up with Harmony, and then we go to real work. It's a pretty technical lesson and goes well until I notice a change in Harmony about thirty minutes in. We've gotten through some of the exercises. Holden has had us working on side passing, which isn't anything too difficult, turn on the haunches and turn on the forehand—all of it to help strengthen both of us from a physical and even mental standpoint. Each movement requires both of us to use our bodies differently. My body cues my mare, and even the slightest bit of incorrect adjusting can confuse her. She may still try and do what she thinks I am asking for, but it won't be correct. I wish for the millionth time that I could communicate as well with horses when I'm riding as when I'm just hanging around. All I can guess is that when we are having a conversation and showing each other images, the focus is completely on that communication. When I am riding her, the focus and the relationship changes some. I am asking her to work, to perform. The focus is on the movement, and it is really concentrated. The way horses are expected to perform is as precise and difficult as any gymnastics or ballet routine out there. I know some might find that hard to believe. But I took gymnastics for a couple of years as a kid, and there was always a ballet lesson or two to go along with it. I can attest to the fact that riding dressage, or any type of competitive riding, requires just as much focus and athleticism.

I am surprised by the shift in Harmony, as she's been working diligently and being so good—on the bit, nice and round, stepping into her tracks, and using her body correctly. Then, when Holden asks us to run through one of our tests, Harmony spooks about five feet to the left and as we make the turn at C past the center line. She just loses it, nearly jumping out of the arena. I half expect her to bolt as I feel all of her muscles go completely taut.

I sit back in the saddle, leg on, but giving her a hard half halt. "Whoa." She comes back to me and calms down quickly.

Holden is laughing. "What was that all about?" he asks.

"I have no idea," I reply. "Maybe she thought she saw something out of the corner of her eye. I didn't notice anything, so I don't know."

"Okay, well, let's put her back up to work and try it again. The sun is starting to set; maybe it was a shadow."

I nod, but have to wonder. Harmony isn't one to spook easily.

"Start the test over," he says.

I do, and we make the left turn at C, the ten-meter circle at E at a working trot—and then I do feel her start to bulge on the right shoulder and tense up. I put my right calf on her and give a little with my inside rein, even scratching the top of her neck for a second. I do this without changing my position, and I couldn't do it at an event, but in this case, it seems like a good idea to give her that extra encouragement.

We continue to work the test, and as we come back around to

the letter M, I feed her the rein to put her on a free walk. Just as we get to the middle of the arena, a group of ducks flies past low overhead. Harmony completely loses it again, and nearly runs out on me for the second time. I have to bring her back and settle her, which at least she does quickly. Oh boy, we are going to be having a conversation! What in the world is going on with my horse? First, she's showing me a dead pony that Melody seemed to have been telling her about, and now she's acting like she's a nervous wreck.

I reach down and with my right hand stroke the top of her neck a little firmer than I had while going through the test. "Hey, what is it?" I try to convey the words and hope that even though I am riding her, I can get through to her. In a flash I see an eye—a horse's eye. Is it her eye? Hard to tell, since the flashing image was so quick, but I think it is. I climb off her and come around to her face.

"What's going on, Vivienne?" Holden asks.

I hold my hand up, cupping my palm over her left eye because the angle of the setting sun is making it hard to see. Holden approaches us. "Do you think she has something in her eye?" he asks.

"I don't know. I just thought maybe it was worth it to take a look, since she isn't exactly a spooky horse."

He nods affirmatively. "You are a vet's daughter, aren't you?"

I shrug. "Have to look at all of the possibilities." I am pretty positive that Harmony wants me to know something about her eye, but I can't exactly say this to Holden. "I don't see anything." He takes a look and agrees. We walk to the other side of her, and it takes me a minute, but I do see something very small. It is on the inside of the eye, almost directly over the pupil. It's a little to the left, and it isn't any larger than the point of a pen.

Holden says, "I don't see anything. Do you?"

I swallow hard and think that I do see something, but I'm not sure I want to say anything just yet. My mom has a special focus on ophthalmology and optometry in her large animal practice, and before I jump the gun and sound any alarms, I want to call her. "Looks good to me," I reply.

"Get back up on her and let's have you both finish on a good note." Holden turns to walk back to his spot under the gazebo.

I scratch Harmony between the eyes. "I'll figure out what is going on with your eye, okay? You have to trust me. I won't allow anything to hurt you. There is nothing to be afraid of here. If there was or is, I would let you know," I say quietly to her. I infuse my body and emotions with an energy that will convey trust and love—my body feels light and warm. I feel like I could walk on air when I express this combination of emotions together. On the other hand, when I'm expressing dark and negative emotions, my body feels heavy and unstable, as if I could easily fall down.

"Okay. Take her over to the mounting block. Let's finish up with a good test, Vivienne."

As I climb back on her, I do think it's possible that the way the sun is positioned made shadows that caused her to spook. I don't know this for sure, but it's one option. The sun continues to shift quickly, and I'm curious if the light might affect her again.

We do as we've done twice already in this lesson and travel down the centerline. We make the left turn at C, start our ten-meter circle at M, and it goes from there. I do feel her tense up at one point when more ducks fly overhead. I speak in soft tones and support her through the physical contact of my leg and my hand, not taking up too much rein but just reminding her that I am very much on top of her. "It's okay. It's nothing scary. I promise." She relaxes into the movement and we finish with a halt back at X.

"That's how you get it done," Holden says and stands up, walking toward us. He shrugs as he reaches out and pats her on the neck. "Spooky today, huh, big girl?"

"Yeah. I really don't know what that was all about," I reply.

"Well, you handled it just fine. Walk her out, and I'll see you tomorrow. Have a good evening, Vivienne. I've gotta run. We have an admin meeting in fifteen."

"Okay. Thank you. You have a good night, too."

Once we get back to the barn and I've taken off Harmony's tack and rinsed her off in the wash rack, I look at her eye again. I can't see anything in this light, which isn't nearly as bright as it is outside. I decide to call my mom, though, and get her take, so I pull out my cell.

"Hey, Schnoopy!" she says, calling me by the familiar pet name she coined for me when I was a baby.

"Hi, Mom."

"It's good to hear your voice. You getting settled back there again? I miss you already."

"I am. I miss you, too. Things are good, but I am so getting an earful from the horses."

"Really?" Her tone changes and sounds a little bit anxious.

I can't blame her, considering that it was my dialogue with Harmony last semester that nearly got me killed. "It's nothing major." I decide not to tell her about the dead pony, or that I think

Tristan's dad could be abusing him. I'll stay in a safe zone. "Well, Harmony is trying to tell me something, anyway."

"What's going on?" she asks.

"She was really spooky today."

"From what you've told me that doesn't sound like her."

"No. It isn't like her. I asked her about it and she *says* it's her eye. I got off and looked in both of her eyes and I did see something, but barely. Holden didn't see it, so I didn't say anything because I could be wrong."

"I doubt your horse would give you wrong information, Vivvie. What did you see?"

"It was about the size of a pen point. I know Holden wears glasses sometimes, and the light was bright, so maybe he didn't see anything because of that."

"You need to let him know."

"What do you think it is?" I ask.

"Without seeing her I can't be sure, but if I had to guess, I'd tell you it's likely a corpora nigra or uveal cyst. I hesitate to say cyst, though, because technically that isn't what it is. It likely does not hurt her, but if it grows, it might block her vision."

"Which could be a problem with jumping."

"Right. But it can be treated with laser surgery. I've done some at the clinic."

"So, she'd have to be completely out?" I ask.

"Yes. Usually. But, it's her eye, Viv, so we don't take chances. There are some vets who will perform this with local anesthetic, but I prefer to have them out cold with a general. The thing is, though, without me seeing her, I can't for sure tell you what you're looking at. The eye is nothing to mess with. I think you need to call in a vet."

"But, Mom, Holden didn't see anything."

"Vivienne, it doesn't matter. You need to tell him what you think you saw, and explain that you think it merits a ranch call by the vet."

"Okay," I reply, knowing that she is right.

"Good girl. Oh, I'm being paged. I have a horse that just came out of colic surgery. I have to go, Schnoopy. Get her checked."

"Okay, Mom. Love you."

"Love you, too."

I hang up the phone and call Holden immediately. He doesn't answer, so I leave him a message to please call me.

I go back to talk with Harmony some more. She's a little distracted as it's feeding time and she can hear the guys rolling around on the golf carts giving buckets and tossing hay. I pat her neck. "Yeah. Dinnertime. So, how is the eye?" I make sure she understands what I am asking by covering her eye with my hand and presenting the mental image. She moves her head away. She bats her eyes at me. She tosses her head around, and the sense that I get from her is that she's genuinely content. I take another close look at the eye, and this time I really can't find anything. Maybe it was as simple as her having debris in her eye and it flushing out by itself. I hate to jump to conclusions and have Holden call the vet out for nothing. I know ranch calls aren't cheap. My mom's words echo in my mind, though.

Luckily, there's not much I can do at the moment. Now that I left Holden a message, all I can do is wait for him to call me back.

I try and continue our earlier conversation about the dead pony and Melody, but about that time the hay cart rolls up, and it's clear Harmony is done talking. I am also aware that at this moment, I won't get much out of Sebastian or Melody, either. But I still have plans to talk with them, because I've got lots of questions I want answered. On top of being worried about Harmony's eye, I want to know what might be happening with Tristan and his father, not to mention the dead pony. I think I owe it to Tristan and the horses to investigate all of these issues further and hear the horses out.

CHAPTER *twelve*

You know those times when you feel like you might come undone? I am, at this very moment, having one of those nights.

Right now, Tristan and Riley are on their way to the bonfire at the beach and into Lydia's lair. I know I shouldn't think like that. I am the one wearing the Tiffany bracelet with a heart on it. But I am still unraveling despite Martina coming back to our room and trying to take my mind off it. At least she is feeling better about things. Going to see her parents was a good thing. I know that Martina has lived a very different life from me growing up, but one of the things I believe we have in common is that we do have normal relationships with our parents. I mean, I have it with one parent, anyway.

"I have to tell you something else," Martina says. We're eating Cheez-Its, beef jerky, and drinking soda—yep, the dinner of champions.

With my mouth full of the cheesy, salty goodness, I mutter, "Sounds serious."

She shrugs. "I, um, well, I met someone."

I nearly spit out the Cheez-Its because she is finally going to divulge. "Oh yeah? Who? Where? How? Tell me!"

"You can't laugh."

"Please. I would never laugh."

"Okay, and you can't question me or judge this."

If she only knew what I know about Riley, she would realize her statement is an unnecessary one. "I wouldn't do that, either." I have to say this is kind of strange, and now I am even more curious about the mystery guy.

She sighs and then smiles. "His name is Raul, and he's here."

"Here? What do you mean he's here? Like he's going to school here, as in a new kid?"

She shakes her head. "No. He, he's one of the new grooms."

My mouth forms the word *oh,* and then I say, "Oh. Oh, so when did you meet him? What's he all about? What does he look like? Wait . . . is he the guy you flashed the bright-lights-big-city smile at when we went to the cafeteria?"

"Slow down, Viv, you might choke on the Cheez-Its. Pass me the box."

I toss it to her. "Come on. Spill."

"Okay, yes, you're right. So, you know how I was coming here almost every day during the break to get your horse and mine out? Well . . . he was here, too."

"Uh-huh." I rub my palms together. "Thought so. I remember him. . . . Keep going."

"I met him while taking Harmony out to lunge the first day after pretty much everyone was out of here. He was walking into the main barn when I walked her out. He stopped and looked at her and told me how beautiful she is. Then, he said that I was beautiful."

I can't help myself from rolling my eyes.

"Vivvie!"

"I agree you are beautiful, but what a player."

"No. He's not like that!"

She looks wounded, and I feel like an ass. "I'm sorry. I know, I'm kind of a cynic."

"You said you wouldn't judge."

"I'm not. Tell me more. I really am sorry."

She hesitates.

"Please."

"It just sort of went from there. We started eating lunches together and he even made me a Christmas present."

"He did? What did he make you?"

She gets off her bed and goes to the dresser where she takes out a long, thin box and hands it to me.

"Open it."

I do and I see a gorgeous brow band for her horse, Jetson. It's black leather with a row of emerald-green stones across it. "Wow. This is incredible. It's beautiful."

"I know and he made it. He makes all sorts of things out of leather."

"Really?" I haven't met this Raul guy yet, but I can't help wondering if he is the real deal. Did he really make the brow band? Because it is quite exquisite, and I know I am sounding judgmental here, but I'm having a hard time with the groom being the awesome-brow-band-jeweler guy. Yes, I am being a bit bitchy, but Martina is my friend, and I just want to make sure this guy is being honest with her.

"Yes, really."

"It's beautiful. It really is, Martina. I want to meet him. I mean, you seem kind of serious about him. It's pretty sudden, don't you think?"

"I guess. But, don't forget how you were last semester . . . so into Tristan all of a sudden even though you wouldn't admit it. I could see it every time you two looked at each other. We're young, and love is supposed to be sudden, isn't it? Raul is sweet, he's funny, and he's gorgeous. You saw him. And, he likes me a lot."

"He sounds great. He does. Have your parents met him?"

She looks down and shakes her head. When she looks up at me, she says, "He's twenty-two."

"Martina! Come on now. That is not, well, you know, it's not legal."

"But it's hot."

"Okay, maybe. But still. Can I ask you something?"

"What?"

"How far have you gone with this guy?"

"I'm not having sex with him. Not yet. But . . ."

"But nothing. That's statutory rape, and your dad would come unglued if he knew. And that is not hot!"

"You're the only one who knows and you can't tell a soul."

"I don't know if this is a good thing, Martina."

"You sound like a mother."

"It's just with older guys like that, I don't know ... Why isn't he going out with girls his own age?"

She doesn't respond for a minute. She stands and grabs her purse off the dresser.

"What are you doing?" I ask.

"I'm going out to see Raul. We planned to meet up. I told you because I thought you would be happy for me. Instead, you sound like a parent. I shouldn't have told you."

"Wait. I'm sorry. You're my friend and I'm just looking out for you."

She's at the door and turns around to say, "Don't bother. I can look out for myself."

She leaves and I'm speechless. I don't know if I should go after her or not. Maybe she just needs time, but I really don't like her going out with a guy that much older. I just find it kind of creepy, and definitely not quite as hot as she does. Yeah—it's definitely creeper material.

I head to the door and out the hallway. I'm in my pajamas and bare feet. She's already gone.

I shake my head and go back into our room, hoping I haven't completely alienated Martina. She's my friend and I really care about her.

I plop back down on the bed and continue to stuff my face. So far, tonight has been a complete disaster. Figuring it can't get any worse, I put in my earbuds and turn on some music and hope that listening to Pink will distract me from my troubles.

CHAPTER *thirteen*

I wake up not feeling super refreshed due to the fact that I tossed and turned all night. I didn't hear Martina come in, but as I pull on my breeches I see her asleep in her bed. I try to be as quiet as possible. I do plan to speak with her later today and make amends. I feel horrible about the way things went down last night.

I'm also not feeling great that I never received a call or text from Tristan or Riley, and I am dying to know what happened at the bonfire. My riding lesson with Christian is early this morning, and I doubt my favorite guy or my best friend is awake yet. Plus, I want to make my way to the barn before there are too many people around. I have a few things on my agenda. The first is to take another look at Harmony's eye to see if anything is in there. I also want to ask her about the dead pony, and I am hoping to get in a few minutes with Sebastian. I feel a little guilty for wanting to do that because he isn't my horse, and what he knows is obviously something Tristan is keeping private. However, Tristan is my boyfriend, and if something terrible is happening in his home, I feel like I have to find a way to help him. I also can't help wondering how Lydia is involved. I just have so many questions, and I am hopeful that these quiet early morning hours will bring me some answers.

I grab a cup of coffee from the coffee hut and walk quickly to the barns. The air is crisp and the skies covered with dark clouds. Looks like rain to me. Smells like it, too. Being an Oregonian, I happen to be sort of an expert on rain. And there goes a big drop right on my head, and then another and another, and the sky opens up and pours down on me as I run to the barn for cover. I peer into Harmony's stall. She's definitely come in from the rain, as her gray coat is wet and sort of speckled looking. "You got wet, too?" I laugh.

Her kind brown eyes follow me as I enter her stall. I notice that Joel's horse, Melody, is also inside and wet, like she just escaped the rain. The only one still standing out in the downpour is Sebastian. Like people, some horses really like the rain, and Sebastian seems to be one of those horses. I have grown up with rain coming down around me all of my life, so I am not super crazy about it. I revel in the sunshine of Southern California. As much as I want to continue my conversation with Sebastian, I do not want to walk back out there. I figure I'll see if I can get any more information from Harmony.

I speak low and softly to her, and start by conjuring up the images she'd revealed to me with the dead pony and the little girl.

All I get back is a murky gray color, which to me indicates that Harmony is confused. So, I flash a picture of Melody first in my mind as I lean my forehead against Harmony's head. Then, I try again with the pony. All I get back is that murky gray. "I know it's raining and icky outside, but come on, we were just talking about this yesterday. Have you forgotten already? What gives?" I sense my own desperation, which I try and fight because the last thing I want is for Harmony to think I am frustrated with her. Then, the murky gray switches to a light pink that transitions into a darker pink and evolves into a heart. I laugh. "I love you, too."

"Vivienne?"

I flip around to see Kayla Fairmont just outside the stall. I hadn't heard her come up. "Kayla, hi. I was, um, just talking to Harmony." I can hear my nervous giggle and want to cringe. Of course, people talk to their horses like they do their dogs and cats, but the thing is, whenever I'm caught doing it, I always wonder if I'm revealing something deeper about myself. I have to wonder if anyone might ever detect that I really do talk to horses, and that they talk back.

"I see that. I didn't mean to startle you."

"Oh. I'm fine. I came down to tack up for my lesson. I would imagine that it'll be in the indoor arena . . . considering . . ." I point to the roof.

She smiles. "Actually we are going to have to cancel lessons today. The indoor arena is getting new footing, and it was supposed to be here last week before you all returned. But there was a holdup, and it won't be here until tomorrow."

"Oh. Bummer."

"Yeah. But it'll give you another day to settle in before classes start again tomorrow."

"True," I reply, but I am pretty disappointed. I wanted to ride, and I also wanted to see what I could learn from the horses. Maybe the rain will allow me to do that.

But then, Kayla says, "Hey, it's supposed to really start coming down. You probably want to get inside. There is an extra umbrella in the office. Why don't you get it and go back to your dorm. I'm just here to give Melody her Regu-Mate. We don't allow students to give it."

"Oh. Okay." I figure, as much as I want to continue on my little fact-finding mission, that I'd better do as the headmistress suggests. I get the umbrella and start back to the dorms, feeling surprised that Joel's horse needs to be on hormones. I didn't know any of the horses here were on Regu-Mate, which is used to suppress estrus in mares and keep them from having "mareish" type behavior. In other words, Kayla is giving Melody a hormone shot to keep her from being a bitch. Melody hadn't struck me as being one, but she isn't my mare, so I really don't know. What I do know is that my mom is not a huge fan of giving hormones to horses unless absolutely necessary. My mom tends to be a pretty conservative vet, and I respect that. Heck, I respect my mom completely. However, I don't know Melody's issues, and maybe her behavior merits being on the hormone. I tell myself that Kayla probably knows what she's doing.

Instead of going straight to my room, I decide to see if Tristan and Riley are around. I rap on their door and wait a minute. Tristan opens it and I take a step back. "Oh my God! How did that happen?" I reach out and lightly touch the big black shiner he has.

"You don't want to know," he says and swings the door wider.

I immediately think of his dad and what I've now become aware of, thanks to Sebastian. But, I can't see how Tristan's black eye could have been caused by his dad. He's hundreds of miles away at home.

"He's your knight in shining armor," Riley says, walking into the front room.

"Thank, Ri." Tristan shoots him a look that tells me he's thinking Riley is "dead meat."

"Someone better start talking." I plop down on the couch and cross my arms, looking up at Tristan.

Tristan sighs. "Harrison Gregory was saying crap that I didn't like. So, I lit into him, and he got one punch in." Tristan points to the eye.

"What the hell?" I ask, not liking the sound of any of this.

Riley sits down next to me. "It was like this. Harrison was making remarks that were about you and sex, and Tristan beat the crap out of him."

"Is that true?" I ask.

Tristan nods.

I stand up. "I don't care what some guy like Harrison Gregory thinks. He's a total tool."

"Well, I care," Tristan replies. "No one is allowed to talk that way about you. Not if I am around to hear it. I think after last night that it won't happen again."

I sit back down, not sure if I should be elated that Tristan cares so much about me that he doesn't want anyone to talk smack, or if I should be pissed off over the fact that he lost his temper so badly that he could have really gotten into trouble. I decide that being pissed off isn't a good plan, but I do think that we should maybe talk about this a little more. Just not in front of Riley.

I sigh heavily. "I guess I should say thank you, but you really don't need to protect me. I'm good at taking care of myself."

Tristan shakes his head.

"Does it hurt?"

He shrugs. "I'm okay."

I kiss his eye as gently as possible. "I'm sorry."

"Don't be." He takes my hand. "Besides, the night wasn't all a bust. Riley did talk to Joel."

I look over at Riley. "And?"

"And, I apologized for being an ass. Told him that I thought we should give our friendship a try again. No hard feelings and all of that."

"And?" I ask, my curiosity piquing.

"He said that he would think about it."

"That's a start. Right? I mean, I think that is kind of the best-case scenario."

Riley nods. "The best-case scenario would be if he'd said that we were cool, no issues, all good, blah, blah, blah, and meant it."

"I agree. But you do have a jumping-off point now."

"True," Riley says. "Maybe your frenemy plan will work out after all, Vivvie."

"Stranger things have happened." I laugh.

"Right. Well, I'll leave you two alone to make out, or whatever it is you do. I need a shower." Riley smiles at me and winks at Tristan. I roll my eyes at him.

As soon as Riley is out of the room and the door is closed, I think about discussing what happened last night at the bonfire, because I am sure there is more to the story. But before I get a chance, Tristan pulls me in and kisses me, and as usual when this happens, I forget pretty much everything else on my mind and find myself kissing him back. "I'm sorry, Vivvie, about Harrison. But the guy was being really obnoxious and I couldn't take it any longer." He takes the loose strands of hair that have come out of my ponytail and tucks them behind my ears.

I lean him back on the couch and kiss him. For this once, I guess I am okay that he came to my defense.

CHAPTER *fourteen*

he weekend passes and school starts. Martina has been evasive and pretty much on a nonspeaking basis with me, and I have to say it does not feel good at all. I've tried apologizing, but she's not having it. She changed over Christmas break. That much is for sure. I know this thing with her parents has her all wound up, but I thought we were the best of friends. I thought we had the kind of relationship that could easily survive stressful times.

Also, it's not like I was *trying* to piss her off when I didn't warm to the idea of her new older boyfriend. I was really just trying to be a good friend and look out for her best interests. She clearly didn't see it that way, and she's not forgiving or forgetting. It's pretty uncomfortable to be rooming with her now that she really doesn't want to give me the time of day, but all I can do is hope that she'll come around. I'm just going to be patient and keep trying to be nice.

I also am a little frustrated that I haven't found out more from the horses. Maybe there's a full moon and it's putting a curse on me or something. Over the weekend, I only got a few minutes with Sebastian, and just like Harmony did the other day, all he gave me was colors—starting with gray, which I think means he's confused. Then, his color communication turns to red and then yellow. I think it's feedback that he loves Tristan.

Harmony seems as happy as she can be and continues to be all sweet and loving. So, maybe I misread things with her eye. But part of me wonders if the horses are shutting down on me for some reason. It's weird how they've stopped communicating images. The only time I've ever felt shut out before is when I first came to Fairmont and Harmony was not willing to share anything. This is different. These horses were communicating with me so well—and then they stopped all of a sudden. Or is it me? I have to wonder if I am losing *my gift*. I don't know what to think. But I noticed there's a full moon, and I plan to blame it on that.

I am happy, though, that I have not seen anything else in Harmony's eye and her spooked behavior from last week hasn't recurred. Holden and I did finally discuss it further, and since neither of us saw anything in her eye when we checked it, and her behavior is normal, we've decided to wait on having the vet out. It must have just been one of those things.

The other good thing I am happy about, other than my horse's eye looking fine, is that classes have started. Yes, I admit that I am happy to be back at a desk. I'm sort of weird like that—I like school. What can I say? Maybe it's because I come from a mother who values academics. But the truth is that the classes at Fairmont are better than what I had back at home. This place has such a different take on course work, and the teachers are interesting. There's a lot of team building and hands-on learning. I like it.

Besides the honors English class I'm in, I think my favorite extracurricular class is going to be Intro to Equine Veterinary Medicine. I'm looking forward to it since my mom is a vet, and I've always loved going on vet calls with her. The first week out, we only attend our core classes—English, science, math, that sort of stuff. The second week, which we are now into, includes the extracurricular course.

I walk into class, and for the first time since returning to Fairmont, I spot Emily Davenport. There's a seat open next to her. There's another one by that jerk Harrison who got into the fight with Tristan.

I sit down next to Emily. She gives me a halfhearted smile. "Hey," I say.

"Hey."

"Did you just get back here? I haven't seen you yet this week."

"A day ago. Actually brought a horse back from Germany."

"Really?"

"Yes."

"That's great," I say.

She shrugs. "He's a beautiful Holsteiner," Emily says. "A lovely mover. Has to be, because he cost a couple hundred thousand dollars." Emily shakes her head. "I don't mean to sound like a spoiled, sarcastic bitch. I like the horse. He's cool. My mom's behind the purchase as usual. If I seriously have to hear the term *lovely mover* again from her, I might lose it. Like completely lose it. My mother thinks I'll ride him to fame and stardom. I just hope I can live up to her expectations."

"I know she's hard on you, Emily. I'm sorry."

She nods. "Not much I can do about it. And, anyway, she's not the only one. I am not having an easy time with a lot of people at school, either. Let's just say certain girls on campus are making me feel less than welcome."

"I was afraid that would happen," I reply. I feel bad about it because if she hadn't helped me last semester . . . But, it had been the right thing to do. "I want you around," I say.

"Thanks."

"No. Seriously. You should start having lunch with me—with us."

She nods and is about to say something, but then Christian Albright walks into the room and introduces himself as our teacher. I glance at Emily and see that she looks as surprised as I feel. I didn't realize he was the teacher. On my schedule it says that it's supposed to be Dr. Billings, one of the local vets.

"Hi, gang, I'm Mr. Albright. You can call me Christian when we have riding lessons together, but I've been told by my bosses that, in the classroom, you're supposed to call me Mr. Albright. I don't care either way. I know Dr. Billings is scheduled to teach this course, but he was just hired on up at Davis and so I am filling in. I am not a vet, but I do have a lot of knowledge about treating various conditions that may affect your horse. However, we have decided to change the title of this course from Equine Veterinary Medicine to Equine Health Care."

I shift uncomfortably in my chair. Not because of the change in the name of the course, but because of my ongoing suspicions about Christian—um, Mr. Albright—and Kayla.

Over the next fifty minutes, Christian goes over what we can expect to learn this semester in his class, and I have to say it doesn't sound nearly as exciting as veterinary medicine, but I have no choice. I'm in the class. At least it sounds like I'll come out of it with an A. Now *I* sound like the bitchy one, but the syllabus indicates that we will be going over some pretty basic fundamentals, like how to correctly wrap a horse's leg and treat certain common ailments. It's not that interesting for me, because my mom is a vet, who taught me how to do most of this stuff by the time I was about eight years old. Oh well.

At the end of class, he makes an announcement. "I know that some of you will be riding with me, particularly those of you in the upper levels, and I recognize some of your faces here, so I want to share with you some very exciting news. Mrs. Fairmont and I are on the board of governors for the scholastic committee for the Young Equestrians Association, also known as YEA. We have been working hard for the past year to create a single competition event that will bring together the best young riders from around the country. The winners of the event will be awarded a spot at the coveted summer YEA equestrian program at Liberty Farms, where some of the world's best coaches teach. We are talking four-star riders, people. I don't have a complete list yet of coaches, but with this kind of teaching and coaching available, those of you who make it will have some serious opportunities. It could take your riding careers to new levels. This program is for students who have the goal of competing at the highest level out there." He looks at me, as if he knows that my brain is swirling. I so badly want this that I can almost taste it! My goal is to one day go to the Olympics, and not just compete, but win the gold. I've wanted it ever since I was a little girl—ever since I can remember.

"What we have come up with will be known as the Scholastic Championship Event. The chance to participate will be extended to students at the country's top six equestrian academies—including Fairmont, which is the best, of course," he says, giving us a friendly wink. "Any former member of YEA who has gone on to a college or university where the YEA program is supported by an equestrian program will be eligible as well."

Harrison's hand shoots up. "Does that mean we'll get to compete against college kids? I'd love to show them up."

Christian smiles. "Sorry, you won't have that chance. The college students will compete in a separate division. All you kids have to worry about is this: only the top six high school juniors and seniors from each school will qualify to travel to the Kentucky Horse Park in Lexington in April, so the competition will probably be stiff. The qualifications are based on how well you and your horse place at the local events as well as your scholastic achievements. . . ." He clears his throat. "In other words, your grades and behavior. The top six students who qualify will have their entry fees and travel expenses to Kentucky paid for. They will also be the chosen students for the summer program out at Liberty Farms."

I look over at Emily, but she doesn't seem all that interested. My own pulse, on the other hand, is racing. This is a *huge* opportunity for me. I'd dreamed of qualifying for the Young Equestrian Championships back home, but I'd always known that attending them was out of reach. My mom never could have afforded all the travel expenses and entry fees that participants are required to pay. Now that the Fairmonts seemed willing to fund a team, pay all the expenses, and cover tuition for the Liberty Farms summer program, I had a shot. If I went, I'd also get to see the Kentucky Horse Park in Lexington. I'd seen tons of pictures and watched the Rolex on TV countless times. The Rolex is the premier four-star competition in the United States, and it's called the Rolex because the company behind Rolex watches is the main sponsor. My mom and I never miss it, but with a three-day event being narrowed into a succinct time slot on television, it's impossible to see all the details. I have always wanted to go out and see the event, but I've never been lucky enough to do so. It has always, always been one of my dreams to go there—and have the opportunity to ride on the same grounds as my idols, like Phillip Dutton, Mary King, Karen O'Connor, David O'Connor, and Gina Miles. Honestly, going to Lexington is a dream I have never imagined might come true.

I hear my heart pound in my ears and realize I've been holding my breath. I'm so excited I think I might hyperventilate.

The bell rings to signal lunchtime and I grab my books and head for the cafeteria with Emily beside me. I just can't wait to find Tristan and tell him my new goal for the semester. Now everything is going to be about getting to Liberty Farms.

CHAPTER *fifteen*

I walk into the dining hall and almost stop dead in my tracks when I see Joel seated across from Riley at our table. Looks to me as if the talk they had at the bonfire a week ago must have worked. I know Riley has been stressing about it because Joel didn't stop hanging out with the DZ after the bonfire. But I know what I am witnessing, and Joel is definitely at our table, so everything must be good between them. I feel relieved for Riley.

Emily nudges me and says, "I haven't met the new guy yet. He's kind of cute."

"Oh. Yeah." I know—so lame, but really, what am I supposed to say? *He's gay and he's Riley's friend, or more specifically, he's gay and he's Riley's ex?* At a loss, I search the room for Tristan, and as I do, the shock of seeing Joel at our table seems small in comparison to what I see: Martina at the DZ table! What the hell is going on? Am I even on planet Earth at this moment? Martina sees me and gives me a glare. This is ridiculous! I turn away. I am going to have it out with her later back at our room. I'm over this big-time!

"Looks like I've been traded for Martina," Emily says. "What is that all about?"

"No clue," I reply. "Not a single clue." I do have a little clue, actually—our stupid argument the other night.

I have to think about gluing my feet to the ground to prevent myself from running away and down to the barns. I really want to go see Harmony. She's the only one who can help me make any sense of this moment. She really is.

I don't see Tristan anywhere. He helps, too, and I could use his down-to-earth rhetoric right about now.

"Let's get something to eat." I look at Emily. Maybe if I get some food in me I can start thinking rationally about this weird situation. Although who knows if that would help, since nothing about what I'm seeing at the moment makes sense.

I pull a turkey sandwich, an apple, and a drink onto my tray, and make my way over to our table. "Hey, guys," I say, trying to act cool. I sit down next to Riley, and Emily sits down next to Joel and introduces herself. It's the first time I have seen this girl light up ever. Oh no. If she only knew. Great. Just great.

"Have you seen Tristan?"

"No," Riley says.

"I saw him over by his locker earlier. It looked like Lydia had him trapped," Joel says.

Weird just dug its heels in and basically jabbed me with spurs. "Really?"

Neither Emily nor Riley says anything, but I notice they eye each other.

Joel finally says, "What?"

"Tristan and Lydia used to go out," I say.

"Oh. Sorry," Joel replies.

"No. Don't be. It's a free world. They can talk. I'm okay with it."

Riley pinches my knee. He probably can tell that between Martina sitting with the DZ, and me hearing that Lydia was chatting up my boyfriend, who remains nowhere to be seen, I'm feeling just slightly upset. The happy buzz I'd gotten from Christian's announcement earlier is obliterated.

"Did you hear?" Riley says. "Did you hear about the championships?" I know my friend well enough to realize that he is trying to change the subject for my benefit.

"I did." I force a smile as I look again over at the DZ table to see if Lydia has arrived yet—no dice.

"If anyone is going to qualify, it's you, Vivvie," Riley says. His words sound kind of forced. I know he is nervous sitting across from Joel, and I appreciate him trying his hardest to make me feel better, but it isn't quite working. I smile at him, though, knowing he is just wanting to calm my nerves.

"I agree," Emily says.

"Thanks. You know what? I'm not so hungry. I forgot that I left something down at the barn this morning. It's my notebook for my next class." I get up and leave. Riley comes after me.

"You suck at lying," he says.

"I need to find Tristan."

"Stop it, Vivvie. Don't go acting like the jealous g.f. You can trust T. He's into you. Believe me. You are all he talks about. Lydia means nothing to him. She's a parasite, and she probably is just trying to drive him up the wall and, in turn, drive you insane. If you go and hunt him down and she's talking to him, she'll know she's gotten to you. You have to trust in him, and you have to trust in what you two have together. You know the other night when Harrison was giving him the third degree about whether or not he was tapping it . . ."

I frown.

"Sorry. That's just how Harrison put it."

"It's okay," I say. "I know he's a jerk."

"Anyway," Riley continues, "a lot of guys would have stood by and let all the other guys standing around think they were getting, you know . . ."

"I know."

"But instead, Tristan kicked his ass for even implying it. I think that should say something, Vivvie."

"You're right." I take a deep breath. The thing is that Riley is right, and okay, maybe there is a piece of me that feels worried and jealous, but I know what's bugging me is bigger than that. What I am feeling at the moment is protective of Tristan. Sure, he can protect himself from Lydia, but I have not been able to get out of my mind what Sebastian has relayed to me—that Tristan's father beat him up while she stood in the background and watched it all. Granted, Sebastian only wants to give me a myriad of colors these days, so I have not had a real chance to "speak" with him and find out more. But something tells me that Lydia has some information that is putting her in a position to hurt Tristan. It's just my gut telling me this, but I have to trust it.

"Come back to the table. Eat lunch. He'll be here," Riley says.

"Fine. By the way, what's the story with Joel? I thought you'd kind of agreed to disagree and keep distance between you." As much as I want to track down Tristan, I also really do not want Riley to think I am some needy girlfriend who has no concept of the word *trust*. On top of that, it isn't like I can tell him what I think I might know, at least not yet. Besides, what would I say? Um . . . Sebastian told me that Tristan's dad abuses him and that Lydia knows? Oh brother! So, I decide the best way to get my mind off it all is to turn the tables and ask Riley about the situation between him and Joel.

He shrugs. "I don't really know. All he said when he sat down at lunch was, 'Can I eat with you?' Then you showed up."

"Interesting."

"Yeah," he replies.

We head back to the lunch table. Both Emily and Joel look up at me. I smile sheepishly. "Looks like I have my notebook after all." I sit back down and pick at my lunch, thinking about whether or not Tristan is in some kind of serious trouble, and if so, is Lydia Gallagher in some way involved?

CHAPTER *sixteen*

ll I can say is, *Thank God for my horse.* After the confusing afternoon, I was able to go and take a lesson from Kayla. We had a jump lesson because Kayla is now doing both dressage and jumping lessons with us. Christian is only doing the jump lessons. From the schedule I got, it looks like a good rotation throughout the week. Holden's main focus is still only with dressage.

Kayla has a softness about her when she teaches. I think she has a softness in general that reminds me of my mother. She is always very encouraging and that is why I hate the idea so much that something is going on between her and Christian.

I try and tell myself that it really isn't my business at all, and no big deal. I am seventeen years old, and even though I will be considered an adult in less than a year, worrying about what could be going on between Kayla and Christian is far beyond my scope and not what I want to think about. If they are having an affair, I am adult enough at this point in my life to understand that it is ethically wrong. But I'm mainly concerned about what might happen if they get discovered. I know these things don't usually end well. I've watched TV, been in school with friends whose parents had affairs that caused divorces. If that happens, what will happen at Fairmont? Most of the other kids here come from the kind of money that can continue to help them build equestrian careers, regardless. They can afford the best horses. They can afford the best training. My mom can't, and I wouldn't expect her to. So I just hope that my worries are for nothing.

Kayla walks over to me as I am cooling off Harmony. "Good riding today. You two have really grown together. Nice to be in sync, isn't it?"

"It is. Thank you."

She strokes Harmony's neck. I notice that she isn't wearing her wedding ring.

My brain doesn't think before I spit out, "Are you and Holden okay?"

Her eyes grow wide. "Yes. Of course. Why?"

"Um . . . I don't know. I just, gosh, I don't know. I haven't seen the two of you together much lately."

"We're fine, Vivienne. Don't worry about us. We're adults and we can take care of ourselves."

"Okay." Given the tone of her voice, I don't have to read between the lines to know that she is telling me in a nice way to mind my own business. I turn away from her and head back to the barn, feeling a little defeated.

After untacking, putting Harmony away, and then cleaning

my tack, I go back to visit her with a handful of horse treats. She eagerly eats them out of my palm. "You and me, we are going to the championships. At least, we're going to try."

I get a reaction from her that doesn't make sense to me. She shows me a familiar image: it's of feed in her feeder. She'd showed me the same image last semester when she'd colicked before our first major event. There is no color involved. No gray, no pink. This vision is clear again. In a way I am relieved.

"Oh no, you're not colicking, that's impossible." I put my ear up to her gut on the right side and listen. She has good gut sounds, which means her digestive track is moving on that side. I walk around to her left side and do the same thing—good sounds on that side, too. As I listen, she puts off a sense of fear. I take a step back. "What is it?" I ask. "What are you afraid of?" I place my hands where her heart is located and experience a new emotion from her. It's fear, yes, and I have sensed Harmony's fear before— but this time it's different. I can't put my finger on why, exactly. She is not the one who's afraid. My brain races. Is she scared for me? For another person? Another horse? And, the image of the feed— the feed that had made her sick. . . . None of it adds up.

Now a fresh image flashes through my mind: Joel's horse again. "Melody?" I say out loud.

At the name, Harmony's fear visibly intensifies as she lifts her head and her eyes widen. She snorts and weaves. I pat her neck and walk out of her stall and into her run. I look over at Melody standing in the corner. She seems okay as she looks over at me, but she doesn't make a move to come any closer. "Hey, girl. Melody." I kiss to her.

She finally makes her way over to me. I have one more treat in my breeches pocket and I give it to her. Harmony walks out of her stall and comes up behind me.

"Don't be jealous; I'm just trying to find out what's up with your new friend," I say to Harmony.

I reach my hand through the pipe corral and stroke Melody's nose. I want to know if this horse is afraid of something. Harmony seems to think she is. But I can also feel myself holding back. In this weird way, I feel like I am crossing a line, or breaching some code of ethics by trying to get inside Melody's head. She isn't my horse. Not that I haven't ever communicated with horses who aren't my own. I did it plenty when I was out on vet calls with my mom and trying to determine what was wrong with a horse, and I did it with Sebastian. But it wasn't as if I had directly tried to get into his head. The dialogue Sebastian had started with me was voluntary on his end. I never specifically asked him anything about Tristan and his father, until after he showed me that one vision.

Talking to Melody is different. I feel almost like I'm a psychiatrist and she's an underage patient whose parent hasn't exactly given me the permission to treat her.

On the flip side, it isn't like I can go up to Joel and say, "Hey, I read horses' thoughts, minds, and feelings, and your horse seems to be afraid of something. I'm just going to find out what that might be and try to help her through it. Don't worry; I got Harmony past some desperately traumatic stuff last semester. I can do this."

Um . . . yeah . . . something tells me that probably isn't the approach I want to take.

"Hi, Melody girl. New kid on the block. I know what that feels like. Kind of scary, huh?" I tap into my own demons and fears as I continue to stroke the mare's face. I express to her through my words and feelings that sense of fear I want to investigate further, mixed with a sense of compassion and love to put her at ease.

Immediately, she shows me an image. It's a stadium, and just ahead is a jump of about three feet. Hard to say, honestly, how high it is, given that I am trying to make sense of the visual memory the horse is sharing with me. What is clear are the emotions Melody is communicating—all fear and anxiety. The other strange thing is that it's as if Melody is traveling in slow motion toward the jump. It must be due to the fact that it is a memory, or that we haven't had a direct line of communication prior to this.

I realize Melody has a rider with her, a rider as small as a child, but it's all a blur. Then, something happens. I don't know what, but Melody and the rider are on the ground. They're down. I see Melody get up and perceive her fear along with the sense that she can't move faster than slow motion. I see Melody looking at the rider, who seems to be about ten years old. It's a little girl. Melody's feelings are traveling through me—sadness, fear, desperation. And, then there is a blur of others running to them both, and someone leads Melody away. I can't see who it is. She doesn't show me.

I am dizzy and I nearly fall to my knees. I've never experienced this complexity of communication from a horse. Harmony senses this and takes a step closer to me, and the dark, difficult feelings I am getting from Melody are suddenly gone, replaced by a sweet confidence that I recognize is coming from my own horse. I gaze at Harmony in gratitude. It is our bond of love that I sense. I turn again to look at Melody, who blinks her eyes a few times as if she is dizzy, too.

I shake my head to clear it. One thing is for sure: this mare is holding on to something traumatizing. And it obviously has to do with what she has shown me. But what, exactly, does it have to do with her owner, Joel?

I push thoughts of him aside as I think about how I can best help Melody. That's what I do. I help horses.

It would be great if I could just ask Joel what his horse is showing me. But again, I don't want to come off as a lunatic. I will have to do a little more delving, particularly into Joel's background. Luckily, I think I have a few ideas about where I might be able to get a little more information.

CHAPTER *seventeen*

My first idea for delving into Joel's past is to find out what his school records say—at the very least I'll learn a thing or two about his family. But getting into the records office and locating his details presents two dilemmas: first, I am not an administrator, so getting into the office won't be easy; second, I am pretty sure that an efficient and organized director like Kayla Fairmont keeps all the records on a computer. So, since that idea seemed daunting, I move straight on to Plan B—Google.

I sit down at my desk in front of my laptop and type *Joel Parker* into the Google search box. There are more than a few hits. First off, the twentieth governor of New Jersey was named Joel Parker. There is a Joel Parker doctor, a few lawyers, a former NFL player, a researcher, even Joel Parker shoes, and umpteen million Joel Parkers on Facebook. Okay then . . .

My brain ticks and I type in *Joel Parker equestrian*. Aha! I click on the link that reads *Joel Parker wins Junior/A-O Jumper High Classic at Saugerties* and proceed to read an article that gives Joel accolades. Turns out he was not riding Melody when he won the event; he was riding a horse named Major Attitude. It must have been a sweet victory, because he'd won a $10,000 class at sixteen. I pause when I get to the part of the article that mentions his trainer at the time—a woman named Tiffany Ferris. The name is familiar but I can't remember exactly why.

So, naturally, I type her name into the search box. What I see next is jarring and brings back the facts: no wonder I remember the name. Tiffany Ferris had been a well-known jumper trainer back east until her career hit a major bump when she came under suspicion of drugging show ponies to mellow them out for their young riders. There had been some type of investigation, and she'd received some bad press in a few of the major equestrian publications, and she'd of course lost a lot of students. I'd learned all of this from listening to a conversation between my mom and one of her clients over the summer. The upshot, apparently, was that Tiffany Ferris had pretty much lost everything. I didn't think much about it at the time other than that the woman shouldn't have been drugging ponies at all. My mom had brought me up believing that if you need to drug a horse to be able to get a kid on it, then it isn't the right horse for the kid to be on.

I look up from my computer and out the window of my room— green grass, horses, and beyond the horizon, the Pacific. Then it hits me! The dead pony. Melody and Joel had been in close proximity to Tiffany Ferris, and must have even been at the barn when that pony died. The pony that turned Tiffany into a villain in the horse world and ruined her career.

So, putting two and two together, I have to assume that Joel trained at some point with this woman—an interesting piece of information to say the least. On top of that, I now remembered that Tiffany Ferris had trained at Liberty Farms in Virginia, a horse farm that is right near Virginia Beach, the town that Joel and Riley are from.

I linked back to the search engine and found articles about the pony-drugging scandal, and a lawsuit that was filed against Tiffany; however, it was later dropped. But, what I discover on the next page, I find even more interesting. "O. M. G." A small article in the local paper out of Virginia Beach with an announcement for the wedding of Tiffany Ferris and defense attorney Jason Parker. I study the photo and there is no mistaking it—Jason Parker is Joel's father. Tiffany Ferris as a new stepmother? No wonder the kid wanted to leave home.

I push back from my computer, feeling somewhat satisfied that I've got a good lead now on what may be troubling Joel. Fear doesn't play into his problems as far as I can tell, but anger sure might. Why wouldn't Joel be angry, given that his dad recently left the family to take up with his former scandal-tainted horse trainer?

The door opens and in walks my mute roomie. "Hey," I say as cheerfully as I can muster.

"Hey," Martina mutters back.

I stand and face her, blocking her from getting past me and going into the bedroom. "Please stop this. Please. I am sorry if you felt judged by me the other night. I'm sorry for being a jerk. I just want the best for you. That's all. Really. You're my friend. Can we please start talking and go back to being friends?"

That's when she pulls an envelope out of her bag and hands it to me. She bursts into tears. "I'm scared, Vivvie, and I'm sorry."

I open the envelope and read the note inside:

I know where you live. I know how to reach you if I want to. I also know your parents have a secret they are keeping from you.

CHAPTER *eighteen*

W hat?" I say. I am totally confused. First, I am confused that Martina has received this and what it might mean, and second, I am confused by her sudden and rapid U-turn back into the friend zone. Not that I'm unhappy about it. I am happy, actually. Just confused. I think we have some talking to do. "Sit down. Hang on." I get a Coke out of our fridge for Martina and grab water for myself.

I hand it to her. "Thanks," she says. "I'm sorry. I'm sorry I was being such a bitch. It's just, well, I did think you were being overly critical, and honestly, I really do like this guy. Then, out of the blue, Shannon Burton invited me to sit at the DZ table, and I did it because I wanted to upset you. How stupid is that? It was so uncomfortable sitting with them, and then I got this note in my locker . . . and . . ." She dissolves into tears.

"Slow down. It's all okay. It is. Really. I get it." I don't completely, but for now I'm going with it. "Let's not worry about what happened between us. We're good. I don't want to lose you as my friend."

A part of me screams that if I am her friend, I need to continue to be truthful with her and share my opinion that going out with a twenty-two-year-old guy just isn't right. But, I can't. Especially now. That will have to wait because what is most important at this moment is the threatening note she's received. I read it again. "This was in your locker?"

"Yes."

"It has to be a joke then. A sick and stupid one, but still a joke." She looks at me. "Why do you think it's a joke?"

"Because it would be very hard for anyone who didn't work here, or go to school here, to get on campus, find your locker, and put that in there."

"I guess that's true."

"Plus, they would have to know your combination, or have the brain power to figure it out. Have you ever given anyone your locker combo?"

"No." She shook her head. "Why would they write this? What if it's whoever is stalking my mom?"

"I doubt that. I really do. Why would that person try to come after you? Your mom is the one who will get them the big coverage in the tabloids. I think we have to chalk the note up to the fact that people can be mean, and stupid, and totally ridiculous."

"I guess they can. Still, what should I do?" she asks.

"Maybe tell Kayla and Holden."

"What good will that do? Besides, I feel like the less attention I bring to myself, the better. Just like Lydia loves to get to you, someone is trying to get to me, and I won't let them."

I give her a hug. "I think that's a good way to play it. You're smart and you're right."

Still, as much as I think Martina's tactic of just going about her business and not letting anything get to her is a good idea, I have some concerns. Martina's question about who would place the note in her locker is bothering me, too, not to mention why they'd do it. I believe what I said about people being mean and ridiculous and all of that. However, I can't help thinking that there is something more to this than just a cruel joke. And as much as I do not want to go there, I can't totally embrace the idea of Martina's new love interest, even now that our friendship is back on. I can't discount the fact that he is so much older. Also, he's a groom, which typically means that he doesn't come from money, and if he did, I seriously doubt it's the kind of money that Martina comes from. I have to wonder if the new guy has some ulterior motive for being involved with my friend. I am thinking the worst, I know, but what if I'm right? Could he be trying to blackmail her family in some way? I don't know. But the fact that I am even thinking this way really, really bugs me.

CHAPTER *nineteen*

aybe because I have so many difficult classes, I find myself almost a month into the second semester without even really noticing how much time has already gone by. There are days when I feel like I live my life in this tight vacuum, and it is one filled with a high level of intensity. A lot of my time after riding is taken up by homework—and spending time with Tristan. His class load is not easy, either, so we have to make time during the week to hang out. We try and do our homework together, but that doesn't always lead to being productive as much as it leads to making out, unless Riley or Martina is around.

I am a little bit at a loss where Tristan is concerned. I have a boyfriend who I care so deeply about that it kind of scares me, but what scares me even more is that I am afraid he has a secret he isn't telling me. I think it's a deep and dark one, too, and I don't know how to ask him about it. I am sure his father is abusive, and I am also pretty sure that Lydia knows about it. I don't know what the deal is with his mother, but that mystery adds to the complexity of it all, and I just wish I could find a way to bring it up and get it out in the open.

Sebastian hasn't given me much more on the few occasions I've tried to communicate with him. Once, he did that dark gray thing with me again that then turns to red, and then yellow. A different time, he once again brought forth the original images that I'd seen the month before. They weren't as clear this time though—almost as if the horse's memory had faded.

I've had the same experience in trying to communicate with Melody. Her favorite color in the scheme of things appears to be blue—turquoise blue, to be exact. She's also only shown me repeatedly what she already shared before—except each time she communicates, it gets hazier. It makes me wonder whether as horses move forward in time, their memories fade.

I never thought they did. I've been around Dean for most of my life, and he always presents things clearly. Then again, Dean's memories were and are many of my memories, so I suppose it's tough for me to base my communication skills with horses on the experiences I've had with the horse I grew up with.

Then, there is Harmony, who is all about pink hearts and butterflies except for the occasions when she replays the scene from when she colicked last semester. I have to say that it's sort of confusing for me, but with as much as I have on my plate these days, I don't have nearly as much time as I would like, or need, to psychoanalyze all of the horses—mine included.

So as another week comes to a close I decide to take Harmony out on a trail ride. I asked Tristan to come along, but he can't because he hasn't finished his English paper on *The Crucible*. I finished my paper yesterday and I feel bad that he isn't done. Riley has a physics test to study for, and Martina is off with Raul. At this point, I've met him twice. He does seem nice and he does seem really into her. She hasn't gotten any more of those prank letters, so I don't exactly know what to think. Maybe I am just too suspicious—period. I have decided that the best course for me where Martina and Raul are concerned is to keep quiet. I don't want to lose my friend again.

I considered asking Emily to go out with us, but her new horse from Germany is a lot to handle. I feel bad for her, because if anyone wanted to know what I think, I'd say he's just too much horse for the poor girl. She seems even more miserable than usual, except for when she is around Joel. She is so obviously crushing on the guy that it makes me feel even worse for her. So many secrets. I know way too much for my own good. First, the horses tell me more than I want to know, and then go all vague on me. Riley has revealed things to me that I can't talk about. Martina and Raul . . . I can't tell anyone. Then, of course, there's the dark secret that I sense lies buried within my boyfriend's head. It's a lot to try and sort out.

So yes, a trail ride does sound good. But the rule at Fairmont is that you can't go out alone. Even though I haven't really gotten to know Joel, despite the fact that he sits at our lunch table, I figure I'll ask him. I wish I could let go of my curiosity—the part of me that wants to find out everyone's little secrets, but I can't help myself. So naturally I want to see what I can learn about Joel. Maybe if we go out on a trail ride, he will say something that will help me understand what his horse is so afraid of.

When I call his cell phone, he picks up immediately. Within a minute, he's agreed to take the trail ride, saying he can't look at his computer screen any longer and will come to the barn right away.

Within a half hour, we are out on the trail.

"It's kind of cute the way my mare is named Harmony and yours is Melody," I say.

"I hadn't thought of that. But it is, isn't it?" he replied. "What's her show name?"

"Harmonious Movement."

"Nice. Melody's is Unchained Melody."

"Ah. After the song?"

"You know it?" he asks.

"My grandma is a huge Righteous Brothers fan."

"Funny. My old trainer was as well." He frowns.

We ride out onto the track that surrounds the cross-country course so that we can do some galloping.

"I think it's really good the way you and Riley have made amends," I say once we are out on the track.

"Yeah. You know, I had planned on shining him. I thought that would be best for the both of us, but it didn't take me long to figure out that the DZ, as you call them—which by the way is so perfect—totally defines them."

"Thank you." I smile.

"Yeah, well, their most intellectual conversation seems to be about which designer purse is better than the other. And the guys who hang with them are not much better. I also kind of thought that since Riley was actually reaching out that maybe I should go ahead and reach back. It's good I did. We've let all of that stuff go and can be friends again. It's good."

"And you don't have any plans to ever say anything about . . ."

"Riley?" He pauses and takes a minute before continuing. At first I'm not sure he's going to answer me. "No. I had something happen to me not that long ago, Vivienne, and it kind of changed me. It made me realize that I wanted to be a better person."

"Oh?" This has piqued my curiosity.

"Yeah. My dad, I think I told you, left us."

"You did."

"He left my mom for my old trainer."

"Oh." I act like I hadn't gone all Google detective on him, and had no idea about any of this.

"It's worse than that, though. See, this woman who I used to ride with, she drugged ponies back home. I was a working student, so I knew she was doing it. She did it for the little kids so that the ponies would be calm enough for them to ride. It was stupid."

"Yeah. Not cool."

"She got found out though, and had some problems because of it. You might have even seen her name in the papers—Tiffany Ferris? She lost her students, some credibility, and most of her money. Luckily for her, she already had my dad. She and my dad had been having an affair for a year, and when she hit bottom, he left us and came to her rescue. He now has himself a new family. And, Tiffany has been able to open up a new training facility with, of course, my dad's money, while my mom is in a huge battle to get what he owes her. After almost twenty years of marriage, I am sure he owes my mother."

"I'm sorry."

"Nothing to be sorry about. He is who he is, and I am working on accepting it. I have to keep him in my life in some minor way at least. He pays my way here."

I think about my own father for a second—not any longer than that.

"The one good thing that came out of it is that I got Melody. I had a horse before her named Major—Major Attitude. He was awesome. He is awesome, but he belonged to Tiffany. God, I almost want to puke when I say her name. Anyway, she sold Major, trying to pocket as much money as she could, but this is a woman who loves to spend money so it didn't last—thus, the appeal of my father, no doubt. I started riding Melody not long after she sold Major. I loved her, and my dad bought her for me—which is maybe the only decent thing I think my dad has ever done for me. Before, she had belonged to a little girl who took a bad spill on her." He looks away for a few seconds. "And the kid was scared, so she didn't want to ride again."

The picture becomes very clear to me now, as to what Melody had shown me—the girl that had fallen off her. I still don't understand why Melody had fallen herself, and don't know if I ever will, but at least I think I can try to convey to the horse that the fall was not her fault, and that I am sure the girl had loved her, and that Joel loves her very much and won't leave her. Maybe if she can understand this, it will ease whatever fears she has.

As we continue with our ride and our conversation turns a bit lighter, I realize that Joel is pretty cool. I like him. Trauma does change people. It just does. It did me, and although I am not happy that Joel has gone through the things he has, it's good that he is choosing to be a better person because of them, rather than a bitter, mean one.

After the ride with Joel, I get back to the room and Martina is there, curling her hair. "Hi," I say.

"Oh hey. I'm glad you're back. Raul has two extra tickets to the Black Eyed Peas tonight. I just talked to Tristan, and he said that you guys are totally in. Get dressed, girlfriend."

"Uh. Oh. Okay."

"You do want to go, don't you?"

I nod. "Of course. I just am surprised. I'll take a shower." I turn the shower on, and okay, I am excited to go to the concert, but I still have my reservations about this Raul dude. Whatever. I guess if anything, I might get a better read on him and find out if he is the real deal or the schmuck I have been thinking he might be. I'll soon find out.

CHAPTER *twenty*

I'm a big enough person to admit when I am wrong, which turns out to be a good thing. After spending more time with Raul, it's obvious that I have been completely off base about him.

He is totally nice and funny, and his cuteness factor can't be ignored. He isn't Tristan, of course, but he's definitely pretty great and clearly 100 percent into Martina. After the concert, which was amazing, our energy is pumping. Even though we know we should go back to school, we stop in at the Malibu Café and order some dessert. We did get permission from Kayla to come in an hour after curfew, after all. Tristan and I share a brownie à la mode.

Chocolate syrup is stuck on the side of his lip and I laugh as I wipe it off. "Messy."

He whispers in my ear, "You were supposed to lick it off."

I shake my head and whisper back, "Stop it. You are really bad."

"I know," he replies.

I smile at Martina and Raul, who are in their own world, sharing a brownie à la mode of their own. It's almost too perfect.

"You guys met over my horse, I hear," I say to Raul.

"Yeah. I saw her—your horse, then I saw her. . . ." He leans his head on Martina's shoulder for a second and smiles. "And that was all it took."

"Stop," Martina giggles.

"It's true," Raul says. "It might sound stupid, but when I saw you it was really like I had been smacked upside the head. It was like I knew you from somewhere else. I can't explain it. Thing is, I was afraid, because let's be honest, we do come from different worlds. And, we can't get around it that I am four years older."

Tristan takes my hand. I wait with bated breath to hear what Raul might say next. "But, I kept seeing her, and we kept talking, and finally I had to ask her out."

When he smiles as he says this, I realize it's impossible not to like the guy. Tristan and Raul get into a football conversation and find serious common ground. Before we realize it, it's almost past the time when we told Kayla we would be back. Finally, once we get back to our room, I bring up the subject of Raul with Martina.

"Seems like the real deal," I say.

"You surprised?"

"Don't get mad at me, but yes. He is older."

"I know, but he is respectful, and he's actually taken an oath not to have sex before marriage."

"What?"

She nods. "Yeah. It's just something he feels is the right thing to do, and it's made it easier for me in some ways because, despite his age, there's no pressure. But, in other ways, it's harder because I am curious. I kind of, well, I just . . ."

"I know," I agree. "I'm curious, too, but waiting is not a bad thing. I don't think so, anyway." I don't know whether now is the time to tell her about the condom I saw in her purse, but then I finally decide that honesty is the best way to go here. "I have to tell you something."

"Yeah?"

I tell her about dropping her purse and what came out of it, and how totally stunned I was to see the condom because I thought we shared everything.

She laughs. "Oh, that."

"Yeah. That."

"My cousins came down over Christmas and the oldest one was getting married. She passed those out as a gag at the bridal shower my mom hosted. My little cousin who is thirteen freaked out and shoved it in my purse. I totally forgot that it was there. I found it, of course, and you know what . . . I didn't throw it away because . . . because I have thought about it with Raul. But he's pretty certain that he wants to wait. Are you and Tristan waiting?"

"I don't know. We haven't talked about it."

"You haven't?"

"No. It's not like we've been together forever yet."

"Yet!" She laughs. "Guess what?"

"What?"

"My parents met Raul and they approve." She claps her hands together like a little girl.

"Really? That's great." I mean it. I like the guy, and he apparently isn't into Martina just to get into her pants, and her parents approve . . . so, well, I made an early judgment call that was off base. I can admit when I'm wrong. Thing is, after hanging out with him tonight, I really can't imagine him doing anything to harm Martina and her family.

Martina and I haven't gotten any closer to figuring out who put the note in her locker, but it hasn't happened again, and fortunately for Martina and her family, the tabloids have laid off, and her parents have been able to work out their differences. Things appear as normal as they possibly could be, considering that Martina is from one of the biggest celeb families around and that a huge scandal was on the horizon.

We say good night because it is really late, and I have one last thought and feeling as I fall asleep. It is relief.

Not only have I made a friend in Joel today, and also discovered I was wrong about Raul, but Lydia Gallagher has not given me any sort of grief whatsoever in the past two weeks. In fact, she seems to not even notice Tristan or me. I still think she is a sneaky little bitch, but she has put all of her focus on a new love interest.

Yep! I am happy as I can be. Lydia has found a new victim to pounce on, and he appears to be loving it—Harrison Gregory. They are always canoodling and playing grab ass with each other. To tell you that I am not a little relieved would be a bold-faced lie. In fact, saying a little relieved is a lie. It's a massively huge load off to know her attention is diverted from me.

I guess I was wrong when I came back from break and thought that second semester might rival first semester at Fairmont.

I have no complaints, and the drama appears to be officially dead around here.

I think.

I hope.

PART II

the missing

CHAPTER *twenty-one*

Time actually does go by quickly, and as unbelievable as it may sound, months pass by without any drama around campus. Then April arrives, and I know the drama will pick up—because the big day is right around the corner when all the students will know who has been chosen to go to the championships in Lexington and score a spot at the Liberty Farms summer program in Virginia, with all expenses paid.

But for all that I can't wait to find out if I'll make the list, I still have one very deep internal conflict going on from January, and it is finding the answer to this question: is my boyfriend safe when he goes home to see his family? The thing is, if Tristan were to tell me that he isn't safe, what would I do with that? Tell my mom? Tell Holden and Kayla? Try to help him on my own?

Things are really great between us, and I want to just ask him about it, but at the same time I have begun to question whether or not the information I receive from the horses is entirely accurate. The last few months of communication between my equine friends and me feels off in some way that I can't put my finger on. I've even wondered if maybe the horses have imaginations like people do, and that what I'd perceived was the equivalent of anxious day-dreams. They obviously feel things, they know things, they understand things. Could they also imagine things that aren't accurate, but are instead a projection of their own insecurities? I don't have those answers.

However, finally the day comes when I know I will be receiving an answer—to the big question I've been waiting for.

I know that I have a good chance. I've qualified well in the events that Harmony and I have been in over the past couple of months. Of the five events we competed in, we always placed in the top five, and we won two of them. If heading to Lexington was only based on event scores, then I know I'd be in. However, the school has other criteria as well—they want the qualification to be about more than just riding. Grades count, as does a vote by all of the instructors. I am hopeful that I am "in." If so, it means that in two weeks I will be heading to Lexington with Harmony. My grades are good, and I think my attitude is always pretty positive—at least around my teachers, anyway. But, my mom is really practical and has always taught me not to "count my chickens," so I've been tempering my hopes. There are quite a few students on campus who could qualify for the championships.

I'm hugely relieved when the bell rings and I can escape my last class, which is math and not my favorite. I bolt out of the room and head over to where Tristan's class is letting out. As I approach his classroom, I spot him walking out the door with Lydia at his side. They're laughing and chatting it up. I feel myself freeze. I am so not good with seeing them act so cozy!

I walk a little bit faster and catch right up to them. The look on Tristan's face is one of surprise. The look on Lydia's is one of amusement. The look on mine, I am sure, is not either of those emotions.

"Hi, Vivienne," she says.

I put on my best fake smile and cough out, "Hello."

"Going to see the standings? See if you made the team?" she asks.

"Actually, yes I am. Aren't you?"

Just then, Harrison shouts to Lydia, "Hey, babe, wait up!"

A minute later she's sliding in under his arm and gazing up at him with those blue eyes shrouded in lush eyelashes. "I'll be there in a few," Lydia says, snuggling even closer to Harrison. "I'm sure I'm on the team, though. Good luck."

Tristan then puts his arm around me. We start walking, heading toward the information bulletin board where the team list is supposed to be posted within minutes. "How was class?" Tristan asks.

"Good. Fine. From the looks of it, not nearly as good as your class."

He gives me a funny look. "What do you mean?"

"Nothing." I shake my head and try to let it go.

"No. What do you mean by that?" he insists, which he probably shouldn't have.

"What I mean is that I just saw you and Lydia laughing it up, your eyes all over each other as you walked out of class just now!"

"C'mon, Vivvie. Don't be ridiculous."

"I'm sorry. You're right. Seeing you two laughing and, I don't know . . . I don't like it. It's been nice the past couple of months that she's been going out with Harrison. She's backed off giving me a hard time, and she seems to have stopped trying to flirt with you. I was surprised to see you acting so chummy, that's all. But you're right. I have way more important things to be concerned about than Lydia." I laugh a little nervously. I do have more important things than thinking about Lydia . . . like . . . whether or not I'll make the team!

Tristan removes his arm from my shoulder and grabs my hand. We are walking past the physics lab and he opens the door and drags me in. He takes hold of my shoulders and backs me against the wall. As I stare into his eyes, an electrical charge shoots through every part of me and then he starts to kiss me. It's this long, luscious, very tempting kiss. I can feel his hand on the back of my head, his fingers intertwined in my hair, and there is this rush that travels through me that makes me feel almost as if I can't breathe, but not in a panicky, bad way. It's a floating, sinking, lovely feeling. The teacher's desk is next to us, and Tristan picks me up and sets me down on it.

"There," he says, looking into my eyes. "Do you have any more concerns or questions about me and Lydia?"

I shake my head and can barely hear my voice as I utter, "No."

He takes my face in his hands and tilts it up toward him where he now gently kisses my lips. "We'd better go before we get in trouble in more ways than one."

"Okay."

We walk out of the lab. I know I have a stupid grin on my face, but I can't remove it. I don't even want to try.

He tightens his grip on my hand as we reach the bulletin board. There is a small gathering in the area. I spot Riley and Joel, along with Emily, and a few of the DZ. Lydia is not in attendance. And, I look around wondering where Martina is. She said that she'd be here.

Riley is standing in front of the board, and when he turns around, he grins and points first at me and then at Tristan. He walks through the other students and over to us. "Looks almost like a dream team," he says.

"Who made it?" I squeal.

"Obviously the three of us . . ."

Joel comes over to us now and finishes detailing the list. "Me, Martina, and Lydia." He frowns.

Riley was right. Sounds like a dream team minus one. Oh well, I suppose I can deal with her for a few days. At least I will have my friends with me. I glance over at Emily, who appears distraught. I excuse myself from the guys and go over to her. "You okay?" I ask.

"Just great. My mom is going to kill me."

I lower my voice so that only she can hear. I have seen Emily's mom in action and she's horrible. "First off, I think you should have made the team. You've had a great year, and we all know you're an honor student."

"Right, well, I know what my mom will say. She'll say that I didn't get chosen because of my attitude. She'll say that I didn't want it badly enough, and you know what? She is probably right." Her eyes water. "At least I'm an alternate. Maybe she'll be somewhat pleased with that." She shakes her head. "Sure. Who am I kidding?"

"I am so sorry, Emily."

"It's okay. It is. She'll ground me for the summer and who knows what else. I really don't even care anymore."

"Have you ever thought about telling her that it's not your dream to be a top rider, it's hers? That instead you want to be a vet someday? If I was your mom and found out that your goal in life is to become a veterinarian, I would be thrilled."

She laughs sadly. "No." She sighs. "My mother wouldn't find that remotely noble. As she would say, *Not very challenging, Emily.*"

"Do you really care what she thinks?" I ask. "Does she know what it even takes to become a large animal vet? My mom did years of school, then an internship. It's not easy at all."

Emily looks down and when she looks back at me, she says, "Yes. I actually do care what she thinks. Don't take offense, but my mom would consider a job as a veterinarian beneath her daughter. She sees it as practically menial. It's not high-class enough for her. She just doesn't consider it on par with her social level."

Tristan calls after me. I tell him to hang on a sec. "That's your mom, and not you. Eventually, Emily, you will have to lay it on the line for her, if you ever want to live life on your terms."

"Yeah. You're probably right. Easier said than done."

"Viv?" Tristan calls out again.

"Go, Vivienne," Emily says. "You should celebrate. Congrats."

"Thank you. I wish I had an answer that would work for you. If there is anything that I can do for you, please . . ."

"I'm fine. I promise that I am fine." She turns and walks away.

And, that is the Emily that I have come to know. She can be sweet and caring, then sullen and surly, and from where I sit, it all revolves around her mother.

As I walk back over to Tristan and Riley, I have this sinking feeling that Emily is far from fine. But I have no clue what to do about it.

CHAPTER *twenty-two*

Iburst through the door of our room and yell out, "Martina! We made it!"

I pause to catch my breath. I ran all the way here because I'm so excited to share the news with her that both of us were chosen to compete at the horse park in Lexington. I still can't believe that in less than a month we will all be in Kentucky.

It takes only a few seconds for me to realize she isn't there.

I walk into our bedroom and see that she has once again been obsessing over that stupid rag *The Hollywood Scene*. The latest copy is sitting on her bed. I pick it up. "Oh no," I say out loud as I read the front page. *More Secrets for the Martín and Lunes Family . . .*

I sit down at the edge of Martina's bed and read the article with a sense of shock. This can't be true. It just can't be. I read it again:

Lies, secrets, affairs and an adoption. Did Erika Martín and Rodrigo Lunes adopt their daughter, Martina, and never tell her the truth? A source close to the family has come forward and revealed that Martina Lunes is actually adopted. Her biological mother was paid a substantial amount of hush money. As further investigations ensue, questions arise as to whether or not Rodrigo Lunes is Martina's biological father and had an affair with Martina's biological mother. Or, as our sources suggest, did the family adopt a baby from a homeless teenager 17 years ago?

Scandal has been an issue of late in the Lunes household as Erika Martín is rumored to be seen around town in intimate situations with Lee Ocean, the producer of the vampire hit series, "Family Bites".

Rodrigo Lunes is reportedly on location in Buenos Aires for his new film, "Vineyard Secret", and has been seen dining with the young starlet Johanna Franz. Seems there are plenty of secrets the family has been keeping.

One can hope that for young Martina Lunes's sake, the truth comes out quickly and as painlessly as possible.

I crumple up the tabloid and throw it against the wall. A wave of sympathy for Martina washes over me. I immediately dial her number but she doesn't answer. I text her and ten minutes, then more, tick past with no reply. I have no idea what to think, or do, for that matter, but I know that I have to do something.

CHAPTER *twenty-three*

This should be one of the happiest days of my life. I am that much closer to my dream. My horse and I are going to Lexington to compete and then will spend the summer in Virginia training at Liberty Farms. The tremendous possibilities that alone presents should be enough to keep me going. But all I can do is worry about Martina.

It's almost eleven at night, and there's still no sign of her and she isn't answering her phone. For hours, Tristan and Riley kept me company, but they finally had to go back to their room because we have a 10:30 p.m. curfew on school nights. They promise to call me if they hear anything.

My big dilemma is that I don't know if I should tell Kayla or Holden that Martina is MIA. If she's just out blowing off steam, I'll get her in trouble if I report that she's off campus past curfew. She could be kicked off the Young Equestrians Team. Yet I just don't like that she hasn't answered my calls *at all*. I could call her mom, but I don't even have her number.

I sit down at the computer and decide that since I don't know what to do, I can work on the paper I have due in equine health next week. I get a couple of pages done and decide that I need a diagram of the horse's digestive system. I go to Google's home page and type what I am looking for in the search engine. I find it and print it. Then I do what I do a lot—I get distracted and start surfing the web—and my first stop is to check the news for the day.

That is when I see the headline: *Celebrity Couple's Teen Goes Missing.* The story just went live two minutes ago. It includes a photo of Martina.

As I am trying to wrap my brain around it, there is a loud knock at my door.

I open it to see Kayla and Holden Fairmont, Martina's mom, and two guys who I can immediately tell are detectives. I've watched my fair share of cop shows, and I have to say, the real-life versions look the same as the ones on TV.

"Hi, Vivienne," Holden says. "We are sorry to bother you, but we have some questions. I'd like to introduce Detectives Develin and Marsh."

"Hello," I reply, trying to suppress the fear in my voice.

"Vivienne," says Martina's mother in a calm voice. I'm struck by her long dark hair and beautiful olive complexion that makes her light-green eyes stand out—it's obvious that she's been crying. "Did you know Martina was gone?"

"She wasn't here when I got back from checking the board to see who qualified for the team. I was so excited to tell her we'll be going together! But . . ." I walk into my room and bring back the tabloid. "This was here." I hand it to her mom.

"Oh no," she says. "I was afraid of this."

"I tried calling but didn't get an answer. I texted her, too."

"Why didn't you come to us?" Kayla asks.

I shrug. "I thought that she needed some space. I really thought she was okay and needed to go and be alone."

Her mother tosses up her hands.

One of the cops, the one with so much dark hair on his head that I am trying to figure out if it's real, says, "We believe that Martina has been abducted, and we need to ask you some questions in private." He glances at Martina's mother.

My stomach drops. "I don't understand," I say. "Abducted?"

"Vivienne isn't a suspect, is she?" Kayla asks.

"No," the detective replies. "But she does live with her and may have information that she doesn't even realize is helpful. But we need to speak with her alone."

I shake my head because I don't like this at all and because I can't believe what they are saying to me.

"Since Vivienne is under eighteen, and she isn't a suspect, I think we should be in here while you question her," Holden says. "We are the school's administrators."

Big Hair looks to the other guy, who is almost completely bald and tall and skinny, too. The bald guy nods his head, and I feel a little bit of relief. At least I can have some comforting faces around me during the ordeal.

"What about me?" Martina's mom asks.

"I think you will need to wait outside, Ms. Martín."

"But this is my daughter we are talking about!"

Baldy speaks in a quiet tone to her and then leads her out of my room.

Big Hair turns to me and says, "Tell me what you know about Raul Torres."

"He's a good guy. He's a groom here and Martina's boyfriend. Why? He didn't take her. He wouldn't do that. Where would they even go?"

"He was with her, though, when she was taken," the cop says. "He is the one who reported her missing."

"What?"

"Yes. Do you know if she talks to any other guys off campus?" he asks.

"No way. She's totally into Raul. She's got a tight-knit group of friends. Martina is a good girl. And I guarantee that Raul would never harm her."

The cop continues to grill me in this vein for an hour. He asks me what I know about her schedule. He asks me if she has issues with anyone on campus. He asks me what she's told me about her family . . . and on . . . and on. By the time he's finished with me, I feel like I have completely betrayed my friend. In front of Kayla and Holden, I have told the police things that Martina and I promised never to share with anyone else—like how she used to be jealous of her mom when she was thirteen. I had to tell. What else was I supposed to say when the actual question they asked me was, "Has Martina ever mentioned being jealous of her mother?"

If I were the type to curse, I'd be swearing a blue streak right now. It's after midnight before I finally get under the covers, and all I can think about is where my friend might be. Who has her? And is she okay?

CHAPTER *twenty-four*

I jolt awake at about 6:00 a.m., amazed that I was able to sleep at all. Eager to find out if there are any more stories about Martina, I start boiling water for a strong cup of tea and turn on my computer.

Sure enough, there are fresh details. What I read online says that Martina was last seen on a surveillance camera just outside a bowling alley, where the footage showed her getting into a van. The video was too grainy to get a license plate, but the police had been able to determine that the girl was Martina and the van was silver.

I'm surprised when I read that she had been inside the bowling alley with Raul initially, but left and got into the van when he'd gone up to the snack bar. The article stated that Raul said that Martina had been upset with her parents. The article then went on to say that *The Hollywood Scene* had printed a very sensational piece about the family with claims being made that Martina may have been adopted and never informed of the truth, and that both of Martina's parents were involved in extramarital affairs.

I feel really sick to my stomach reading all of this.

The news is saying there is much speculation about what might have happened to Martina Lunes, and that it is widely believed that she knew the person who she left with in the van. In addition, the reports imply that she most likely ran away because she believed the derogatory information that was being spread about the family, and wanted to escape and clear her head. And maybe even make her parents suffer.

That part I do not buy. For Martina to do something like that is so out of character for her. Or is it? When I expressed my doubts about Raul in January, she'd gone bananas on me, and didn't speak to me for almost a week. I would have never thought her capable of that, either. Maybe I am wrong in this case. But my gut says that I am not. I think I have to trust that.

After my last class, I make it my mission to go find Raul. I know that I'm on limited time here because I have to be tacked up and in the arena in an hour. I know the implications of being late, especially with the championships approaching. I probably should let the police do the detecting. But I also know from being raised by someone who is analytical in the extreme that sometimes the experts miss the obvious. Since I am far from being an expert, I might be exactly the right person to try and find out more.

Thankfully, it doesn't take me long to locate Raul. He's with Martina's horse, giving him a bath. If he really did have nothing to do with her disappearance, then he's probably going through something similar to me, probably worse. After all, he is the one who was with Martina when she was taken, and he's her boyfriend.

"Hey, Raul," I say.

He turns off the water spigot and the hose dies down. Jetson stands patiently in the wash rack. "Hi, Vivienne." Raul glances at me while taking the scraper to Jetson and scraping off the excess water.

"Giving a bath, I see." I don't know what I should say. I feel horribly awkward and can't think of a worse type of situation to be in.

"Yeah. I want him clean for when Martina comes back. I'll be doing Harmony for you if you'd like. She's on my schedule today."

"I have a lesson, so I'll rinse her when I'm done."

He looks down. "Sorry. I should have gotten to her earlier. I'm not getting my work done as quickly as usual today."

"It's fine. I understand. I really do."

He nods.

Finally, I decide to address the elephant in the room head on. "Hey, I know you've probably been questioned to death, and I am sure talking to the police and Martina's parents hasn't been easy."

"No. It hasn't. I had to face her mother. Her father is on his way back from the movie set in Buenos Aires. I'm scared he's going to come see me, too. But I really don't know what happened to her."

I frown as I recall the article and its insinuation that Mr. Lunes was unfaithful to his wife with the actress Johanna Franz. Is that gossip really what sent my friend over the edge and into some stranger's car? I still am having a hard time understanding what Martina is thinking.

"I had nothing to do with her going missing, Vivienne. I know a lot of people don't believe that because here I am, the lowly groom, and she is who she is, but I really care for her and it's driving me crazy not knowing what has happened to her. I'm just relieved that the Fairmonts believe me. I can't lose this job. I am the sole provider for my family. My dad isn't in the picture. My mom is severely diabetic and can't work, and I have a little sister to care for."

"That is a lot to carry."

He looks away from me.

"I admire what you're doing for your family. And, I believe that you didn't have anything to do with Martina being abducted."

"Thank you," he replies.

"I hate to ask you to talk more about Martina now that she's gone, but I feel a little desperate and I want to do something. I'm kind of good at piecing puzzles together and obviously this is a big one. Can you tell me in detail what happened yesterday when she disappeared?"

"You going all cop on us, huh?"

"No. Maybe. Yes. I don't know. I just want to help."

"I'm sorry," he replies. "Sure. I can tell you, but I don't know how it will help." He unhooks Jetson from the cross-ties. "He's due on the grass, if you want to walk and talk."

"Great."

We lead Martina's horse out of the barn and make our way down to the pastures. "As you probably know, after Martina read that tabloid article, she called me," Raul says. "She was upset."

"Right."

"I came and picked her up because she said she needed to get away. We talked and we drove."

"What did you talk about?"

"What do you think?" he asked. "We talked about the article and if it was true. We talked about whether it was possible that her parents had been lying to her for all of this time, and if it did turn out to be true, how she should handle it."

"What did you tell her?"

"I told her that no matter what, her parents love her. That they have acted like her true parents because they raised her. End of story. I told her that if they kept the truth from her maybe they did so because they're so well known in Hollywood and around the world. Everyone knows who her family is. I tried to make her see why they might have done this. I also told her the most important thing she needed to do was visit with her mom and talk it out with her. I offered to drive her."

"She said that she needed to think, and then she said that she needed not to think. That she wanted to go and do something fun."

"That's when you wound up at the bowling alley?" He looks a little surprised, and I feel very Nancy Drew that I have this piece of information.

"Yeah. I like to bowl and I got Martina into it, and it's what we do for fun." He looks away as if embarrassed. We make it to the pasture gate. He opens it and lets Jetson off the lead and turns him loose. The horse runs and plays for a few minutes and then quickly does the obligatory roll on the fresh grass. Then he stands up and goes directly to do the other obligatory thing that horses do on grass—eat.

"I like bowling, too," I say. "My friends back home and I used to go all the time." A quick memory flashes through my mind of Austen being his silly self and purposefully wearing bowling shoes three times bigger than his actual shoe size. I realize with a pang how much I'd always loved his sense of humor and the way he seemed to feel free from other people's opinions. "Yeah. I have had some good times bowling."

"Cool." He leans both arms on the pasture fence and stares out at Jetson. "I wish I knew what happened. I wish I could tell you why she left the alley but I can't. It's like I told the police, I asked her if she wanted something to drink or eat. She said that she wanted nachos and a Coke. I needed to use the restroom first and, after that, I went to the snack bar and ordered. I thought she was waiting. But as we all have heard by now, she wasn't, she was leaving. I saw the footage from the surveillance camera outside the bowling alley that shows her getting into that silver van."

He's clearly distraught and I reach out and pat his shoulder.

"At least from what I've read, it doesn't seem like she was pulled into the car against her will. It doesn't look like she was threatened in any way. She just got in."

"Maybe the guy had a gun," he replies.

"Maybe, but I really don't think Martina would just get into a van, even if a guy had a gun trained on her. She's tough and smart." I shake my head. "Maybe someone was threatening her mom, or her dad, and she wanted to find out more."

"I don't think so. She isn't five, and she wouldn't fall for that." He shakes his head hopelessly.

"There is another possibility," I say.

"What?"

"That the driver was someone she knew."

"Like who?" he asks. "You think another guy?"

I shrug. "I don't know. Has she ever mentioned any friends she had who didn't go to Fairmont?"

"No. I think she was pretty sheltered by her parents. She only ever mentioned you and the crew you hang out with."

I nod. "Right, well, to me, she only talks about you."

I'm glad that at least this brings a smile to his sad face.

"I wonder, though, if maybe there is someone we don't know, a secret friend she has who she went to hang out with. So she could have some time to think."

"She was pretty much calmed down by the time I asked her if she wanted a Coke. She'd decided that talking to her mom was a decent idea. I can't see her deciding to just take off. I can't see her leaving me and going with someone else. At the least, given her mood, it seems like she would have told me."

"I agree, but when people feel desperate they do desperate things. Maybe she wasn't as okay with all of it as you thought. Did she take any phone calls when you were out together?"

"No. In fact, she turned off her phone because she didn't want to take calls from her parents or anyone."

"She didn't answer my texts. The whole situation is weird." I look at my watch and see that if I don't get a move on, I'll be late for my lesson. "I've gotta run. Maybe we can grab a coffee tomorrow and see if we can't come up with any other ideas. Call me, please, if you hear anything at all."

"Okay. Sounds good." He looks miserable and kind of scared.

"It'll be okay. It will. She'll come home."

He looks away and I say good-bye. He holds up a hand and tries to smile, but I know this is eating him up. We just have to find Martina.

CHAPTER *twenty-five*

"V ivienne, come here, please."

It's Christian and we have been having my jump lesson, which I will admit is not going so well. It has nothing to do with Harmony. My head is just not in the game. I know that. I am tense and I'm holding onto her face, meaning my contact on the reins is too heavy, and I know it. Yet she's totally taking care of me and jumping regardless. I've dropped her one too many times in front of the fence. My timing is off, and all she is trying to do is make up for it and please me. I have begun to really understand this horse—almost as much as I understand my Dean boy back home, and I know that in time I will understand Harmony just as well as I do my gelding. What's clear about my mare is that she wants to make me happy. She wants to please, and she has been trying to do this for the past forty minutes during this lesson, and I am completely letting her down.

We walk over to Christian, who is standing next to the oxer in the middle of the jump arena. We had been doing a triple bounce exercise, and then a small course. None of it had worked out so far.

When Harmony comes to a halt near Christian, he places a hand on her neck and looks up at me, his blue eyes squinting in the sunlight. "I'm sorry about Martina," he says.

As he says it, I feel this surge of emotion go through me, and tears spring to my eyes. I haven't cried yet over this, and I am not sure why I want to right now. I believe that she is coming back. I really do, but it's been a full day now, and there is this part of me that is completely freaking out.

"I know what it feels like to lose someone I love. You know that," he says.

I think of how his fiancée, Dr. Miller, was murdered last fall, and I nod my head.

"But, I want you to remember that Martina is not lost yet. The police believe they will find her and that she will be fine. You have to believe that, too. There are a few reasons why you need to believe it. The first is that she is your friend and you care about her. You have to have faith in a situation like this. The second reason is purely about you."

"What? I don't think I understand." I weave my fingers through Harmony's short silver mane.

"You have been given a major opportunity, Vivienne. Huge. It is something you have worked for, and it is something that you deserve. Going to the horse park in Lexington to compete in the championships is a stepping stone to your ultimate goal." I must look at him in surprise because he says, "Yep, I know about your Olympic dreams. Kayla and I have spoken about it."

The mention of him and Kayla discussing my dreams is in one sense flattering, and in another it's kind of distressing, because it reminds me of my suspicions about the two of them. The idea of their affair—which could potentially lead to an implosion of the Fairmonts' marriage and, who knows, possibly the demise of the school they started together—bothers me. A lot. "Oh." That is all I can muster. Lame. But that's it.

"And, you are on your way. I believe it. Kayla believes it. Holden believes it. But if you allow the world to get in your way, and it will, it will constantly try, then you won't be able to make it, kiddo."

I must give him a funny look, because I really don't entirely understand. Don't we live in the world? I mean, how do you not allow it to be a part of who you are?

"What I mean by all of this is that you are one of the most talented young equestrians that I have ever come across. You have a major and bright future ahead of you, and if you let the negative things in life disrupt your focus, your goal will become harder to achieve, possibly even unattainable. Today is a perfect example. Let's face it. Your riding today was way below par. You can't be perfect every day, but you don't want to make a habit of riding poorly. Sure, there are some rotten things going on. I can completely understand how Martina's disappearance is messing with you. But, you have to always keep your eye on the ball. Keep your focus on your dreams, kiddo, and you will go far. I promise you that."

All I do is smile and nod. I agree with what he's saying and understand wholeheartedly. But, my friend is missing, and if all I do is focus on my dreams and goals, well then . . . what kind of human being does that make me?

In this very moment, I simply do not have the answers.

Yep. For once I don't have any answer, right or wrong.

CHAPTER *twenty-six*

Tristan has left two messages on my phone and both of them start with, "Hey, baby, where are you?"

I have not been answering because I have been thinking, and God knows that boy can distract me pretty much like nothing else.

The third time he calls, I pick up. "I'm sorry," I say. "I had a lesson with Christian and it didn't go so well. Then, I came back and took a shower."

"You and a bad lesson with Christian is not good. At all. You in a shower . . . that sounds very good."

"Tristan!" I feel myself heat up and I am sure I'm blushing.

"I'm sorry, but I'm just being honest."

"And, honesty is a good thing." God, I am so bad at this flirting thing, and I am so bad at knowing where the two of us are headed. I am not stupid. I'm seventeen. Girls my age have sex all the time. Girls a lot younger than me have sex all the time. And, trust me, there is this part of me—a big part of me—that is super curious and kind of into it. Then, there is this other part of me that is so scared to take that big of a step and commit to one person in that way. I think Tristan is the right kind of guy, but that doesn't make such a major decision seem any easier.

My thoughts about having sex are interrupted as Christian's words from the jump lesson run through my head. Is this situation with Tristan the kind of thing Christian's talking about? The kind of distraction that can take me out of the game?

"Earth to Vivienne," says Tristan.

"Oh yeah, I'm here," I say.

"You want to meet me in the cafeteria and have some dinner? We could go and see the movie after. It might help take your mind off Martina and everything else."

Tonight is movie night, and we always go to movie night. Tonight is actually *Silver Linings Playbook*, and it's junior and senior night only because of the R rating on the movie. Normally, I would say 100 percent—absolutely. But tonight, I really want to try and sort out what may have happened to Martina, and I am going to need some peace and quiet to do it. However, one must always eat.

"Tell you what, I am game for dinner. But I might have to skip the movie. I didn't sleep at all last night, and I'm hoping to get some sleep tonight. I'm sorry."

"Oh. Okay. So, how about dinner in fifteen minutes?"

I can hear the disappointment in his voice. But I have to do this. I just have to. "I'll be there." I hang up the phone and go into overdrive on trying to make myself as presentable as possible as I am still in breeches and my polo. I finally decide to just say, *Screw it*. It is not getting better than this. I will wear what I have on. I wet my hair and slick it straight back in a ponytail and then spray some hairspray on it, hoping that I don't smell like helmet head. Helmet head is awful—it smells like a mixture of sour sweat and horse. Sorry. Just is what it is.

I wash my hands, freshen up with a face wipe, and then reapply some blush, mascara, and lip gloss. Yep. Good as it is going to get. I take another look in the mirror and realize that the hair looks totally hideous. It really does. I find my Fairmont Academy cap and place it on my head. Oh yes—so attractive. Unfortunately, I am out of time.

Walking up to the cafeteria, it hits me: I told Tristan that I showered after my lesson. There's no way he'll believe that when he gets a look at me, not to mention a whiff. It's embarrassing, but I have no choice but to be honest about my little white lie.

I make it to the cafeteria and spot Tristan. I smile, not in the *I am so happy to see you* way, but in the, *Oh my God, I am completely mortified* way.

"Hi," he says as he kisses my cheek. "Nice attire."

"I know. I've got some explaining to do," I reply.

He shrugs and looks at me as if to say, *Okay*.

"Okay, here's the deal. I did have a rotten lesson with Christian. It wasn't him, or my horse . . . it was me. I have been distracted over Martina's disappearance, and everything else. After the lesson, I sort of checked out. My brain was on how and why . . . and what happened to our friend. You do care about what happened to our friend . . . don't you?"

"Of course I do," he says. "But don't you think you're obsessing a little?"

"I'm sorry. It's just that I can't pretend to ignore the situation like everyone else. Martina is gone, and she may be in serious danger."

"She may be. But I doubt it. I think she is with someone she knows. Why would anyone get into the car of someone that they don't know?"

"She could have been threatened. We don't know. We don't know what happened to her." I realize that I am sounding nearly hysterical right now.

Tristan reaches out and touches my shoulder. "I know that she is one of your best friends, but, baby, you can be naïve. I think that Martina is with some guy right now. Hanging out. Dealing with her stuff. I really do."

I take a deep breath. I look at Tristan. He looks amused as he smiles. I sigh.

"I don't think that is the case," I say, my voice trembling with the effort of remaining calm, "but I will take a step back and consider your point of view."

He pauses. "That is very mature of you, Vivienne Taylor."

Really?! Really! Is he trying to get to me? "Thank you." I try and say it as sweetly as I possibly can, but I sort of want to smack him upside the head.

"Let's get something to eat and try and move on. Okay? I get why you told me you showered. You felt pressured and you wanted an easy excuse. And, you know what—it's fine. Plus, I liked the visual. But, you can always tell me the truth. I wouldn't have cared."

"You're not mad at me?"

"Nope. Let's eat."

We both get the lasagna for dinner. As we put the food on our trays, I try hard to take his advice about Martina and stop worrying so much. We sit down and he asks me what I'd like to drink. I tell him an iced tea would be good.

As I watch him go up to get our drinks, I see Lydia making a beeline for my boyfriend. I'd been so absorbed in our conversation I hadn't even noticed her. What the hell does she want from him at this point? The sight of her just makes me sick.

I get up and go over to them. "Hi, Lydia," I say. Of course her makeup is perfect. Her long blonde hair is curled, and she is wearing a nearly see-through white blouse. Why does this girl always look like she just stepped out of the pages of a Victoria's Secret catalog? It makes me that much more self-conscious of the way I am looking right now.

"Hello, Vivienne." She gives me a disapproving once-over.

"Where's Harrison?" I ask.

"Oh, he's putting his horse up. He had a lesson. I'm hoping he makes it to the movie. You guys are going, aren't you?" She directs this at Tristan.

"Yeah," he says.

"I might," I reply.

Lydia's expression is amused. I am sure that I look disgusted.

"You can always sit with me, T, if Vivienne can't make it."

"Thanks," he mutters.

"I decided I want lemonade instead of iced tea," I say.

"Oh, okay." Tristan fills up my glass with lemonade.

"Hope you can make it, Vivienne," Lydia says as we walk away with our drinks.

When we sit down, I look at him and say, "What is it with her?"

He sighs and looks down at his dinner. He finally says, "Vivienne, there is something that you should know about Lydia."

My stomach sinks. I don't like the sound of this at all. "Okay," I reply.

"I can't tell you everything because I don't ever want you to get hurt."

I definitely do not like the sound of this. "I don't understand."

"When Lydia and I went out, I told her things about my family that I wish I hadn't. What she knows could cause us a lot of problems, and if she talks to the wrong—or should I say the right person—about these things, it would be very bad."

I swallow hard, and my mind is racing. "I really do not understand, Tristan. I mean, what could you have told her that could cause us problems?"

I think I know, of course, given the communication I got from Sebastian, but I'm not sure what to say.

He takes both of my hands now and doesn't look at me. "My father is not a great man, and he has been involved with some illegal things. Lydia knows this. I was stupid enough to tell her the details."

"It's natural to tell people things when we feel close to them. You were going out then, so it's understandable. Now, you can talk to me."

He shakes his head. "I want to. I really do. But I care too much about you. I don't ever want you to be harmed. I am sorry. I can't explain it."

I am confused that he opened up to Lydia about something horrible in his personal life, but won't to me. Ironically, though, I believe him. His secret is obviously so dark that he wants to protect me from learning it. I waver between getting upset with him and throwing my arms around him.

"I'm grateful that you want to protect me, and you're worried about my well-being, but we are a couple. I'm here for you. I understand if you can't talk to me about whatever it is now, but please be open to it. Please understand that I am here for you, and I would never betray you. Ever."

"I know." He kisses my cheek and looks back at his dinner.

We finish eating in silence. I am not upset or angry with him, but I am growing more furious with Lydia every second. Could it be that she's blackmailing Tristan? Would that explain why she's always sidling up to him and making strange comments about his family, to remind him of what she knows? If so, I have to wonder what she is getting in return.

We leave the cafeteria and I turn to Tristan and blurt out, "Is Lydia blackmailing you?"

"No," he replies a little too quickly. "Vivvie, I want to tell you everything, but I have to keep you safe. I need to think about my next move. Okay?"

I nod. But it isn't okay. I'm worried about him. I'm irritated that Lydia knows something about him that I don't. For sure, I am more suspicious than ever of Lydia.

"I don't think I'm going to the movie," he says. "I'm tired, too, and have some stuff to sort out."

"If you need to talk, please call me."

He kisses me, but I notice that it lacks his usual passion. He seems to be in as much of a strange mental space as I am, and since he won't talk to me about what he's hiding about his family, I decide to go to my room and see if there is anything I can do to locate Martina.

CHAPTER *twenty-seven*

Where to start? The first place I can think of to begin looking for clues to Martina's whereabouts is the tabloid articles. I know that Martina tossed most of them, but there's the one I'd crumpled up and thrown against the wall. Now I pick it off the floor and smooth out the pages. I read it and reread it. The thing about her possibly being adopted stands out to me. But, so does the stuff about her parents cheating on each other. Heck, what doesn't stand out as nastiness in this article? Maybe Tristan is right and Martina did find someone to hang out with until she could get herself together.

I don't have any other articles, but I do Google searches of the family name until I have all of the gossip from the past year in front of me—from the mystery stalker who started going after Martina's mom last fall to Martina getting into the van at the bowling alley and disappearing.

I go over the articles a few times, and before I know it, I am blurry eyed and realize that I still have not showered. It's almost eleven o' clock. I jump in the shower and am halfway through washing my hair when it hits me. Sometimes answers come from the most unlikely sources. At least—answers, where I am concerned. I need to go and see Martina's horse. It's possible that Jetson might be able to give me a piece of information. If Martina is like me, she may have actually talked to her horse. We do tell them secrets. Even people who don't have my gift talk to their animals. I think they do, anyway.

I know that I am not supposed to break curfew, but I also realize that late at night is the perfect time for me to try and communicate with Jetson. I throw on sweatpants and a sweatshirt, and pull my wet hair back into a ponytail.

I'm down at the barn in five minutes. The lighting is dim, but I know this place like the back of my hand. I go into Jetson's stall and say, "Hi, big guy."

The first feeling I get from him is sadness, which seems normal since his kid hasn't come to see him in the past day.

I run my hands all over Jetson's face, neck, and back. I stand to the front and then move to the side of him and place a hand on his neck. "I know you are missing Martina," I say. "I am trying to find her and bring her back here." I picture her face in my mind. I picture her walking away and then going out of focus, and I am hoping that he can understand what this means. I am trying to convey to him that we can't find her. That she walked into the dark, so to speak. I don't know how well he can understand this, but I have to start somewhere.

Then, without even making me wait, he does it. He tells me something. He shows me Martina reading something. It's a note. I connect with the image. I can see that the note is on the same type of paper as the note that she found in her locker. Her face looks upset and irritated and I see her stuff the note into the tack tote on the ground next to her.

I pet him and say, "You are a good boy!"

I leave Jetson's stall and turn the combination lock to get into the tack room. Once inside, I open up Martina's trunk and find her tack tote. I rummage through brushes, a bottle of fly spray, a hoof pick—and then, at the bottom of the bag, I find the note.

I read it in the dim lighting.

I have information you want. I will be in touch soon.

I feel a rush of adrenaline as I realize the note could very well lead to whoever took my friend. But the crazy thing is that the person who wrote it had to be someone on campus. To come onto Fairmont's grounds you have to sign in. The gate doesn't just open for anyone. Of course, one of the students or staff could have given someone the gate code, which would have allowed them access to the grounds. But, we notice strangers around here. An unfamiliar face at the barn would surely be reported by the grooms or the students.

I wonder if there are more notes like this that Martina never told me about. One thing I do know: I've been one of the only people who believed that she is in real trouble, and this note proves it.

CHAPTER *twenty-eight*

The next morning, in between second period and my third-period study hall, I decide to go up to the main office to talk to Kayla and Holden.

Hopefully, my thinking is sound, although I'm not sure. I didn't sleep much again, for obvious reasons. Between wondering about Martina's disappearance, worrying about Tristan, and hearing Christian's lecture on achieving my goals echo through my brain, I am pretty much wiped out. But it seems only right to tell Kayla and Holden that Martina was receiving these notes and that someone left one for her in the tack room. Not to mention that at least one note was inside her locker, meaning that someone found out her combination. I had forgotten to tell the detectives about the initial note left in Martina's locker. I'd been pretty overwhelmed when they'd questioned me. I really don't want to talk to the cops again. I think it is best to let the Fairmonts know and they can take it from there.

I open the office door and my jaw about drops to the floor. Guess who is working the front desk?

Um . . . Nate Deacon. Yep, *that* Nate Deacon. The one who runs the "scholarship girl bet" every year, which revolves around betting big money on which guy will be the first to sleep with the new scholarship girl on campus. He'd hoped I'd be his victim fall semester, but I'd managed to turn that on its head.

"Hey, Nate."

He turns toward me from the filing cabinet. "Oh hey, Scholarship. What's up?"

I stare at his beefy face in disgust as my brain works overtime. What is he doing here? And why would anyone trust him to work in the office?

"Not much. I just came by to talk with Holden or Kayla about Martina."

He nods. "Huh. They're not here right now."

I smile. "So, how long have you been working in the office?"

"This is my study hall." He frowns.

"Let me guess, you got busted for something?"

"I might have been a little loud or something."

"Oh, you know, I think I do remember. It was more than you just being loud, wasn't it? Didn't you actually put some poor freshman in the trash can?"

He smirks. "You're a pain in the ass, Scholarship."

"And, you are an ass."

"Thanks. I take that as a compliment," he replies.

"You would probably never do a thing like find out what other students' locker combinations are, would you, Nate?"

He gives me a stone-cold glare. And, I know that I have him.

"What in the hell are you talking about, Scholarship?"

I pull the note from my backpack and hold it up.

"You're a weird chick. What's that?"

"It would so suck for you if I were to go and spill the beans all about your little poker games and your sick bet, wouldn't it?"

"What do you want?"

He looks genuinely scared, and I am so loving this moment that I don't want it to end.

"What do you think I want, Creeper?"

"I have no idea."

"I want to know why you left these notes for Martina."

He doesn't say anything. He just stares at me.

"I'm waiting, Nate. I will tattle just like a little girl if you don't start talking."

He sighs. "Fine. I didn't have anything to do with Martina running away or whatever happened to her. I swear. So, let's just get that straight right off the bat."

I shrug. "Whatever. But you did leave the notes."

"Yeah, I did, but I was being paid to do it."

"Priceless. Keep talking."

"Okay. Like back in January, right after I got busted in study hall and I had to come work in here, some lady showed up saying that she was interested in sending her kid here. Kayla and Holden were out of the office, and I told her that. She asked me all sorts of questions about the school and stuff." He picks up a bottle of water off the desk and takes a long sip.

"Okay, so far you've given me nothing." I look at my watch.

"God, I am getting to it, Scholarship. I answered her questions and then she asked me if I knew Martina. I said that everyone knew everyone around here. She asked me if I liked money and I told her, 'Who doesn't like money?' She asked me if I was good at keeping secrets for money. I told her that I was the best at it."

"Oh, so you can tell the truth sometimes."

"You are so exhausting, Scholarship."

"Sorry. I couldn't help myself." Sometimes these things just seem to come out of my mouth. What can I say? "Continue."

"This lady paid me a lot of cash to leave the notes."

"How much?" I ask.

"A thousand bucks."

I can't even say anything for a solid thirty seconds. My mind is processing all of this and seriously having trouble believing it. "Were there more than two notes?"

"Nope."

"I know when you left the first one. You must have just left this second one the other day. What gives? Did the lady come back here?"

"Nope. She called me."

"She called you?"

"Yes."

"She called you?" I know I am repeating myself, but this is insane. "Do you have her number? And, did she tell you what to write in the notes?"

"Her number comes up as UNKNOWN on my phone and yeah, she told me what to write, genius."

I shake my head. "What does this lady look like?"

"She was hot. Like maybe thirty—you know, a hot cougar type."

"You are so gross. Just tell me what she looked like."

"A chick. I don't know. A hot chick. She had long dark hair and a good body."

"What color eyes? How tall was she?"

"Dude, I don't know. I just noticed the hot bod."

"Don't ever call me dude. Ever. And, if I were you, Nate, I'd start remembering exactly what she looked like, because if I had to put money on it, that 'hot cougar type' is going to be in serious hot water. She has to be the person Martina is with right now—or maybe it's someone associated with her. Either way, she's involved. And, I am pretty sure that you don't want me to go to the police and let them know that you're an accomplice to Martina's abduction."

"Please, your little friend was so not abducted. Everyone knows she got into the car with some guy she's probably banging because she's all stressed out over her parents now that their embarrassing family crap is all over the place. Don't be stupid."

I walk around the desk and I get right into his face. I am not about to let anyone talk like that about Martina, much less the guy who tried to destroy my reputation during my first semester at Fairmont.

"You'd better figure out how to save yourself real quick, because whether or not you grasp it, you could be in some real trouble here."

His eyes narrow as he glares at me.

"I am so not bluffing, Nate."

He sighs. "There is a security camera in here." He points to the corner of the ceiling.

"Ah, well. I think you have a project," I reply.

"What?"

I smile. I have beaten him. "You are going to find the section of video that shows the woman who paid you. And then you are going to give it to me."

He shakes his head. "Seriously? I could get into so much trouble for that."

I almost start laughing. Almost. "Right. Not as much trouble as what you could be in when I fill in Kayla and Holden and Martina's parents on your story. Oh, and let's not forget, I still have other ammunition to use against you. Do you want to try me?"

"You are such a bitch."

"Thanks. I take that as a compliment," I say, echoing his line about being an ass. "I'll see you in the library at seven tonight. You should have what I want by then." I walk out of the office feeling like I'm a little bit closer to finding Martina. And I have to admit that it feels pretty good knowing that I just got the best of Nate Deacon.

CHAPTER *twenty-nine*

Sitting in the library alone, I check the clock on my phone for the third time. It's ten after seven and no Nate as of yet. I crack open my physics book. I'm glad Tristan bought my story that I needed to study by myself. It's kind of true, actually, but waiting for Nate is making me too anxious to concentrate on homework. What if Nate is blowing me off?

He knows the consequences. And, I will follow through on my threats. I was not messing with him when I made them.

"Scholarship."

I look up to see Nate standing over me. He tosses an envelope onto the table.

"I think this is what you were looking for."

I give him my biggest, most sarcastic smile, and say, "I sure hope so. For your sake."

He places his wide freckled hands on the table, and I realize just how tall and strong Nate Deacon is in this moment. "Don't continue to threaten me, Scholarship. I will make your life hell around here. I can do it, you know."

I pull myself up to my full five foot three inches. "Bring it on. I am not afraid of you," I say, but I am shaking on the inside. My heart is pounding like crazy.

And then, a savior shows up. Riley slaps Nate on the shoulder. "Are you bothering Vivienne?"

Nate takes a step back and looks from me to Riley and back at me again. "Nah, man. We were just having a conversation." He holds his arms out wide. "Weren't we, *Vivienne*?"

"Oh yeah, definitely. Just a nice little chat."

"Chat over," Riley says. "Vivienne and I have some studying to do."

Nate raises his eyebrows. "Your boy Tristan know you're *studying* with his chick?"

"Go play mean somewhere else, Deacon," Riley says.

"We good, Scholarship?" Nate says.

"I think we probably are," I reply and sit back down as Nate leaves the library. I sit on my hands for a minute trying to keep Riley from seeing them shake. "I hate that guy," I say.

"What was that all about?" Riley asks.

I stand back up and take his hand. "Come on. I'll show you."

"Vivvie?"

"Trust me. I think I am going to need your help."

"We can get in some trouble for whatever we're about to do, am I right?" he says.

I don't answer.

"Any time Nate Deacon is involved, there's trouble," Riley says. "What kind of serious shit are we getting into here, Vivvie?"

"What's in this envelope here might actually help bring Martina back. It's worth the risk."

He stares at me in silence for a full minute.

"Okay, I'm in," he finally says. "What about Tristan?"

"Maybe we should include him, too."

"Trouble does love company." He laughs.

I point a finger at him and wink and say, "True story."

But when I call Tristan, it goes to voice mail after a few rings.

"Looks like we are the only ones partaking in trouble," I say. "He's not answering."

We get to my room and open the envelope. Inside is a disc. I pop it into my computer and a minute later we are watching a woman talking to Nate inside the office. He was right—she is quite attractive.

"Hey, Vivvie, what are we watching?"

There's no audio and we can't hear what the two are saying, so I fill Riley in as we watch.

"Seriously? Nate took money from this lady to write those notes to Martina?"

"Yeah." Something is bothering me as we watch. As the woman finally leaves the office, I know what it is. "She didn't hand him any cash there, did she?"

Riley shakes his head. "Nope. I didn't see her hand him anything."

I think about this for a minute. "Which means that Nate had

to have met her either off campus or somewhere on campus where they weren't noticed. Come on," I say, standing up.

"Where we going?"

"Where do you think?" I ask.

"To have another *chat* with Nate?"

"Bingo."

CHAPTER *thirty*

"ey, Creeper," I say as Nate opens the door to his room.

"Oh God. What now? I gave you what you wanted. Can't you just shoo like the little fly you are?"

"Funny . . . and no, I can't."

Nate looks at Riley. "Why do you hang out with this chick, man?"

"We didn't come here to trade insults," Riley says. "Vivienne has brought me up-to-date and there's one thing we want to know—when the woman gave you the money."

"What are you guys, like all *CSI* now?"

"Just answer the question," Riley says.

"Fine," Nate says with a shrug of his huge shoulders. "She said to meet her at a coffee shop the next day. But when I got there, some other lady was there to give me the money. Not a hot one, either.

She was kind of short and fat. She sat down across from me at the table I was at and handed me an envelope with the cash in it. Then she left."

"Did she say anything?" I ask.

"Just, 'Here is something for you.'"

"That's it?" Riley asks.

"Yes."

I look at Riley and then back at Nate. I think he is actually being honest. "What coffee shop?" I ask.

"Vick's down in Malibu."

Riley puts out a hand to Nate. "Thanks, man," he says. "Thanks for telling us."

Nate shakes Riley's hand but shoots me a look. "Scholarship, just remember, we're done."

I narrow my eyes at him in disgust.

"What are you thinking?" Riley asks, as we walk away.

"That clearly there are two women involved in making Martina disappear, but why, I don't know. I do think it ties into the tabloid articles, but how and why, I don't know." I repeat myself because sometimes that seems to get my brain working.

"I have an idea," Riley says.

"What's that?"

"Did you see if all of those articles in *The Hollywood Scene* were written by the same reporter?"

I shake my head.

He smiles. "I say we check it out."

I think I know what Riley is thinking, but we need to do a little research first. Back at my room, we look up the articles on the computer. Sure enough, it's the same reporter on all of the stories—a woman named Tracy Sanford.

"Do an image search," Riley says.

I do, and when an image of Tracy Sanford pops up, we both look at each other and simultaneously say, "No way!"

"Field trip?" I ask.

"Yep," he replies.

"We need a car," I say.

"Tristan?"

I nod.

"You gonna tell him why?" he asks.

"I probably should. He's going to ask."

"Yeah. But he's going to think we're nuts."

"Probably," I reply. "Definitely. I mean, if we had been able to bring him in on it from the get-go when I tried calling earlier, but now . . ."

"Tell you what, I'll handle it. We'll go after class tomorrow."

"What are you going to say?" I ask.

"Don't worry about it, Vivvie." He winks at me and leaves my room.

Honestly, sometimes guys drive me insane.

CHAPTER *thirty-one*

The next day at lunch, I notice that Joel is really quiet in his seat at the end of the table. As usual, Emily is trying to get his attention. Tristan is also kind of distant, but he's holding my hand under the table. Lunch passes by in such a subdued atmosphere that it's clear that each of us is in our own world contemplating our own problems. I, for one, am focused on finding Martina.

When the bell signals that lunch is over, Tristan kisses me on the cheek before heading off to class. "You and Riley doing some shopping this afternoon?"

"Uh, yeah." I restrain my eye roll. Couldn't Riley have come up with something better than that lame excuse? "I have something special that I want to get you." That is sort of lame on *my* part, but I can't have Tristan being suspicious about what we are really up to.

"You don't need to do that," he says.

"I know. I want to." I kiss him back and wave, then chase down Riley.

"Shopping?" I say.

"At least I came up with something, and I got us a car, so chill, you little pill."

I frown at him. "Fine."

"Be at the Jeep after school." Riley peels off to head to study hall as I walk toward English class.

When I arrive at Tristan's Jeep at the requested time after school, Riley is already behind the wheel. He says, "Look up the address for *The Hollywood Scene*."

"Look at you. I do believe we have gone all Sherlock and Watson."

"Which one are you?" He laughs.

"Either."

"Okay, then, Watson."

"Actually, it does kind of matter," I reply. "I'm Sherlock."

"Fine. Take all the glory, but if you remember anything, remember that Watson did all of the work. And, Sherlock had that problem with drugs. Was it cocaine or heroin?"

I roll my eyes at him. "You are kind of rotten, you know."

He grins at me. "That's why we are such good friends. Takes one rotten egg to know another one."

"Riley!"

"You know I'm kidding, Vivvie. Now find me an address."

The address for the offices of *The Hollywood Scene* pops up on my phone, and forty-five minutes later once we get through traffic, we are in Hollywood and looking for a parking place. We finally find one.

"How are we going to play this?" Riley asks.

I look at him. "I have no idea. I thought you would have the answers, Watson."

"Not a one."

"Great. Well, here's to winging it," I say as we walk through the glass doors of the tabloid's offices.

A blonde girl who's probably not too much older than Riley and me is behind the reception desk. She looks up from a computer screen. "Hello," she says. "May I help you?"

"I sure hope so. See, my brother and I just took a road trip because we wanted to check out some of the colleges here in LA." I am putting on what I hope sounds like a Midwestern accent because after doing a little research on Tracy Sanford, I learned she is from Chicago originally. "And, Nate here was like, we should stop in and see our second cousin Tracy. And, I really want to be a journalist, and I know she is one, but I couldn't remember where she worked, so we called our mom, who told us, and here we are. Is Tracy Sanford here?"

The receptionist eyes us suspiciously. She is so not buying this.

"What did you say your names were?"

"Oh, tell Tracy that Martina and Nate are here."

"I'll see if she is available." The receptionist picks up the phone and dials an extension.

Riley gives me this shocked look and mouths the names Martina and Nate.

I nod. "She's a tabloid reporter," I whispered to him. "She will figure this out pretty quick, I am sure, and she will be right . . . here."

The woman who Riley and I saw online when we did our research materializes in front of us practically a minute after the receptionist calls and relates our lame story. Yep, it's for real. Tracy Sanford the reporter is the same woman who appears in the video that Nate gave me. "Nate and Martina. Hi. So good to see you. Why don't you come into my office?" she says.

"That would be so great," I say.

Poor Riley looks like he might puke.

"Come on, Nate," I say. "Let's go check out our cousin's office."

"Great."

We follow Tracy back behind some cubicles and down a hall and on into a small corner office. She shuts the door and immediately says, "Who the hell are you two, really? And what the hell do you want?"

"We want to know where Martina Lunes is."

"I have no idea. Who are you? I am going to call the cops."

"I wouldn't do that. We know all about the thousand dollars you paid to Nate Deacon at Fairmont Academy and the notes you had him leave for Martina."

"Nooo. I didn't pay Nate that money, and I had nothing to do with writing the notes to Martina."

"But you know the woman who did, don't you?" Riley says.

"What are you two after?" she asks.

"We want to find Martina," I say. "She's our friend."

"Don't you think you should let the police do that?" she says.

"Funny thing is, I am pretty sure the police would want to hear about the fact that you came to our school and asked all sorts of questions about our friend, then had Nate write the notes and offer to pay him. I am sure they would love that," I say.

"Fine. Here's the deal. I'll tell you what I know if you'll just go away. So, this woman came to me about a year ago and said she had some information about Erika Martín and Rodrigo Lunes. She gave me all sorts of photos of them and told me details about the stalker situation—she was bringing me tabloid gold."

"And she became your source," I say.

"Yes."

"Who is she? Why did you trust her?"

Tracy stares at us. "Look, I'm not writing for the *Los Angeles Times*. I don't exactly do a background check on my sources."

"So you just take the word of anyone who offers you revealing personal photos and a bunch of gossip?" I raise my voice. Riley shoots a look my way and I take a deep breath.

Tracy stares at me as if I am a lunatic. "Pretty much."

"Our friend is missing," I say. "I'm worried she's in trouble. You should be, too."

"Your friend is with some guy. Everyone says so," Tracy Sanford replies.

"You're wrong," Riley says.

"Who is your source?" I ask.

"Why should I tell you?"

"Because it will be your fault if something bad happens to Martina."

She sighs. "God, you're annoying. But fine, I'll tell you. My source was the family's nanny, once upon a time. Says her name is Felicity del Rey. I don't know."

"When did she work for them? Martina is seventeen—it had to have been a long time ago. Why would she still be holding a grudge? If I had to put money on it, I'd say your source is a liar. What was her deal with the notes and money?"

"I can't believe I am telling you guys this."

"You can tell us or I call the police," I say. "Which will really eat up your whole afternoon."

"Sit down," she says and points to the two chairs opposite her desk. Riley and I follow the order. "Tabloid journalism is, how should I put this delicately . . . ? Well, we don't write award-winning journalism. We write stories that sell papers. And, sometimes that means the truth gets slightly exaggerated."

"Slightly?" I say.

"This Felicity del Rey came to me and said she had some dirt on Erika Martín. I didn't have to pay her a ton to spill the details. She seemed to know quite a bit about the family. A lot of her info did check out, so I took her word for it that she had been their nanny at one time. She continued to give me sporadic information over the past year, and she always had photos to back up her stories. Finally, recently, she told me that Martina was not her parents' biological daughter, and that with a little help from me, she could get proof."

"What kind of help did she want from you?" I have a sinking suspicion that I already know.

"She asked me to find a kid at Martina's school who knew her. She told me to tell the kid that I'd pay him or her to drop Martina a note or two. I didn't ask what the notes would say. I just did as Felicity suggested because her stories had already sold a lot of magazines."

I shake my head. "You do realize that those stories are probably the reason that Martina Lunes is missing," I say.

"I am just a writer," she says. "That's all."

"No. You have no soul. You're not a real writer." I really want to punch this lady. "Where does this Felicity live?"

Riley places a hand on my arm.

"I don't know. I didn't get that close to her," Tracy says.

"You must know how to reach her," Riley says. "Don't bullshit us."

She sighs and leans back in her chair. "There is a number that she gave me. It always goes straight to a recording. I leave a message and, within a day or two, she calls me back. Usually, though, she is the one who reaches out first with new information. I've only called her a few times to make sure I have my facts straight."

I laugh at this. "Facts," I say, rolling my eyes. "Please."

I know that I need to get myself in check here, but this woman is on my last nerve. "Here's what you're going to do: call her and set up a meeting."

"I don't think so," she says.

I stand. Riley looks up at me. "Come on. We're out of here. I am sure that the detectives who interviewed me for over an hour about Martina's disappearance would love to hear about this. Especially the way you bribed an underage student to place threatening notes in another student's locker. I am sure there is criminal intent in that."

"Who are you?" she asks again. "I still don't get why you care so much."

"I am Martina's friend and roommate, and that's all you need to know. Now, I will ask you one more time—call Felicity del Rey. Tell her on the voice mail that you want to meet her tomorrow afternoon at Vick's Café in Malibu at 3:00 p.m. Do your best to sound convincing. If she isn't there tomorrow, we are going to the cops."

We walk out of *The Hollywood Scene* offices. I don't turn back to see Tracy Sanford's expression, but I am hopeful that I made an impression on her.

"What do you think?" I ask once we are outside.

"I think you are one scary chick when you want to be. You're a badass, Vivvie."

"No. I'm not. I'm just scared for Martina, and fear brings out the mean side in me."

He laughs. "I wouldn't call that mean. That was pure badass."

CHAPTER *thirty-two*

iley and I stop at Beverly Center, where I buy Tristan a gift and get back to school just after dinner. It's not much, because my mom isn't able to give me a ton of spending money at school. It's just a box of chocolates. But everyone likes chocolate.

I'm happy to say, while curled up on Tristan and Riley's couch, popping a raspberry chocolate truffle into my mouth, that he seems happy with the candy.

"You didn't need to get me anything," he says.

I sit up and cross my legs. "I wanted to. You know I have some things I need to work on within myself, and the big one is the trust thing. I haven't ever gotten over my dad leaving us." I'm thinking that maybe if I open up more to Tristan about my family that he might feel more comfortable talking to me.

"I'm sure you haven't," he says and takes my hands. "Do you ever talk to him?"

"No, but what is really hard is that I do see his picture sometimes in the equestrian magazines. He's well known on the East Coast as a trainer. That part is tough."

"At least he's back east and not teaching here."

"That's true. But I do have a fear that one day I will see him at an event, and if I do, I will have to figure out how to deal with it."

"And you will deal with it. And I will be right there with you," Tristan replies.

"Thank you." I kiss him lightly, but he returns it more intensely. I know that we could get carried away here, but I also know that Riley could walk in any minute.

A moment later, I pull away, laughing a little. "I'm embarrassed to admit this but I'm worried that Riley will bust us," I say, shaking my head.

Tristan laughs, too. "I hear you," he says. "Roommates are a buzz kill. I guess I'll have more chocolate instead." He reaches for the candy box.

"There's something I've been wanting to ask you," I say. "Have you noticed Joel acting weird at all?"

I change the subject because I'm realizing that Tristan is not just going to immediately open up to me. Whatever his secret is, he seems to be pretty terrified of sharing it. All I know so far is that I think his father is abusive—then there's the thing he mentioned about his dad doing something illegal. I'm going to take baby steps. I figure talking about other things is a good way to go for now.

Tristan taps me on the side of my head with his finger. "You are a funny girl. Always curious, always worried about others. No.

I haven't noticed, but I kind of think that Joel always acts a little weird."

"You do? Why?"

"I don't know. He acts like a guy who has something to hide."

"Yeah. He's hiding the truth of who he really is so he can protect Riley. I don't think that's strange. I think it's a good thing."

"Can we go back to making out?" he asks. "I don't want to argue, and I don't want to talk about Joel and Riley."

I smile at him. "Okay. This time, I will let you get your way."

Just as he leans in to kiss me again, Riley comes walking through the door. "Hey. What are you guys up to?" he asks.

"Just hanging out," I reply, probably a little too quickly and in a high-pitched tone.

"Sure. Whatever. I already figured you guys are swapping spit."

"Riley!" we both exclaim at the same time.

"Anyway, check this out," Riley says. "I just spotted Joel and Emily down by the horses, and they were holding hands, and it looked cozy."

"What? But he's . . ." Tristan says.

Riley shrugs. "I don't know what to think, but yeah, it kind of struck me as odd, too."

"Maybe it was a 'just friends' moment," I say.

"Or maybe he isn't gay," Tristan says.

Riley frowns. "It isn't like that, T. You know the saying that leopards don't change their spots? We don't just wake up one day and decide we are gay, and then the next decide that we aren't."

"I'm sorry, man. No offense," Tristan replies.

I sit back on the couch thinking this all over. I have another theory but am not voicing it until I have the chance to confront Joel about it first. My guess is that he's using an innocent Emily to gain Riley's goodwill, and that is just plain wrong.

I stand. "I think I'm going to go and see my horse."

"Vivvie . . ." Tristan replies in a warning tone.

"What? I just want to go and say good night to Harmony. You can join me."

"I've got homework to finish, and you are not a good liar. You may want to say good night to Harmony, but I think we know you have ulterior motives named Joel and Emily."

I shrug. "I'm curious, is all. I'm off. See you tomorrow." I kiss him on the cheek and wave good-bye to Riley.

I'm at the barn in five minutes but I don't see Emily or Joel. I'm annoyed because I must have just missed them. So, instead, I go inside the barn to give Harmony a kiss good night on the nose. It's our routine. She does this thing where I kiss her nose and then she pushes her nose in my face again as if to say that she wants another one. We play this game for a couple of minutes and I laugh. I throw my arms around her neck. "I love you," I say.

I feel the love back for me, but as I hug her I immediately sense her communicating a wave of fear, and once again she starts showing me images that don't make sense to me. She shows me a needle, and a hand, and the neck of a chestnut horse I don't recognize. I see the needle go into the horse's neck. Then I get a glimpse of the horse's face. It's Melody! I'm amazed at how clear the image is since so much of what I've been getting over the past months is vague clouds of color.

"I see," I say. "So you and your friend have been having some more girl talk. Anything else?"

She reaches out with her nose again, but I get no more communication. I give her one last kiss.

Before leaving, a rush of curiosity sends me to Melody's stall to see if she might talk to me, too.

I start by stroking her neck. "You and Harmony have been having some serious talks, haven't you?" Then I deliberately place my hand on the area on her neck where a vet would put a needle. I decide to go easy on her because I don't know this horse like I know my own horses, and I already suspect that she has been traumatized. I start the communication by showing her images of Harmony. Then, I put Joel's image out there and say, "Joel loves you very much. He would never hurt you. But I think that someone did." That's when I picture the needle, and I feel her immediately tense. She gives me back the color blue. The blue quickly fades to gray. Why do the horses keep reverting to colors?

Then, the gray diminishes, and I see a distinctive-looking watch on a man's hand. Melody switches the imagery. I feel like I'm watching a movie pieced together from rapid clips that are hard to understand. They are scenes without sound. She shows me the dead pony again, and then herself and the little girl on the ground.

"Wait a minute," I say. "You were drugged, too." I think that is what she wants to convey. I need to find a way to get across to her that Joel wouldn't do this to her. Again, I try through my imagery and communication to show her Joel and his love for her. But she doesn't relax, and I keep getting the same images over and over like they're on a loop for her.

It hits me that Joel might be the only one who can heal her. This poses a serious question and a problem for me. The question is, should I take a chance and tell Joel my secret and risk him thinking that I am crazy insane? Not to mention risk that he might expose me to everyone? For some reason, I think I can trust Joel. I see the lengths that he has gone to to keep Riley's secret—although if he really is leading Emily on, I think he's going in a bad direction. But still, his horse needs some healing. Melody is hurting, that much is obvious. Questions run through my head. Can I somehow heal her without telling Joel? Or, is it possible for me to teach him how to heal her? It all comes down to whether sharing my so-called gift is a smart thing to do.

The truth is, though, I don't know what is smart at this point. After saying good-bye to the horses, I head back to my room and dive in to the boatload of homework that's waiting for me. Once I'm finished, I climb into bed, send Tristan a good-night text, and then turn off my light. But soon enough, I find that I can't fall asleep. I toss and turn in bed. After a half hour of trying to sleep without luck, I get up and turn on the computer. Something about Tracy Sanford's story is bugging me big-time.

I go to my standby Google search engine and type in *Felicity del Rey* plus *nanny*. I get nothing. Then I type in *Martina Lunes* plus *nanny*, and I do get one little item. It's a small piece from *Today's Star* magazine, which I don't think is even printed any longer. However, here it is on the eternal Internet. It's a page on celebrity "tiny tots." It's from fifteen years ago, so Martina would have been two years old. It shows a photo of Martina as a toddler at the beach in Malibu with a caption, "Little Lunes starlet hits the beach with nanny Isabella Garcia." The picture shows a woman who seems to be in her twenties, short dark hair, a little frumpy, but a big grin on her face as she builds a sand castle with Martina, who is adorably chubby and all smiles.

I spend more time on the Internet and eventually find some interesting articles in a local newspaper based in Hemet, California. They date to seventeen years ago and give me a hunch as to who Martina is with and why.

CHAPTER *thirty-three*

What are we going to say to this Felicity del Rey if she shows up?" Riley asks.

"Oh, we aren't going to say anything," I reply.

"What? I'm confused."

"If this woman does have Martina somewhere, she isn't going to tell us that."

"Probably not," Riley replies.

"We have some good clues as to what the woman looks like. Nate told us that much, at least."

I don't tell Riley that if my hunch turns out to be correct, I'll be able to spot her easily.

"So are we just going to hang out and watch her once she comes in here?" Riley asks.

"Something like that." I take a sip of the Coke that I ordered.

"Vivienne," he says. I can tell from his voice that Riley is growing increasingly frustrated with me. I seem to sometimes have that knack with people. I should probably work on it.

"I'm sorry. So here's the deal. . . ." I stop mid-sentence because I spot who I am sure is the woman calling herself Felicity del Rey—and whose real name is Isabella Garcia. She's short, a bit on the plump side, probably somewhere between thirty-five and forty years old.

"Don't look now," I say, nudging Riley. "But it's her."

I watch the woman look around and then gaze out the large glass windows that face the Pacific Coast Highway.

"What are we going to do?" he asks.

"Just follow my lead."

I watch the waitress take her order. The woman is facing me, and I can tell that she seems a bit tentative and nervous. "Wave the waitress down and order something," I instruct Riley.

The waitress comes back by our table and I order an ice cream sundae. Riley follows suit. Felicity-slash-Isabella checks her phone.

Just as the waitress returns and sets down our desserts, I see Felicity get up, put down a couple of dollars for her coffee, and leave. "Come on."

I toss down enough money to cover the ice cream. "Let's go," I say.

"Hey, I can't even stay for a bite?"

"Really. Really, Riley?"

"Sorry."

We climb into Tristan's Jeep. "She got into that Volkswagen over there—the black one pulling out. Follow her."

Riley clicks his tongue. "Now your master plan is coming into focus for me."

"Is it now? And, what is it?" I ask.

"We are going to follow this lady back to her house, where hopefully, we find Martina."

"Bingo! And that is why you are one of my most favorite people in the entire world, Riley Reed."

"And why is that?"

"Because you know me so well, and you are terribly intelligent."

"Not as well as Tristan. I mean, I don't know you as well as you and he know each other."

I don't respond to that right away. I finally say, "I don't know about that. I think that Tristan is keeping something from me." Heck, I know he is. He's even admitted that he is.

"Oh, Vivvie, you aren't still worried about him flirting with Lydia, are you?"

I sigh. "No, it's not that. There's something else he isn't telling me. And, I do think it has to do with Lydia. Not about him being into her, though, but about her knowing some secret. I've seen them talking a couple of times and it looked kind of tense."

I wonder if Riley can tell I'm fishing here, trying to find out if Tristan has possibly talked to Riley about any of this.

"What you're probably seeing is him blowing her off, and you know how she is. She doesn't like being blown off."

I look out the window as the blue waters of the Pacific roll by. The ocean is calm and peaceful, unlike my nerves at this moment. I finally say the words out loud. I let it out. "Do you think that maybe Tristan has a difficult home life?"

"Don't we all?" Riley says.

"I guess to some degree, but for him, I'm just wondering if maybe he, um, well . . . I think maybe his dad abuses him."

Riley glances sideways at me. "I don't know, Vivvie. That would be a big deal. I can say that when he talks to his dad on the phone, he does sound different."

"What do you mean?" I turn down the radio.

"He sounds nervous and he always leaves the room so I don't overhear."

I sigh.

"You know, though, Vivvie, I don't know how you'll find out the truth if something that awful is happening. That's a hard question to ask someone, even someone who is your boyfriend."

"I know, but I want to help him if I can."

"I think you have to let him be the one to tell you something like that," Riley replies.

"Really? Because what if he gets hurt? Besides, I think he told Lydia at some point. So why can't he tell me? What I do know is that his dad has done something illegal that Tristan refuses to tell me about because he's afraid I could be hurt by knowing it."

"You want to know what I think?"

Riley directs the car from Highway 1 to the 10 East.

"I wouldn't be talking to you about this if I didn't want your opinion," I say.

"I think that you should do as Tristan asked you to do. I think you need to leave it alone and back off. I know for a fact that the guy never cared about Lydia the way he cares about you. So, if he's asking you not to worry about it, or ask him about it, then I think that you need to listen."

"Yeah. Maybe so." I know that he probably has a point, but I can't help feeling like there are answers that I need and want from

Tristan. I am also really afraid of what Lydia knows and how she might use it against him.

"Hey, she's turning right," I say, seeing the woman's blinker start up. We follow her car into a residential area. "Keep a little distance."

We drive slowly down a tree-lined street. The houses are cute, cottage style, like maybe they were built in the 1950s. Their lawns are trim, and many have rose gardens in the front. It's a little slice of serenity in the middle of the big city.

We find a place to park and get out. Riley looks at me and says, "Do you have a plan?"

"I'd like to say that I do, but yet again, I do not."

"No?"

"No." I shake my head. "Just going to wing it. It worked the last time, didn't it?"

"Perfectly," he replies. "Just perfectly."

"Sometimes these things are better off just done on the fly, my friend."

"You're officially nuts. You know that, don't you?"

"Yeah," I answer, knowing that he is right. I probably am a little bit crazy.

We see the woman we have been assuming is Felicity del Rey climb the front porch steps and go inside the house. I'll admit that my nerves are jangling and I can pretty much feel the blood rushing through me.

Riley and I walk up to the porch. I bring my fist up and knock.

A minute later, the door swings open. There stands the woman we've followed here. "I'm sorry," she says. "I don't buy candy bars, or magazines, or whatever it is you kids are selling." She starts to shut the door and I place my hand on it, pushing back. "Excuse me?" she says.

"Hi. I'm Vivienne Taylor and this is Riley Reed."

Her eyes widen just a tad. There's some recognition there, and I spot it. She knows who we are. "Do I know you?"

I smile. "Maybe. I think you do. I at least think you've heard of us."

"No. Sorry. Why should I have?"

"We're friends of Martina Lunes. She's my roommate at Fairmont Academy."

"Okay."

"We know that you are Tracy Sanford's source. Those stories you fed her caused Martina a great deal of pain, and now she's missing—I'm guessing you have something to do with it. Why else would you have given the payout to Nate Deacon to leave those notes for Martina?"

"I don't have anything to do with her going missing. That's all on her parents."

"Really?"

Riley glances at me. The poor guy is as pale as a sheet.

"Is it? Is it really all on her parents? You didn't have any choice at all to go to Tracy Sanford and feed her a bunch of lies about the family?" I say. "You know what I think, Felicity—or, should I say, Isabella? I think that you are Erika Martín's stalker. I think you put this whole thing together. I'm not sure why you did it. My guess is money."

I was figuring that Isabella lived modestly. She didn't seem to have much. I couldn't completely understand why or how she'd given Nate a thousand bucks, but then again, maybe she saw it as a means to an end. The van she'd taken Martina in had obviously been rented because we had just followed her in her Volkswagen bug—unless she had another car or had stolen the van. Heck, she might have even stolen the grand that she paid Nate. Isabella wasn't exactly coming off as sane, and crazy people do crazy things.

I don't have all the answers, but I'm confident that I have some of them. And, I am positive that what I've learned has led me to Martina. I'm not leaving without her.

Isabella stares at me with a stunned expression. "That is not true. You don't know anything . . . uh . . . What did you say your name is?"

"Vivienne Taylor." I chuckle a little and shake my head.

"Miss Taylor, I suggest you and your friend here go on back to school and be a good boy and girl."

"I'd like to do that. I really would. But, I can't."

"Yes, you can." She starts to close the door again, and again I push back, only harder.

"I can, if you send Martina out here and she comes with us."

Now, her eyes really widen. "What? You're crazy."

Riley gives me a glare that says he completely agrees with her.

"I don't think so. See, I enjoy solving little mysteries, especially when my friends are involved. And, I've been delving into you." I feel bad now that I never brought Riley up to speed on what I'd discovered last night—I guess I am a bit of a Sherlock, wanting the glory for myself.

"You would not believe what you can find out with a little ingenuity," I say. "See, I know that you ran away from home in Hemet,

California, and came to LA and got hooked on drugs. Your parents posted all sorts of flyers around your small town to bring you back—even put a notice in the paper. You were, what? Seventeen? Same age as Martina is now. I also know that you gave up a baby for adoption twenty years ago and that you eventually got sober and then became a nanny. You were Martina's nanny when she was a baby." I am guessing at the facts, but I can see from Isabella's stricken face that I'm right.

"Why are you doing this?" she whispers.

"Because I believe that either Martina is here, or you know where she's at. I believe you owe her the truth. I also know that she has two parents who adore her and who are worried sick about her. Martina is not your daughter, Isabella. You've created that in your head. If you're hiding her, what you're doing is against the law."

"Leave. You both need to leave."

That's when I hear a girl's voice come from behind a closed door down the hallway. "Is it true?"

A moment later, Martina steps out where we can see her. I'm guessing that Riley might pass out. Even I feel a little faint.

Isabella nods. "Yes."

Martina looks at me and then Riley. She now stares at the woman who has been sheltering her and who obviously had the hopes of creating some kind of mother-daughter bond with her. Her face is full of disbelief.

"Why would you do this, Izzy? For three days you've been showing me photos of an infant that was supposedly me. You've been telling me that you're my biological mom but you gave me to my parents to raise, so I'd have a better life. But you've known all along that I'm not your daughter. I trusted you. That's why I'm here. I loved you so much as a little girl. I don't understand why you would do this."

Isabella looks dazed. Her eyes have dark circles underneath them.

"You tried to blow my world apart," Martina says. "You told me things that I started to believe." She turns to me and Riley. "Thank you guys so much for finding me. I know you probably hate me, but can I go with you?"

I pull her into a hug, and a minute later, all three of us are outside the house.

"We don't hate you at all," I say.

"Martina," Isabella calls after her, "please, let me explain."

"You've done enough damage," Martina replies and keeps walking.

I sit in the backseat with Martina, who leans her head on my shoulder. Other than an occasional sob from Martina, we drive in silence back to Fairmont.

CHAPTER *thirty-four*

artina sits on her bed facing me. She's waiting for her parents to arrive. She hasn't said a lot because I think she's in a bit of shock. "Why do you think she did what she did? Isabella, I mean. Do you think she really thought I could be her daughter?" she asks me.

"I don't know. But I do know that your mom is your mom. I also think that Isabella is crazy, no matter what."

"Yeah. I think so, too. She wasn't like that when I was a little girl. I loved her and we always had fun together. She stopped working for my family when I started middle school. My mom didn't think I needed a nanny any longer. I just don't understand why she would do this."

"Can I ask you what happened the other day outside the bowling alley? Why did you go with her?"

"I guess I owe you that much," Martina replies. "Well, I actually owe you a lot more than that. Isabella had called me the day before the bowling alley to say that she knew who was stalking my mom. She also said that she couldn't tell me over the phone and didn't want me to say anything to my parents until she knew the facts for sure. She said that she wanted to meet with me. I wasn't sure if I believed her, but remember, she was someone I had known since I was a baby, so I had no real reason not to trust her. Then, the other day—the same day I saw the story that claimed I was probably adopted—she called. She said that she definitely had proof of who my real mom was. She said that I could meet her, and that she would call when she had a date and time. She asked me again not to tell anyone. I wanted to say something to you, but I needed to find out on my own if any of it was true or not. Then, I went to the bowling alley with Raul. I saw her phone number come up on my cell while we were there, and Raul was off getting drinks. I took the call, and she asked where I was. I told her, and she said that she was close by and could meet me out back in a couple of minutes. I figure now that she must have followed Raul and me. I went out there, and she said that she could prove the identity of my real mom. She said that all she needed was for me to get in the van so she could show me. I got in the car. I wanted to call you. I wanted to let Raul know, but she handed me a file folder as soon as I got in, and there were pictures of her with a dark-haired baby girl in the hospital. She showed me my mom's signature and my dad's on some paperwork, and then she claimed to be my real mother. I was shocked, Vivvie. She said that my parents allowed her to be my nanny and that she wanted to die when they fired her when I was twelve. She said the only reason she didn't take them to court and get me back was because she knew they loved me and could give me a rich girl's life."

"Did she explain to you why she was coming for you now? After so many years?"

"She said she wanted me to know now so that when I turned eighteen, I had the option of having a relationship with her. She also said she was very disturbed by all of the events she'd read that were happening between my parents. She said that she wanted to keep me from having to deal with that kind of pain if possible."

"I can understand that, but what I don't get is why you would just believe all of it so easily, and why you would go with her, and on top of that, why you wouldn't let any of us know that you were okay."

"I don't really know." She wipes tears from her face. "I think I sort of snapped. It's not easy at all to have your family's dirty laundry aired all over the place. I didn't know what to believe. I think there was this part of me that wanted to be normal. I wanted to feel normal. I guess I thought if I had a normal mom like her, who lived in a normal house and wasn't some big celebrity, then maybe all my problems would go away."

"Interesting that Isabella struck you as *normal*," I say.

Martina laughs a little. "Yeah, seriously. I guess she was probably the stalker, too."

I'm amazed to realize that my friend with celebrity parents has been so sheltered that she could be this vulnerable and trusting. "I think so. She knew too much about your family and she's pretty twisted."

"The thing is, through all of this, Isabella was really sweet to me, just like when I was little. For those few days I wanted to allow myself to be that normal kid."

"But people were looking for you. We were all worried."

"I know, and I'm sorry. I made a huge mistake, but I was so mixed up. I still am."

I nod and try hard to grasp her point of view, but honestly, I don't completely understand it. "Have you called Raul yet?" I ask.

"No. I need to."

"I can go in the other room if you want me to, so you can call him."

"Okay," she replies.

I walk into our common room and grab a bottle of water from the fridge. I plan to call my mom tonight and just let her know how grateful I am that I was born into a "normal" family. Let me rephrase that—I am the daughter of a normal parent who lives a normal life.

Ah, who am I kidding? What is normal, anyway?

CHAPTER *thirty-five*

I help Martina pack the last of her things. I can't believe that she's leaving. I fight back the tears as she talks on the phone with her mom, who is on her way, along with her dad. She hangs up the phone and turns to me.

She shakes her head. "That was my mom."

"I thought so."

"It's crazy. I mean, Isabella was . . . is crazy. She's the one who has been stalking my mom. She's a fraud. Completely." Tears well in her eyes and, like me, she is fighting them. "My mom says that Isabella confessed to the police. What you said was true. Isabella did run away from home, and she did have a baby twenty years ago and gave it up. Then, she became obsessed with our family when she worked for my parents as my nanny. She's been collecting information on our family ever since my mother let her go, and she became so sick in the head that she really believed that I was her daughter."

"That is crazy."

"Yeah, but I kind of feel sorry for her," Martina replies. "Because, apparently, she tried to locate the baby she gave up, and learned that the girl was killed in a car accident at sixteen. I guess that made her snap."

"Oh my God," I say. "That is awful. Here she had been looking for her long-lost daughter for all of those years, only to discover that she was no longer alive. Meanwhile, the only child she ever did have a maternal relationship with belonged to someone else."

"Exactly. I guess it drove her over the edge. So, she created this lie in her head and convinced me it was true. I mean, my parents really are my real parents."

I walk over to Martina and give her a hug. "I'm sorry that you went through this, and I am really sorry that you have to leave."

She hugs me back. "I know. Me, too. But I will be back. Promise. I wish I could go to Lexington with you, but I think being with my parents now is the right thing to do, and it's what we all need to heal. I can't help but feel like the ground has kind of shifted from under me."

I nod and now I can't help the tears. "You'd better be back," I say.

She's crying, too. "I promise. I will. Now stop it. What you have to do is focus on the championships! You go out there, Vivienne, and kick some ass."

I wipe my face. "I'll try."

"No trying. You do it, and you'd better text me, and e-mail me, and call when you can! I want to hear about it—every single thing."

I swallow the lump in my throat.

A knock on the door signifies that her parents are here. I help them carry her things to their car, and before I know it, I am waving good-bye and watching my friend leave for how long, I don't know. All I know is that good-byes really suck.

CHAPTER *thirty-six*

After Martina's departure, I make a conscious decision: to stop prodding and prying into the lives and minds of both the humans and horses around me. I'm still doing the day-to-day—going to school, hanging with my friends, and spending any extra time I have with Tristan. However, I don't talk to him about his secret and I don't talk to his horse, either. I keep things light, and as much as I hate to admit it, our relationship seems to be feeling far more physical than anything else. I don't mean like we're having sex, or even traveling down that road. I just mean that we seem to make out more than we talk these days. And, it is kind of getting to me because I enjoy talking with him. I think also that if I admit it, I'm hurt by the fact that Lydia was trusted with whatever it is he is hiding, and I haven't been. Wanting to protect me, or not, it still bothers me.

Weeks pass this way with me being ultra focused on working

with Harmony. Christian's words continue to echo through my head—and help me make my goals the first priority.

I'm hoping it all pays off. After weeks of waiting, we are leaving for Lexington in the morning. Emily Davenport has replaced Martina on the team. I don't think Emily is thrilled by this, but she's going with it. I do think she is happy that Joel is on the team. The bad part about that is obvious . . . and it's something I have not confronted Joel about, but it has become apparent around campus that those two have become a thing. I'm also still trying to sort through how I should and can help Joel's horse. But, like I said, my focus for now needs to be on the championships.

I go over my list of what to take for a fourth time and finish packing, feeling excitement course through me. In the morning, our horses will be loaded onto the trailer going to the LA/Ontario Airport where they will then board an airliner specifically designed to transport horses. Our grooms will fly with the horses, and the riders and coaches will fly on a commercial airline out of LAX. I wish I could go with Harmony, though. She means the world to me, and I can't help wondering how she will feel about flying. At least Raul will be with her. After everything that's gone down with Martina, I put in a request that he be my groom on this trip. Typically at events, students have to do their own grooming, but since this is the championships and we are headed to the horse park, the Fairmonts are allowing us each our own groom. I think it will be a good break for Raul, who feels he should let Martina and her family work through everything before he sees her again.

I just finish zipping up my bag when there is a knock on my

door. I open it to see Tristan standing there with a dozen red roses. "What?" I say. "What are these for?"

"What . . . what?" He smiles. "I wanted to give these to you before we leave tomorrow. I know I probably should have done this earlier because we're about to leave and now you'll just have to leave them behind, but I don't care. I wanted you to have them because you mean everything to me. I also want you to know that I'm proud of you. I know you are going out there to win."

"Thank you, but what about you? You're going out to win, too."

"Maybe, but winning doesn't seem quite as important to me right now. What seems important is that I am crazy falling in love with you."

I look at him probably like an idiot for several seconds. I'm rethinking this focus thing because what he has just said is seriously the sweetest thing ever. I mean—really? I'm a little stunned. Our relationship has seemed physical rather than emotional lately, so it's just interesting that now is when he's declaring his love. I can't deny that I have some very strong feelings for Tristan, and I guess I hadn't realized how strong his feelings for me are.

I pull him into my room, set the roses down, and kiss him. How can you not totally make out with a guy who brings you a dozen roses and says some of the sweetest things in the world to you? Right? Right!

His hands are around my waist when he stops kissing me. "What was that for?" he asks.

"For you being you."

He kisses me now and we move farther back into my room. I know I should stop this. But, I don't want to at all.

We are next to my bed, and I am sure he is thinking pretty much what I am thinking as we continue a make-out session that seems to be leading to something else.

"Vivienne?" Tristan says my name.

And, there is another knock on the door. "They'll go away," I say.

The knock comes louder and I hear Holden's voice. "Vivienne?"

"Oh no." I look at Tristan. He's wearing a grin like the Cheshire Cat's from *Alice in Wonderland*, which happens to be one of my all-time favorite Disney movies, even though it's an old one. I wish he could pull a disappearing act like the cat manages.

Instead, Tristan sits down on the couch, and I go to the door after straightening my blouse. "Hi," I say as I open the door.

Holden looks past me at Tristan. "Hey, guys. Ready for tomorrow?"

"Yes," we both reply.

"Good. We do have a problem, Vivienne."

Oh no. I wonder if he can possibly know what Tristan and I were on our way to doing. "We do?"

"Yes. Raul broke his ankle this afternoon. He tripped over a rake on the ground. It's a bummer. What it means is that you will get a new groom for Harmony in Lexington, but you don't have one to fly across country with your horse tomorrow morning. How would you feel about being the one to fly with her?"

"Poor guy, that's awful! Is he okay?" I know what it's like to break an ankle. Mine still has pins in it.

"He'll recover just fine. It wasn't a bad break, but he can't travel tomorrow, and he'd be useless as a groom. What do you think? Want to fly with her?"

"Yeah. Definitely. I don't want her to go alone." I feel horrible for Raul. I'll need to give him a call and just let him know that I'm sorry. I'm sure he's pretty bummed out, too. He'd finally smiled for the first time in days when I asked him if he wanted to groom for me.

"There will be other horses and grooms on Harmony's flight. She'll be in good hands if you decide not to join her, but I know you and how you feel about your horse, so I wanted to give you the option."

"Thank you. I want to go with her."

"Okay. You'll need to be ready to go at five in the morning with the transporter and other grooms. And dress warmly. It's freezing on those planes. Tristan, want to walk back to your room? We all have an early morning and now Vivienne's is extra early."

"Sure." Tristan winks at me and then gives me a kiss on the cheek. "See you in Kentucky, baby."

"Yep. Safe flight."

Holden and Tristan leave, and I am breathless and caught between states of bliss, confusion, numbness, and delirium—yep—all of that.

PART III

the event

CHAPTER *thirty-seven*

The morning—or should I say 5:00 a.m.—comes quickly. I gather my things. Walking out the front doors of our dorm building, I spot Christian in a golf cart in the darkness. "Hey, kid. Thought you might want a lift. I can help with your things. I heard you're flying with the horses."

"I am. Thanks. You're up really early," I say, shivering. It's mid-April but spring mornings this close to the coast are always chilly. It's so early, in fact, that the sun won't be up for almost two more hours.

"I'm always up early, and Holden filled me in on your situation, so I figured that I'd see if I could help you out. You have a warm jacket, don't you?"

"Yeah. It's in my bag there."

"Make sure you get it out. I am sure Holden told you that the plane will be really cold. Here." He hands me a brown paper sack.

"What's this?" I ask.

"Your lunch. The accommodations on board are a bit rugged. I suggest you take a bathroom break before getting on. Also, I have a folding chair for you in the back of the cart."

"Lunch? Thank you. You didn't have to do that, though. That's great, I mean, I really appreciate it. I hadn't even thought about that. Why the folding chair?" I know that I may be talking too much, but sometimes Christian makes me nervous. It's because of what I think is going on between him and Kayla. However, I try hard to keep that out of my mind and just look at the fact that he is here to help Harmony and I handle the trip.

"I made you lunch because you're a good kid, and also because I have faith that this coming week is going to be yours to own. I don't want my star student starving or getting sick. The folding chair is for the plane. You'll be able to sit in front of Harmony's stall with it. It's a small space, but I've done it before. Once the horses are loaded and secure, just set your chair down, open up a good book, snack on some of the food I packed, and before you know it, you'll be in Lexington."

I am not even sure how to respond to this. It is really flattering, but at the same time it does add an element of pressure on top of what I already feel. "Thank you," I finally say, because that is what my mom has taught me—she drilled it into me so it's almost a reflex, and right now with my eyes feeling bleary, I'm glad about that.

"I'll make sure your bags get onto the truck, and I'll let the driver know to help you get them checked through security at the Ontario Airport. You ready for this, Vivienne?"

"I think so."

"Get ready, because this is your time. This is your opportunity to go out there and really shine. You've got what it takes. See you in Lexington," he says as he brings the cart to a stop. "The hauler is already here parked on the backside of the main barn. Grooms should be loading horses any minute, so if you want to get Harmony, you can do so."

I climb out. "Thanks. I will. See you there." I look at him and add, "I really do appreciate this."

"No problem, kid. I am just happy to see this happening for you."

My stomach twists and knots in a way that makes me know I'm both anxious and feeling pure excitement. I can't believe this day is here. I want to call my mom, but realize that she's probably still asleep.

"Hi, baby girl," I say, going into Harmony's stall. She doesn't look exactly pleased that I'm intruding on her sleep, and I think she's also curious if I'm planning on feeding her at this hour. "We have a long day ahead of us." I put her halter on and lead her out of the stall and back behind the barn. Melody is already there with her groom. The horses are being taken to the airport in a semitruck and trailer by a professional hauler. When the Fairmonts decided to make this happen for us, they weren't messing around.

Sebastian is loaded first, then Melody. Next up is Emily's horse, Fleur de Lis, and then Riley's horse, Santos. Then it's our turn, and I walk Harmony up the loading ramp and get her clipped in. There is already a flake of hay in the feeder, which makes her happy as she begins eating. Lydia's horse, Geisha, goes on last. Within fifteen minutes, all the horses are on the trailer, and we are ready to roll out.

An airport shuttle arrives to pick up the grooms and myself and we follow the semi out of the Fairmont grounds. I take my iPod out of my bag, put my headphones on, and lean back listening to a little Justin Timberlake—what can I say? I like my hip-hop.

I am really on my way. *Harmony and I are really on our way.* I doze off until we reach the airport. The sun is barely breaking over the horizon. We drive straight onto the tarmac. Our driver unloads our stuff and it's handed off to someone from security. I'm told it will be scanned and then loaded onto the planes. The truck with the horses pulls directly alongside the airplane. A utility truck pulls in next to the airliner, which has the words *First Class Air Travel* painted across it in red lettering.

The head steward comes down the airplane ramp and introduces himself. "Hi. I'm Joe Pierce." He has dark hair and a kind smile. "I fly horses every day, so I promise this will be easy. First thing to do is lead your horse up the ramp. Then, me and possibly another handler will turn him to the side and back him into his stall. The stalls are set up as each horse comes on board. They will be bedded, and each horse will have its own hay net. This is a Boeing 727 that's specifically equipped to transport these animals. They will never have to touch the tarmac because you will be taking them directly from the truck up the ramp and on board, and it will be done in reverse when we land. This ensures safety for the horse."

I nod to myself, glad to be reassured that he knows about the danger asphalt can pose for horses wearing shoes; it's so slick they can easily slide and get hurt. I remember an episode my mom told me about in which a dressage horse worth several million dollars lost her life because inexperienced handlers unloaded her onto the tarmac and she'd flipped out.

I tune back in to the head steward's words as he continues, "The pilots on board are experienced with flying horses long distances, and they're very sensitive to weather conditions; they'll avoid turbulence as much as possible. The plane holds up to eighteen horses going three wide and six deep. We will be having a full flight as we are taking the Fairmont team of six, and the other twelve stalls will be filled with racehorses returning to Lexington. You can set a chair out in front of your horse and travel with him. However, if the plane does run into turbulence, you will be asked to take your jump seats. Any questions?"

No one seems to have any. Joe says, "Okay, since the Fairmont horses arrived first, we're going to start by loading them. Ready?"

There is a cohesive mutter of "Yes."

The first horse out is Lydia's. She leads easily and goes up the ramp with no trouble. Next is Harmony. I get a thrill from starting to walk her up the ramp and into the plane. Never in a million years would I have thought we'd have this experience together. I am so excited, I can actually feel the adrenaline pumping through me. I look east and see the sun rising and casting a shimmering golden glow across the sky, and suddenly I find myself fighting back tears. This is the first time I will ever experience anything like this—and I just hope it isn't the last. This is what I want for my future: to go and compete in the most amazing venues around the world, always aiming to win the highest honors a rider and horse can achieve. If my entire body could smile, it would right now. Instead, I just have a huge grin plastered across my face that probably looks ridiculous.

A few steps up the ramp, Harmony does a little sideways jig. I pick up on her anxiety, but can't tell if she's afraid or if maybe she is just as excited and thrilled as I am. "It's okay. I'm here with you. You're safe." At my words she loses some of her nervousness. At the top of the ramp, Joe takes the lead rope and turns her to back her into the stall that two other guys are finishing putting together. She backs right in, and is hooked in with a short pair of cross-ties. The quarters are really close. Each "stall" is about the same size as a horse trailer. Joe ties in her hay net and she takes a bite of hay. She still has a slightly nervous look in her eye, but for the most part she seems to be settling in.

Boarding the rest of the horses happens efficiently and with no real upheaval. The racehorses Joe told us about are loaded after our animals, and all of us are asked to take our jump seats. Between the Fairmont grooms, and the ones traveling with the racehorses, there are eight grooms total. Then there's me, Joe, and two other professional handlers. I'm the only girl.

True to what I was told by Holden and Christian, the plane is really, really cold. In fact, as we take off, I am thinking that the plane takes the term *frozen tundra* to an entirely new level. There aren't any windows—so forget about a view. After takeoff, I get out of my jump seat and set a folding chair in front of Harmony. Joe Pierce is seated in a folding chair next to me, in front of Geisha's stall. The grooms spread out and the handlers also have folding chairs they set out.

"You one of the grooms?" he asks.

"No. I'm one of the riders for Fairmont."

He gives me a curious look. "Why aren't you with the other kids? Aren't they leaving out of LAX?"

"Yeah, but my groom broke his ankle yesterday, and I don't know . . . I was given the option to go with my horse or not."

"She's special, huh?"

I smile and nod. "She is the most important thing in the world to me, other than my family."

"I get that. I hear it a lot in this business. They are family, aren't they?"

"Very true."

We talk about how long I've been riding and the reasons I got into it. He tells me that he's been doing this job for ten years and that he loves it. I'm relieved I have someone to talk to, because it makes the flight easier. When I'm talking, I can ignore that I'm freezing cold and nervous about flying in a massive plane with eighteen horses on board.

About two hours into the flight, just as Joe is in the middle of telling me a story about flying with the royal horses of England a few years ago, we hit a pocket of turbulence. It's not horrible but it's rougher than any of us would like. A few of the horses start to whinny and I can hear a couple of them scramble. Harmony looks at me with a wild eye, and I stand up and place a hand on her face. "It's all right." We hit another big pocket of turbulence and I lose my balance. Harmony scrambles for a minute. Joe looks at me, "Why don't you take your jump seat."

"I think I'll stay with her."

One of the other handlers comes over. "One of the two-year-olds up front needs some sedation."

The plane tilts slightly to the right. "Vivienne, you need to take a jump seat." I can tell by the tone of his voice that he isn't messing around, so I give Harmony a last pat and tell her again that it will be okay. But I don't want to leave her. All the horses including Harmony are becoming more agitated.

I realize that I probably look totally beside myself when one of the grooms looks at me kindly and says, "Don't worry. This happens. These guys have it under control."

I take one of the jump seats and strap myself in. I can't see Harmony from where I am at, since she is up front. I can hear the men talking. A horse whinnies loudly, and I recognize the sound as one of fear. The scraping of hooves echoes through the airplane.

The plane hits another patch of turbulence and my stomach lurches. I want to get up and go be with Harmony. I start to unfasten my belt. One of the other grooms looks at me and says, "Stay put." The way he says it tells me that he's also scared.

A few more whinnies ring out and echo off the metal of the plane. One of them is Harmony's. I know how she sounds. I close my eyes and picture her in my head. I don't have any idea if this will work or not, but I flash image after image of the two of us together. I breathe in and out in as calm of a state as I can. I can feel her energy as I do this. It's innocent, kind—almost like a small child's energy. I feel her calming down and as I do there is a shift throughout the plane. All of the horses seem to settle just in time for the plane to level out, as if it has emerged from the storm. I take a deep breath and realize with surprise that I've just discovered something new. Of course, it's impossible to know if it was really me who had the calming effect on the horses. But I know *for sure* that I can't communicate with airplanes, so I'm wondering if reassuring Harmony somehow translated to the rest of horses.

We get the go-ahead to take our seats back near our horses, and everyone leaves the jump seats to return to the folding chairs. Joe comes back and takes the seat next to me. "Everything okay?" I ask.

"Yes. One of the racehorses got pretty nervous there. We gave her a sedative, so she should be good the rest of the flight. I spoke with the pilot and he said that looks like the only rough patch. You okay?"

"I think so." I'm relieved to know we don't have much longer to Lexington, and we land without any more events occurring. I am pretty happy when it's time to get off the plane. I think Harmony is, too, as she's the second to the last horse off. I get her into the trailer and step out to see a van waiting for me.

I know it's going to take me to some fancy-sounding place called the Cardinal Manor and Estate. The horses, meanwhile, are being taken to the horse park along with the grooms.

As I get in and fasten my seatbelt, I almost want to pinch myself. I made it. I'm here. Harmony is with me. I can't tell whether I want to laugh, burst into joyful tears, or have a nervous breakdown.

CHAPTER *thirty-eight*

My first views of Kentucky—a place I've dreamed about—come as we leave the airport in the overcast afternoon. As we drive, the famous racing grounds of Keeneland stretch out across from us as we make a right onto Man o' War Boulevard. Once we drive beyond the city limits, I begin to see nothing but long stretches of green pastures, hemmed in by wooden fences. The grass is a color that instantly makes me think of the term *bluegrass*, since it shimmers with just a hint of a subtle, amazing blue that I've never seen in nature before.

Along with the abundant grass, horses are everywhere. Since it's spring, there are brood mares with their foals in all the pastures, and I catch glimpses of them eating, playing, and taking naps. It is incredible.

The silver gray sky allows only slivers of the sun to reflect through the clouds. As we drive farther, raindrops begin to sprinkle the windshield. I badly want to open my window and breathe it all in. In a way, Lexington conjures up memories of home with all of its expansive green pastures and rural feel. The difference is that there are certainly no mountain ranges like the Cascades in Kentucky, and back home the houses aren't massive, sprawling estates. The barns that we keep passing are all at least three times larger than the home I grew up in. And they're beautiful.

My heart beats rapidly inside my chest as I take it in. I'm here. I am really here. I'm in Lexington headed to compete at the championships. I am here with a couple of my best friends, and with Tristan. This moment can't be beat.

The driver turns onto a cobblestoned road set between ancient-looking stone walls. As we wind up the road, trees with light pink flowers arch over the drive, and I almost feel like I am back in some other time or even in some other country. It feels very Old World to me, and I'm enchanted.

The driver pulls into a circular brick-paved drive, and yep—the enchantment continues.

I see barns in the distance, and more of those lush green pastures, but directly in front of me is a huge mansion. Or maybe the word is *manor*, or *estate*, or *villa* . . . I'm not sure what to call it other than huge—and impressive.

I get out of the van, and as I am taking it all in, two airport shuttles pull in behind us. My heart jumps to know that Tristan is here. And, Riley, Joel, Emily . . . and What's-her-name. . . .

I race over to their shuttle. Joel climbs out first, then Riley, then Emily, and then I am confused as my mind tries to make sense of Tristan stepping out with Lydia right behind him, a huge smile on her face as she says to him, "Thank you for being so sweet to me on the plane, Tristan."

I notice his face turn red and I glare at her.

"Oh, hi, Vivienne. How was your flight?" she asks.

"Great." I flash my fakest smile back at the snooty b, and stare at my boyfriend, who won't even look at me. He finally gives me an awkward kiss on the cheek, and says, "Hi, babe."

"Hi."

The second van opens up and out climb the Fairmonts and Christian.

"Okay, you guys. Let's head in." Holden checks his watch. "We'll get your rooms and then we have an hour to meet out in the stallion shed for the welcoming reception. We got really lucky with the housing draw, I think." He smiles.

I totally agree. I can hardly believe how beautiful the place is as, next to Tristan, I head up the stone path surrounded by immaculately kept rosebushes. As Holden opens the front door, we walk into a marble-floored entry. There is one of those huge staircases in front of us. To the right is a large room, and I take a peek. It looks like a library. To the left is another large room with a massive fireplace and it's paneled in a dark wood and furnished with cushioned leather sofas that look incredibly comfortable to me.

An elderly lady greets us. "Good day, Fairmont Academy," she says with a slightly Southern accent. "I'm Hannah Hill. I am one of the caretakers of Cardinal Estate. We are pleased to have you with us for the week. Feel free to treat this as your home. Breakfast will be served at seven per your instructors' request in order for you to get over to the horse park in a timely fashion. However, if you need to eat earlier, there will be pastries and coffee prepared by six a.m. The kitchen is behind me down this hall, and the dining area will be off to the left. Feel free to explore at your leisure. I know that right now you all are on a schedule, and I'm sure you are weary from traveling."

I have to say, my first experience with Southern charm bowls me over. Hannah Hill is like the grandma I've always wanted.

"Each of you will receive a key to your own room located on the second story," she continues. "I will give Mr. Fairmont the keys and a roster."

She hands Holden a sheet and sets of keys, and he turns to us with a stern look in his deep-set hazel eyes. "Okay, gang, you know the rules. What goes at Fairmont, goes here." He calls out our names and hands us each a key to our room.

Once everyone has gotten their room assignments, Kayla reminds us of how little time we have before the gathering at the stallion shed.

"I can't be ready for a party in an hour," Lydia whines. "I mean, we just got off a plane."

"You'll look great, I'm sure," Kayla replies.

I shake my head in disgust that all Lydia is thinking about is her looks. I just want to soak this all in. My room turns out to be as spectacular as the rest of the place. It's painted a light yellow and has a dark wood four-poster bed. The comforter is simple and white, but the framed photos on the walls get me—all horses. I look at them each in turn, wishing that I could have gotten Harmony settled myself. After the flight, I wonder how she's doing.

I take a quick shower in the bathroom connected to my room, and then I pull out one of the two dresses that I packed. I choose the one that Martina told me I had to wear. I even seem to hear her voice as I pull it on. It's a little bit tighter than what I might usually choose and I'll admit there is a plunging neckline—not that I have much to plunge into. I am no Lydia Gallagher. Shaking my head, I grab the padded bra that Martina insisted I buy to wear with the dress. It's as if she's in the room with me. *A padded bra can be a flat girl's best friend.* I laugh out loud when I picture her saying this to me. I slip the black dress on and at least feel happy that I have a flat stomach—and that thanks to the bra, my cleavage is at least not as flat as my stomach.

I put on a little blush, eyeliner, mascara, and lip gloss, and brush my hair. It's gotten really long, so it hangs half way down my back. I figure since all I ever do is wear it pulled back that maybe I will wear it down for once. I blow it out and put on silver hoop earrings—another loan from Martina.

I walk out of my room and descend the stairs. Tristan is already waiting for me. No one else is in the entry yet. As I make my way down to him, he gives me that ever-so-sweet dimpled smile and my heart actually flutters. I swear it does. "You look beautiful. Wow, Vivienne."

I do a twirl for him and am almost disgusted at myself for the girlish giggle I let out—almost.

"Not too bad yourself." I like what he's wearing; a blazer strikes the right balance between upscale and casual.

He grabs me and pulls me in tight against him and I catch my breath. He kisses me and that heart-flutter thing does a repeat.

"Oh God," says a girl's voice. At the words, Tristan releases me. "Get a room," the voice adds.

I turn and look up at the stairs to see Lydia coming down. My stomach sinks. I guess I was hoping that for once she would look hideous since she didn't have an entire day to get ready. But who am I kidding? This is Lydia, after all, and she looks as insanely hot as usual. I hate her. She has no deficiencies where a plunging neckline is concerned, and I have to wonder if her super short red dress with the neckline down to, well, pretty far down, should be illegal. Her outrageously high do-me heels match her plump red lips. I look at Tristan. Is he salivating? He puts an arm around me and I breathe a little easier—a little.

"You look really cute, *Scholarship*."

I've just accepted her stupid name for me and have recognized that she calls me it because she's acutely jealous. Tristan's arm tightens around me as he says, "Vivienne is more than cute. She's hot. Gorgeously hot."

"You guys are so sweet," she replies in a syrupy, super sarcastic way.

Before I say something that gets me in trouble, I am saved by the charming Riley Reed bounding down the stairs. His smile is wide as he takes the last three stairs with a flying leap and yells, "Booyah."

Tristan high-fives him. "Ooh, Miss Taylor cleans up pretty nicely," he says. Then he turns to Lydia. "Wow. You're so very Ke$ha tonight. Minus the glitter."

"Thank you," she replies. "I'm planning on finding the other hot guy in the room," she says and looks at Tristan. "I'm sure one of the college guys will fit the bill."

"What about you and Harrison?" Riley asks.

"Oh, I'm bored with him," she replies. "Ke$ha, huh?"

"Totally," Riley says.

I can tell by her tone that for once she's uncertain and doesn't know if she should take it as a compliment or not. I am certain Riley didn't mean it as in, 'you look Ke$ha glamorous.' Pretty sure he was going right for, 'you look Ke$ha slutty.' I love that he might have just insulted her. But this is tempered by my disappointment that she's broken up with Harrison. Bummer.

Before long the Fairmonts show, and so do the rest of the team, and we make our way through the unbelievably perfect gardens down to the stallion shed. It's a huge covered arena, all done in cherrywood paneling. Along the outside of the arena are countless windows, so it isn't entirely enclosed. The whole place is meant for buyers so that they can see how a particular stallion moves if they're interested in him. It gives buyers or owners of mares who are looking to breed with a stallion a better idea as to how the horse moves.

As we enter the arena, the air smells like I am walking through the woods after a fresh rain, and I am once again blown away. The place is lit up by miniature Chinese lanterns strung across the high wood beams. The tables are covered with white tablecloths and floral arrangements that would make my mother go completely gaga. They're made of gorgeous yellow roses and lavender hyacinths, which are starlike clusters of flowers that I only know about because they happen to be my mom's favorite.

There is a stage up front with a guy playing bluegrass on an acoustic guitar, which sets a fun, soulful kind of mood. A buffet table lines one wall, and servers are filling flutes with what I figure must be sparkling cider, as I doubt many of us here are of legal drinking age. More riders keep filing in and the place quickly fills up. Excitement and anxiety race through me with the anticipation of the week to come and the realization as to how huge this is, and how lucky I am to be a part of it. I can't help but feel like I almost want to cry some seriously happy tears.

Tristan says, "We should grab a table."

I nod. We find one closer to the stage. Riley and Joel sit down with us, too, but on separate sides of the table, and I can't help but notice they aren't really saying anything to each other. Wonder what this drama could be about? There are some empty seats left, but I am sure that Lydia won't be joining us. Like she said, her plan is to hunt down the hottest guy in the room besides my boyfriend.

We take our seats. Tristan leans into me and whispers, "Can you believe this? I'm so happy I'm here with you."

His words are sweet and his breath in my ear sends tingles down my spine. I smile at him and say, "I couldn't think of anyone else that I'd rather be with."

As he kisses my cheek, I hear a voice say, "Vivvie?"

I look up. *Oh. My. God.* "Austen."

"Hey." He walks around the table. "I didn't know you'd be here."

I nod, and the nod turns into a shake of my head as I muster a smile. "And crazy, but I didn't know you'd be here, either."

Austen flashes his smile, dimples on both sides of his cheeks, his blue eyes dancing in the candlelight as if he has a secret and one he is happy about. He runs a hand through his wavy dark hair and looks pointedly at Tristan.

He opens his arms, and I awkwardly break away from Tristan to stand up and hug him. Even though there is plenty of noise and a lot of people, I suddenly feel like I am on some deserted island with no escape. I can feel Riley's, Joel's, *and* Tristan's eyes on us as we hug.

I turn to the guys and say, "This is Austen. We rode at the same barn at home growing up. We've known each other since we were, like, eight."

Austen stretches out his hand and each guy does the obligatory handshake and introduction. He reaches Tristan last. "Hey, man, nice to meet you," Tristan says.

"Tristan. The boyfriend," Austen says, bobbing his head a little too enthusiastically. "Can I sit down? Is this seat taken?"

"It's all yours, man," Tristan replies.

Can someone please rescue me? I wish.

I should really watch what I wish for, because right then Lydia sidles up and says, "Oh, hey, guys—looks like you have an open seat."

I feel like I'm going to be sick for sure as she pulls out a chair on one side of Austen and introduces herself. Where is Emily? She could have taken that seat! I stare at Lydia in disgust. Yep, she did it. She found the other extremely hot guy in the room.

CHAPTER *thirty-nine*

Lydia is doing her best to get Austen to fall madly in love. Between the eyelash batting, the giggling, and that neckline, she's going all out. Worst of all, he is responding. I even see him touch her hand at one point. . . . Yeah, I don't miss much. Even I have to admit that, at the very least, Austen is already madly in lust.

Riley at one point gives me the raised eyebrow, bug-eye look that I understand means, "What the hell?"

I return the look with a smile and a shrug. I imagine he's in his own kind of shock. As soon as Emily arrived, she pulled up a chair and started fawning all over Joel, who is responding with his usual totally fake romantic interest. I try to focus on the prime rib and au gratin potatoes—and Tristan—but the whole night feels off kilter.

As I take the last bite of my dessert of chocolate mousse, I see Christian Albright head to the podium. Guitar guy takes a step down as a DJ sets up behind him. Christian goes to the microphone.

"Excuse me, riders. Excuse me, I need your attention for a few minutes."

People start hushing one another, and once the chatter dies down, Christian addresses us. "I'm Christian Albright, and on behalf of the Young Equestrians Association board of directors I want to extend a warm welcome. All of you in this room are here because you've worked hard, you've gotten the grades, and your instructors in the classroom and the arena have faith that you are high achievers. So, we want to congratulate you. We are in for an exciting week in Lexington. Tomorrow begins your journey toward the event next weekend that will change your lives. It's going to be fun, and you will be challenged. I encourage you to get to know some of the riders from other schools and make new friends, because we all have one thing in common. We love our horses, and we love eventing, which we all know is the best sport on the planet."

A loud cheer goes out, followed by applause. Everyone quiets down for another minute as Christian adds, "And the most important thing to remember is to be safe. So, riders, let's get set for the week and get it done. Now, I want you to enjoy the rest of your evening."

More applause is followed by the DJ starting to spin some Jay-Z. Tristan takes my hand and we head to the dance floor. I notice that we are followed by Austen and Lydia.

My guy can dance. End of story. And, I find that for the first time since I saw Austen this evening, I can relax and enjoy the party as I lose myself in Tristan and the music. I want to warn Austen about the viper he's chosen to bump and grind the night away with, but I remind myself that he is a big boy who can make his own choices. But then I also remind myself that he is my friend and *only* my friend. I would want a friend to tell me if I was about ready to hook up with a snake.

Rihanna and Mikky Ekko sing "Stay." Tristan's arms go around my waist. "What's the story between you and Farm Boy?"

"Farm Boy?"

"Yeah. Your buddy Austen. He looks a little rugged, you know, like he grew up on a farm."

I laugh. "Yeah. His dad raises pigs."

"Ah, see, I can peg them."

"But he's no hick, I can tell you that," I say. I'm surprised by how defensive I sound. "And what do you mean 'what's the story'?"

"Well, it was hard to miss the way he looked at you over dinner, and the way you glared at the flirting going on between Lydia and him. I think there is something I may have missed."

I stop dancing and pull away. "What?"

"You and Farm Boy? Were you ever more than friends?"

I can't say I'm surprised that Tristan has picked up on some truth here. Although, what is the truth? Austen is my friend and we shared one kiss, plus a moment over Christmas break that I wanted never to end. But so what? Mainly what I feel about Austen is confused. That's not something I should have to explain. But I can tell Tristan is waiting for me to talk.

"We have always just been friends. The guy is a goofball. He's part of my group back home. Trust me, most of the time the guy grosses me out making pig noises or just acting stupid." Yes, I am laying it on thick. But it's true Austen did gross me out when I was, like, ten.

"He doesn't seem to gross you out now."

I pull away slightly and my hands go straight to my hips. "Excuse me? I just told you that we have never been anything more than friends. I don't want to be more than friends. The guy is all over Lydia, so it's obvious to me that it goes both ways. I don't know what you think you saw, but it's in your head. But you know what isn't in mine? The fact that when you and Lydia got out of the van today, she was all smiles and made that remark about how sweet you were on the plane!"

"She hates flying. I was only trying to make her feel better. We hit some turbulence. She grabbed my hand. I let her. It was no big deal."

"Guess what? We hit turbulence, too, today. Horses were going nuts; one had to be sedated . . . I had no one there to hold my hand, though!" I shake my head. "I need some air." I turn on my heel and head outside, fighting back tears. I take a walk over to the closest barn. I walk inside. It's dimly lit, and I hear the sounds of horses eating. The smell of the hay calms my nerves. But then I hear the sound of someone crying. Not sobbing, but sniffling. I recognize crying when I hear it. It's coming from the end of the barn. I walk down and have to do a double take.

I see Joel on the ground, slumped against one of the walls.

CHAPTER *forty*

oel?"

He startles and looks up. He immediately wipes his face. "Oh hi, Vivienne."

I sit down next to him knowing that my dress is getting dirty but whatever. I am not in the mood for partying at this point, and I can see that he is upset. "What's going on?"

He shakes his head. "Nothing."

We sit in silence for a few minutes. He finally blurts, "I kissed Riley, and I think he hates me again."

"What!?"

"I know it was stupid. I can't blame him for being mad. I didn't mean to do it. It just happened. The worst part is that I think Lydia may have seen us."

"Oh. That is bad," I say. "But I don't think Riley hates you. He isn't like that. Is that why he's giving you the cold shoulder? When did this happen anyway?"

"You picked up on the fact that he's giving me the silent treatment? Yeah, well . . . it happened last night in the tack room at school. We were packing our trunks, and I don't know. It just happened, and then he pulled away. The next thing I know, Lydia is walking into the tack room, and maybe she was at the door the whole time. It was stupid and I have to make this better again. I have to. There's just stuff that we . . . there's stuff that I told him about that I can't tell anyone about."

I'm not sure what he means here. "Want to clue me in?" I ask.

"I can't." He shakes his head and there are more tears coming down his face. "I really can't, Vivienne. It could cause you harm, and I've done enough where Riley is concerned just by sharing things with him that I shouldn't have."

What is it with everyone not wanting to reveal their crap, in order to keep me safe? Jeez, you'd think I was some dainty little girl. It's starting to really get to me! But, Joel is so upset that I don't argue this point with him right now. "I'm here for you if you want to share. I'm sorry you feel so stuck, or down, or whatever is going on. God, I don't know what to say."

"There is nothing to say. I just can't talk about any of it, and I would appreciate you not saying anything to Riley or anyone."

"I won't. I promise." I hug him. "You're a good guy, and you're strong. Whatever it is . . . it will be okay. And, Riley has a big heart. He'll get over it. I think if Lydia had seen you then she would have already done her best to spread the word." I try and reassure him, but I have to wonder if I am speaking the truth. I honestly don't know. I know that Riley will do whatever he needs to do to keep his secret of being gay under wraps, at least until he graduates. He's counting on being able to move away with Santos and start a new life.

"Thank you," he replies.

"I have to ask you, though, what are you doing with Emily?'

He doesn't answer.

"Joel . . . it's wrong. I know why you're leading her on, and now it really makes sense. You're protecting Riley and I respect that, but it is really unfair to Emily. She's into you."

"I know. I do. But I have to protect Riley, and she keeps throwing herself at me, and it just has made everything easier."

I sigh. "It's a no-win situation. You're going to have to get out of this at some point, and it won't be good."

"I'm planning on breaking up with her at the end of the year, and that's less than a month away. I have to keep up this act for now. There's so much you don't understand."

"Then tell me," I say.

"I can't. I wish that I could, but I can't. Trust me that it is for your own good."

"Want to go back in? Maybe try and have some fun?" I want him to confide in me, but pushing the issue doesn't seem to be working.

"Sure."

He stands and holds out a hand, which I take. I brush myself off and we go back into the party. I scan the area looking for Tristan, knowing that we need to talk. Maybe I need to get over my crap, and maybe he needs to get over his. In the big picture, petty jealousy is just stupid.

I spot him sitting at the table by himself, looking as miserable as I feel. Joel and I start to head over to him when suddenly some guy steps in front of us. He's tall, lanky, and looks like he may have had a broken nose once. His dark eyes narrow into slits as he says, "Joel Parker." He smacks him hard on the shoulder. "How are you, buddy? Long time, no see. And who is this lovely specimen you're hanging out with?"

He turns his attention on me. I look at Joel, who has gone paler than a white horse. Tall, lanky, jerk guy says, "I'm Christopher Haverly."

Haverly?

"Pretty little brain at work. Yes. *That* Haverly, of Haverly Watches. We sponsor this event."

"Splendid," I say. "And you know Joel?" I ask.

"Oh, we rode together at Liberty Farms." He smacks Joel again, clearly a little too hard.

"Good to see you," Joel says. "We'll have to hang out. We were just heading over to our table." I think I detect a tremor in his voice.

"Right, but not before you introduce your pretty friend here."

I'd kind of like to kick this pompous jerk in between the legs at this moment.

"Vivienne Taylor, obviously, this is Chris Haverly."

I force a smile and shake his sweaty palm. He does one of those weak-ass handshakes that no girl likes. "Nice to meet you. Come on, Joel, let's get Tristan. I think we need to get back soon. It will be an early morning."

Joel nods as if on autopilot. I wipe my hand on my dress as we walk away, and ask him, "What was that?"

"What? Haverly? He's an ass."

"I got that much. But why are you freaked out by him?"

"I'm not."

I sigh. "Okay." It's clear that Joel isn't in the mood for an intimate tell-all talk tonight, so I will let this go for now. But, I am positive that Joel *is* freaked out by Haverly. I am pretty sure what I spotted in Joel's eyes was genuine fear.

I look over at Tristan again and he sees me. He stands and walks over to me. "I'm sorry," he blurts. "I was being stupid.

I throw my arms around him. Joel says, "I'm going to go talk to the Fairmonts for a minute."

"I'm sorry, too," I say.

"You okay?" he asks.

"I am now."

CHAPTER *forty-one*

The next morning, I get up too early. I know I should sleep longer because the trip out was tiring and there's a three-hour time difference, but I'm too excited. I can't wait to get over to the horse park and see Harmony. I shower and am more than ready for breakfast by the time the team wakes up and gets going. We all eat together. I pick up on some tension between Riley and Joel, and I am sad for the both of them. I wish Joel had confided what he is so upset about and what secrets he is keeping, but that is between him and Riley. I just liked it so much better when we were all one big, happy family.

Tristan puts an arm around me as we walk to the van, and I realize that for once Lydia is being quiet this morning. Emily is hanging on Joel's every word. I have also noticed that Tristan has not given Lydia the time of day and vice versa. This makes me happy.

I lean my head on his shoulder as we drive down the road. Once again I am mesmerized by the beauty of our surroundings. We are at the entrance of the Kentucky Horse Park in a matter of ten minutes and I feel my heart racing. The sign at the entrance is green with gold lettering and has a painting of a mare with her foal running alongside her. It's beautiful, and I can hardly register the enormity of being here. As we drive through and up the lane, there are pastures all around—draft horses in one, and minis in another. There is a pond with swans and ducks. To the right, I can see administrative offices.

We are directed to make a left turn and follow the road until it winds around to the barns. Holden has already told us where our horses are, so as soon as the van comes to a stop, I bound out to find Harmony. Tristan calls after me, "A little excited?"

"You could say that," I shout back over my shoulder.

I find my horse. She takes a second to rub against me and then goes right back to eating. "What do you think of this place?" I say. "Can you believe we are here?"

She looks at me as if to say, "Really?! I'm eating, sis! And, I am kind of tired."

"I know," I say. "Long plane ride and all that." I place a hand on her neck and she shows me an image of the tiny makeshift stall on the plane. I laugh. "No. You don't have to ride in a plane for another ten days. Promise."

I hear Joel before I see him. Then, I see him on the phone. I duck inside the stall because I'm nosy like that and want to hear what he is saying. "Dude, leave me alone. Look, I don't want any problems. All of that is behind us. I did what had to be done for myself, and I am sorry, but you had to do what you had to do. I have no plans on talking to anyone about that day. So, drop it and leave me alone."

I peer out of Harmony's stall to see him hang up his cell phone. What is going on with Joel?

Then I hear him say out loud to himself, "Oh crap. As if it can't get any worse!"

"Joel? Is that you?" I walk out of the stall.

"Geez, Vivvie, you scared me."

"Sorry. I just heard you say something about can it get any worse?"

"That's all you heard?"

Hmm . . . *to lie or not to lie*? "Yeah. Why? You okay? Dumb question after . . ."

"Last night." He finishes my sentence.

"Right."

"Totally okay." He raises his voice. "Just happy as I can be. My dad just sent me a text saying that my soon-to-be stepmonster is driving down from Virginia with my soon-to-be stepsister to watch me compete. Isn't that great?"

I can tell by his face that it's the opposite of great.

"Can he really expect me to act as if we are all some happy family? After everything that went down?" He shakes his head. "You know what, Vivvie? Sometimes I wish that I could just go to sleep and never wake up."

I touch his arm and squeeze it. "Stop it. You don't mean that."

I see the tears well in his eyes as he replies, "Yes. Yeah, I do. If I didn't have Melody, I am pretty sure I'd either go insane or jump off the nearest bridge."

"Stop talking stupid talk. You have friends. We are not going to let your future stepfamily get in the way of what you have to do this week. You are a freaking rock star, Joel Parker, and we are going to keep you focused."

"Yeah. Okay."

"No. That is not good enough. I want to hear you say, *I am a freaking rock star.*"

"You're kidding me, right?"

"Do I look like I am kidding? Look at this place! Will you just take a look around here? This is a place for freaking rock stars like yourself. Say it." I laugh.

"Okay, if I say that, then you have to say, *I am Vivienne Taylor and I am a pain in the butt.*"

"No problem. I am very aware that I am Vivienne Taylor and I am a pain in the butt. And, you know what, I am actually proud of it."

This gets a smile out of Joel, and I am happy to see him have some sunshine in his face. "Your turn," I say.

"I am Joel Parker and I am a freaking rock star," he mumbles.

"Really? That's it? No. That is not going to work. I want enthusiasm. I want to feel it!"

He sighs and repeats the phrase.

"Better. But like this." I yell out, "I am Vivienne Taylor and I am a pain in the butt!"

I hear applause at the end of the barn aisle and then I spot Austen. "And I am Austen Giles and I second that! Vivienne Taylor *is* a pain in the butt!"

I feel myself turn beet red and wish more than anything that I could go crawl under a rock.

"Tell her what she wants to hear, man, and say it the way she wants to hear it. The girl is persistent, and she's known for getting what she wants," Austen says as he walks toward us.

I shove my hands into the front pockets of my breeches.

"Hey, Joel."

"Austen."

"Mind if I steal Vivvie here for a few?"

"No. Go ahead."

"Thanks. Can we take a walk?" he asks.

I look around to see if Tristan is nearby. He must be already tacking up Sebastian. I know that he is one row over. I'm not sure if I should go with Austen or not, but like me, he can be persistent. I know from growing up with this guy that he is also one who doesn't typically take no for an answer.

I can't imagine what he wants, but I figure if it's a talk I might as well get it over with. "Um, okay, let's go."

CHAPTER *forty-two*

usten and I walk out of the barns. "Let's check out the foals over there," he says.

I am confused and curious but he stays silent as we casually stroll next to the fenced pasture that houses a handful of colts and fillies with their mothers, all eating the grass that spreads out underneath them. There is a mist in the air and I pull my sweater tighter around me.

"You cold?" he asks. "You can have my jacket."

"No. I'm okay." I am getting good at this lying thing. I stop walking and so does he. Austen shoves his hands into his pockets and rolls back and forth on his heels ever so slightly. I have seen him do this many times with our old trainer, Gail. He's nervous. "What is it? Why did you want to talk to me?"

"It's about your friend."

"My friend?"

"Lydia."

I can't help but laugh. "She's not my friend."

"She isn't?"

"Uh. No. Not even close."

"She seems to think you're friends. In fact, she speaks rather highly of you."

"Oh please." I roll my eyes at him. "So typical."

"What do you mean?"

"She'll say anything to snag a guy—even that she and I are friends, I guess. I promise you that she and I are the opposite of close. I know Lydia is every guy's dream come true, especially when she wears a dress like the one she wore last night. But I can almost guarantee you that if you get tangled up with her that she will become a high-maintenance nightmare who takes over your life."

"Do I detect jealousy, Vivienne Taylor?"

I cross my arms, look down at the dirt, dig my boot into the ground, and shake my head. "No. What you detect is the truth."

"Then why did she do nothing but sing your praises last night? All she talked about was how cool you are, and how great of a rider you are."

"Are you that stupid?!" I cross my arms.

He takes a step back, stops rocking on his heels, and stares at me. "What does that mean?"

"She's manipulating you. She knows you and I are friends. And, if she can make you think that she and I are BFFs, then that just gets her that much closer to her goal, which from what I could see last night is getting you hooked on her."

"You're being ridiculous."

"And, you are being blind!"

"I don't know what your history is with Lydia other than she used to date Tristan, but I am pretty sure that is what this is all about. You are ugly possessive. I brought you out here to ask you if there is anything at all between us. I can see that you have Prince Charming, but, Vivvie, I know when we kissed last summer before you left for Fairmont that there was something there. When you were home over Christmas, there was something there between us, too. I wanted to be sure that you and I aren't missing something, before I move forward with asking Lydia out."

"What? First off, let me tell you something, Austen." I know the tone of my voice is awful, but I can't seem to stop myself from continuing. "Lydia and I are nothing alike, so if she's the kind of girl that you think you want, then go for it. I won't stop you, but don't say that I didn't warn you. As far as what happened between you and me, it just happened. So what? It's behind us now. And I'd never hold you back from going after something else, because I already have a boyfriend who I really care about. Finally, why are you even thinking about asking someone out while you're here? Everyone is just going to go back to school after this . . . different schools. Shouldn't the focus be to ride?"

There is a part of me that immediately wants to take it all back, but his stupid accusations of possessiveness and basically not being open-minded toward Lydia have set me off. I can't believe that Austen, of all people—the Austen that I grew up with, who I always thought was smart and had good instincts, would actually be interested in Lydia Gallagher. Then again, I am reminded that Tristan was her boyfriend for months. Guys are so stupid. And so easily played!

Austen turns and starts walking back and, as he does, he says, "Thank you, Vivvie. I got my answers."

I watch him walk away and there is a pit in my stomach. I just wish so badly that Lydia would go away. Go find another girl's life to make miserable. Leave my boyfriend alone and let him be, no matter what she knows about his family. I just know she is up to no good, and now she has her hooks in my friend. I definitely wish she would climb under a rock and stay there forever. Since that isn't going to happen, I am realizing that the time to confront my enemy is growing increasingly closer.

CHAPTER *forty-three*

I push the conversation I had with Austen out of my head as best as I can, and walk back to the barn to start tacking up. Today is going to be super busy, as we are to just get our horses out on our own and do some flat work with them in order to get them acclimated to the change from being away from home.

As I reach the barn, I see Tristan standing at the end of the aisle with a halter in hand. He looks like he's waiting for me. "Where were you?" he asks.

"On a walk."

"With Austen?"

Something tells me that lying this time would not be in my best interest. "Yes. I did take a walk with him. He was asking me about Lydia."

"That's it?"

I nodded. "Yes." So, a partial lie is told.

"Why?"

"He's interested in her, is all, and he wanted to know if she's a good girl."

"Why is he asking you?"

"I don't know," I snap. "I guess because we are friends."

"What did you tell him?"

"Oh my God. What is this? Am I on the stand here? I told him that she was fine. I don't care if he goes out with her. It's not my business."

He nods. "I would have thought, though, that if he's such a good friend that you might let him know what she's really like."

I walk into the barn and grab Harmony's halter off the rung. "It's not my business. The last person I am going to care about or think about while I am here is Lydia Gallagher."

"Do you care about me?"

I stop and face him. "Insecurity is not nice on you. Don't ask me such a stupid question. I think Sebastian is waiting for you."

He turns and heads down the barn aisle and I stand there feeling exhausted, as if someone has stuck a big sharp pin into my happy, excited little bubble.

I walk into Harmony's stall and wrap my arms around her neck. A flood of love comes over me. This horse knows me. I start to back away from her when I get something from her. She wants to tell me something. She shows me Joel standing outside her stall, and next to him in the image is Chris Haverly. And, for the first time ever while communicating with Harmony, I can actually hear the conversation the two are having. "I am warning you, Parker. If you say a word, you're dead."

Then, I see Joel's face more clearly, and he has that fear in his eyes that I have seen a few times since he came to Fairmont. It's intense.

The image that Harmony shows me fades, and I am totally baffled and at the same time elated in a strange way over the fact that Harmony was able to share with me an actual conversation happening between two people. And, this was no ordinary conversation.

I sigh as I hook the halter onto my horse and realize that the week's focus may not be just on winning. I am getting the big picture that I have a friend in trouble and that he needs my help.

CHAPTER *forty-four*

I need a favor, V." Joel is mixing Melody's bucket for the evening feeding. My surprise as to who this guy is always kind of amazes me. I had always pegged him as one of those rich kids who allow the grooms to do everything for his horse, but Joel loves his mare like I love mine and he seems to enjoy taking care of her himself.

"Sure," I say. "What?"

"I need you to go to dinner with me tonight."

I look up from Harmony's bucket after dumping in some ground flaxseed. "Okay, but I had planned on going to the social. What's the deal?"

"We can make the social. I promise. The deal is that my future stepmonster and crew have arrived and they want to have dinner."

"You couldn't have just said forget it? I mean, it isn't like they don't know there is tension between all of you," I reply.

"True." He sighs. "But it's complicated. Tiffany apparently wants to make amends and meet some of my friends. My dad is insisting that I go. You know how family is."

"I do. But, your dad is a jerk and he left your mom. You don't owe these people anything."

"Actually, I do." He nods his head toward Melody. "If my dad wasn't footing the bill for her, then sure, I guess that I could walk away. But I can't. This is all I have. My horse. School. You. My other friends. So, I have to go tonight and I have to play nice. But, I need some backup. You in?"

"Sure. I'm in, but I really do want to make it back for the social, and we have to get to bed early. Tomorrow is the beginning," I reply, referring to the jog-out.

"No worries. It'll go down that way."

"Okay." I finish fixing Harmony's bucket and bed her stall. Joel finishes up. I check my watch. The vans will be here in fifteen and I don't know where Riley and Tristan are. As I walk over to where we are supposed to be picked up, I see Riley up ahead and I walk over to him. "Hey, where have you been?"

"I went over to talk to Christian about Santos. He just felt a little off today, and I wanted Christian to check him out. I don't want him to get spun at the jog."

Riley is referring to when we do our jog-out in front of the judges and vet tomorrow. If the horse is lame at all, it won't be permitted into the competition. No one ever wants to get spun at the jog-out. "That doesn't sound good. But I didn't see you come back to the barn. Did you guys get him out? What did he say?" I ask, concerned for Riley and Santos.

He shakes his head. "I don't know what to do, Vivvie."

"What do you mean?"

"I'm worried about my horse, but there's also something else. I saw Christian and Kayla Fairmont kissing—like really going for it. It was not a *you're my friend* kiss on the cheek."

I remain silent.

"Vivienne? What should I do?"

"Nothing. There is nothing we can do," I reply.

"Are you kidding me? She's married to Holden. That guy has to know."

I sigh. "Look, I have suspected something between Christian and Kayla for a long time, but I had no real proof."

"You suspected the two of them?"

"Yes. I saw them hug fall semester in a way that looked like they were way more than friends, and Tristan and I saw them down on the beach one evening having this intense conversation."

"You didn't tell me?"

"I keep secrets."

"Yes, I guess you do." He looks away from me.

"Let's be real, Ri. What can we do about this? I think it's wrong, too, but it isn't our business."

"But they coach us, and Holden is such a great guy."

"I know, but come on, think what would happen if this all came out. If Kayla and Christian are having an affair, then things might really change at Fairmont. In fact, Fairmont might cease to exist. I don't want to risk that."

"I see your point, but it's still wrong."

"Yeah, it is, and I really don't know the right thing to do, either."

As we make it to the van with this heavy dilemma weighing us both down now, I see Austen up ahead with Lydia—hand in hand, and all giggles. Nothing like taking things slow.

CHAPTER *forty-five*

The restaurant that Joel and I meet his soon-to-be stepfamily at is delicious, but as the clock ticks on, I am beginning to worry that we won't make the social. The whole scene is really awkward and I want to leave—badly.

So here's the deal. Tiffany is the scandal-tainted jumper trainer who worked with Joel and who had also broken up his parents' marriage by running off with Joel's father. Her daughter is named Paisley, a name that fits her perfectly. She is oddly quiet and feminine in a lithe, almost ballerina, way. Paisley doesn't say much at all. Her boyfriend, James, is at dinner, too, and he puts off a weird vibe.

I am pretty sure that Joel's stepmom is paying for the dinner. I hope someone is paying because I looked at the prices and my eyes about popped out of my head.

Joel, meanwhile, is acting like the arrogant kid he seemed to be when I first met him. He's also using words such as *splendid* again, which totally annoys the hell out of me. Tiffany is having her share of wine, and before the main course is ever set in front of us she's slurring her words.

"Your father and I have been thinking that Melody is such a special horse. Look how far you've taken her." I watch her with curiosity, as she seems very close to drunkenly knocking over her full glass of water.

"She truly is, Joel," James says, in his seriously affected voice. I wonder why Paisley wants him as a boyfriend. "I remember her at Liberty, and frankly, I was shocked that your father would have purchased her for you, and then allowed you to make an event horse out of her." James takes a sip of the tea he's ordered.

"Thank you, I think, Tiffany. I'm not even going to respond to you, James, other than to say that Melody is all heart and a perfect event horse," Joel replies. "We've worked hard."

"Yes. However, we are questioning whether or not her true forte is being an event horse," Tiffany slurs. "James does have a point. She is a fine animal."

"Excuse me?" Joel says. "What's going on here? And, who is this ass"—he points to James—"to even have a say in anything?"

I shift uncomfortably in my seat and focus for a few seconds on the crystal chandeliers in the room and my breathing. I really don't like where any of this is going.

"Yes and, well, she is a fantastic jumper," Tiffany says, ignoring Joel's question. "But cross-country is so . . . hmmm . . . hard-core. We think that Paisley should have Melody, and we will find you a suitable horse for your sport."

Joel is staring at her. "What? No. No way! Melody is my horse, and there is no way that I am letting her have my horse!" He points at Paisley, who looks down at her plate. "This is why you came here? You didn't come here to cheer us on like my dad said. I knew it. He didn't even have the guts to come down here himself, so he sends you to tell me that you're taking Melody away! You are not taking her. There is no way. I'll die before that happens!"

"I don't think that's for you to decide," she slurs. "We pay for Melody. It's our say."

"You're a drunk, a home wrecker, and a gold digger!"

I want to help Joel calm down, but I understand why he's losing it. They are threatening to take his horse from him. On the other hand, he is kind of off the Richter scale with that comment. I reach out to touch his arm, but he pulls it away and continues, "You don't pay for Melody. My father does. You won't be taking my horse home. My parents are still legally married, and I will be calling my mother. She owns half of Melody, and I am sure she will side with me on this. If you want to try and do this, I will do everything that I can to make sure my parents' divorce stays in the courts for as long as possible, until every last dime of my father's is spent."

"Calm down, Joel. Don't speak to Tiffany like that, and I suggest you never insult Paisley again. I think you need to be reasonable here," James says.

"Shut up. You're a douche bag and everyone knows it, and there is a lot I know about you, if you remember correctly. I'd get off my high horse and go back to the rock I crawled out from under, *dude*."

James stands up. "You'll regret speaking to me that way."

"I'm scared, man. Really scared."

As I watch this spectacle go down, I'm feeling kind of impressed. Wow—it's a seriously smart move on Joel's part to bring his mom and the divorce in on this. He does have some lawyer in him. But there are strange aspects of it, too. What is Joel talking about with this James kid?

Tiffany cackles. "Good luck with that, son. Your threats are so not scary. I am not troubled in the least."

"Don't call me son. Ever."

"A trailer will be here on Monday morning after the competition is over, and Melody will be going back to Virginia with us," says Paisley, finally chiming in.

"That's where you're wrong," Joel says. "My horse is going back to California with me." He looks at me. "Come on, Vivienne. Let's leave the cretins to their dinner."

I think about saying thank you for the dinner, and then rethink it. This woman doesn't deserve a thank you from me.

We leave the restaurant and get a taxi to take us back to Cardinal Estate. Joel is breathing heavy and fast. I can't blame him.

"What are you going to do?" I ask. I decide not to bring up James or Paisley and how odd they seem. I can't put my finger on what makes James seem so weirdly unpleasant, but maybe it's that he talks like he's some highbrow socialite from yesteryear. Even though he's clearly eighteen, he acts like he's fifty—and not in a good way, but like some obnoxious, rich, good old boy. I wonder what kind of info Joel has on James that set the guy off.

I feel like giving Joel a hug. He has clearly had enough for the evening.

"Whatever it takes to keep my horse," he replies. "No matter what that is. I will do whatever it takes to make sure she never goes back to Tiffany."

CHAPTER *forty-six*

We get back in time to make the social, but I have the feeling that Joel doesn't want to go in. I offer to stay with him.

"No," he sighs. "You go in and have a good time. I am going to go call my dad and see what I can do to talk some sense into him, and if I can't, I'm going to call my mom and find out what she can do on her end."

"Okay. If you need me, you know where to find me." I hold up my cell phone.

"Thanks. Thank you for going tonight. I'm sorry you had to see any of that."

"Don't worry about it. That's what friends are for."

"Have fun, Vivvie."

We both get out of the taxicab. I give Joel a hug. "Please call me if you need anything, like just to talk. . . . I don't care what time it is. You can call me at three in the morning."

"Thank you." He kisses my cheek. "You are a really good girl and friend, Vivvie. I hope Tristan appreciates you."

Joel waves good-bye and heads for his room as I start my walk down to the stallion shed where the social is taking place. It's dark, but the pathway is illuminated by tea lights set on either side of the path. I make it halfway down the path when I hear my name. It's Tristan and he is sitting on a bench next to a koi pond. "Hey, you. What are you doing out here?"

"Waiting for you," he says. "How was the dinner?"

"Strange. I feel bad for Joel, but I don't really want to talk about it right now."

"Good. I don't want to talk, either."

"You don't?" I ask. I sit down next to him.

"No." When he leans in and kisses me, heat sears through me from my lips all the way down through my body. I begin to feel hot all over as the kiss grows and his hands wrap around my waist. I am not going to lie; there is a part of me that wants this to go farther—much farther.

"I haven't stopped thinking about the other night before we flew out here," he says. His fingers reach around my back and slide under my shirt. He stops kissing me on the lips and whispers in my ear, "We'd better stop." Just his breath and voice in my ear sends another jolt through me—and this one shoots down my spine and starts this sweet, delicious tickle that travels all through me.

"Maybe we shouldn't stop."

"Don't tempt me, Vivienne."

I pull away and in all seriousness look up at him. "I mean it. Maybe we shouldn't."

He shakes his head. "No. Tomorrow is a big day and you need to focus. We both do. I just wanted to kiss you all day, and I've been waiting here for the past hour for you to come back from dinner with Joel, and God, that kiss was worth waiting for. Trust me, there is nothing more that I'd rather do than take this to another level. Believe me, I would really like to find somewhere safe and quiet and where we can . . ."

"But . . . ," I say, completing his thought.

"But, only if you really think you're ready for it. I don't want to push you. . . ."

"You're not pushing me into anything," I reply.

He sighs. "It's your virginity. And, I want you to be a hundred percent sure, and this isn't the place. It just isn't. We need to make it special."

"How did I get so lucky?" I ask.

"Because you deserve it."

Oh my God! Sweet, sexy, smart, and sensitive.

"Really? How did I get so lucky? I am serious," I ask him again.

"I'm the lucky one. Want to go down to the party?" he asks.

"No. I don't. I think I want to be here with you."

"I was hoping you'd say that."

He wraps his coat around me and we spend the next hour or so just talking horses, school, and our hopes for the event. In between the talking, there is plenty of kissing, but we have established something: that if we are going to take this to the next level, then everything about it has to be just right. And, we both know with such major days ahead of us that waiting a little bit longer makes more sense. I just wish it felt easier. However, I don't know that I exactly want to be living by common-sense rules right now.

"It's getting late," he says. "We'd better get back."

We walk up to the house hand in hand and as we turn the corner to the side of the building, we both stop as we see Austen and Lydia all over each other. I am not going to be upset, or care, or want to throw up. I am not feeling any of that. I am not. I am with Tristan, who I adore, and who I nearly begged to sleep with me an hour ago. So, yep—I am just totally fine with this.

They don't even hear us as we start to walk on by. At least I don't think that they hear us, until Lydia says, "Oh, hi, you two."

"Hi," I say, almost too loud and too enthusiastically.

"Hi," Tristan says.

The way he says it sounds like he feels about as out of place as I do right now. "Good night," we mutter as we walk past them and into the house. Tristan leaves me at the door to my room.

"I'd come in, but that's probably not the best idea tonight." He gives me one last kiss and a hug.

I slip through the door and throw myself on the bed, and despite the many thoughts racing through my mind, I manage to fall asleep.

CHAPTER *forty-seven*

The next morning after checking in on Harmony and seeing that my groom, Charlie, has everything under control, I go to the bathroom near the event space and put on some makeup, and dress in the outfit that Kayla helped pick out for the jog. I'm wearing a cute pair of capri khakis with a fitted white blouse underneath a cropped red jacket, and a pair of flats. The jog-out has everything to do with presentation, so the typical attire of breeches and a polo isn't going to cut it here. I am feeling pretty J.Crewish at the moment.

As I'm finishing curling my hair, Lydia walks in. "Hey, Scholarship. Don't you look cute."

I don't even comment.

"I kind of like your old boyfriend. He's a really good kisser."

I continue to ignore and curl my hair.

"I guess I'm just going to call him *hot*. Like h.o.t." She spells it out and I want to gag. "I do think there must be a story there," Lydia digs. "One between the two of you."

"You think wrong. Austen was never my boyfriend."

"Uh-huh."

I set the curling iron down and face her. "What do you want? I mean, really? What do you want from me? We aren't friends. It's perfectly clear to both of us that neither one of us likes the other. I think that maybe we should just stay out of each other's way and leave it at that. Austen is a great guy, and it's too bad that he can't see through who and what you are. But I think he'll figure that out soon enough."

She crosses her arms and lowers her voice, staying eerily calm. "You know what it is, Scholarship? It's that you nearly ruined my family. My brother is in jail because of you. My mother won't get out of bed, and my dad is so busy trying to get an appeal for my brother that he couldn't even make it out here to see me compete."

"Wait a minute. You're blaming me for your brother's crimes? Give me a break. Figuring out the scam your brother was running with Newman and realizing that Newman murdered Dr. Miller almost got me killed along with Riley and Emily last semester, so I hate to tell you, but I am not taking the blame for this at all. Here's the deal. I say that we agree to disagree and stay out of each other's way."

"Sure thing, Scholarship. Besides, I am not too worried about you getting what is coming to you. Since you seem to pride yourself on being Little Miss Detective, let me give you a heads-up—maybe you should go digging in your boyfriend's closet. I'm thinking there may be a skeleton or two."

I look straight at her. I take a chance here, but I think it's time that I do so for Tristan's sake. "I know about Tristan. He told me that he told you about his dad."

She looks shocked at this, and for once I see that Lydia is speechless.

"Yeah, but the kicker is that he didn't tell me what it is that you know. It must be something so bad because he is afraid I could get hurt. My gut tells me that you know all about whatever it is, and in some way I think you're blackmailing him. I don't know what you're getting out of it, but I am pretty sure you're hanging something over his head, and you're rotten for it. You really are. Why don't you just let people live their lives and leave them alone?"

"Huh," she laughs. "Hate to tell you, Scholarship, but it goes both ways. Have you ever thought that maybe Tristan's little secret has a bit more to it than just the fact that his dad is a bad guy? Maybe he's not telling you because he just doesn't want you to know. You don't really believe it's because he wants to protect you, do you?"

I have no comeback. Nothing. She gives me a cold smile and leaves the room. I start gathering my things furiously. I know she wants to wind me up. I get that. But I can't let her distract me. I need to be jogging Harmony in a half hour, and this is just Lydia's sick and twisted way of trying to blow up my world. I tell myself over and over that none of that is really about me. It's all about her.

Once I get outside, I'm glad to see Christian walking toward me. He is all smiles. "Hey, kid, you ready? You look great."

"Thank you. I think I'm ready."

"Your head in the game?"

"Yes." Can he tell that I have just been shaken up by Lydia? He's right. I have to get my head straight. I am here, and this is where it all begins.

"Good. Your horse is ready."

I go and get her. I take a rag and wipe down her face again. I run a hand over each leg—her legs are nice and tight. I hear the jog being announced.

I see Tristan and the rest of the team on the lawn jogging their horses, prepping them for the jog-out. This part is for a few reasons. One aspect of it is key because this is where we make our first impression. The judges will check us out. Are we neat and clean? Do we present well? However, the most important aspect of the jog is that the judges are making sure the horses that are going to be competing are sound, meaning there are no lameness issues or any other prospective health issues that may need to be addressed.

I am only five minutes away from my turn to present when I see Riley go up to the jog path with Santos. My mind needs to be solely on my horse, but knowing that Riley was a little concerned about his horse yesterday, I have to watch. I see Santos take a few borderline steps and watch as the officials ask Riley to wait. This means he will have to go through a second pass after the other horses go. The vets will be checking Santos's legs as well. My nerves are set off by this. I want to go up to Ri and support him, but I know that isn't an option.

In a couple of minutes it's my turn to present Harmony. I make a kissing sound to her as we start into the jog. There is a spring in her step that I don't think I've ever seen before. I almost laugh as we trot down the pathway. It's as if she is saying to everyone, "Look at me. I am here! Look at me!"

The judges thank me when we finish and that means we have passed. The rules dictate that we are not allowed to wait at the finish for anyone else because it'll back up the lineup. It's frustrating because I so badly want to find out if Santos passed.

I take Harmony to her stall, and as I am putting her away, I see Riley coming back with Santos. He doesn't look completely devastated so I think this must be a good sign.

"Well?" I ask.

"We were spun," he replies.

"What? Really?"

"Yeah. He's sore. I don't know why, or what's going on. Christian is going to have one of the vets come and take a look and see what we can figure out."

"Oh, Ri, I am so sorry. I am really, really sorry. That sucks."

"It's okay," he replies. "These things happen. It's not our time, but it is yours. All I want is for my horse to be okay."

"Want to get some lunch?"

"Yeah. That sounds good."

Once he's finished, we walk down to the food stands and order a slice of pizza and a soda. We take our food and sit on the grass facing the lake. "Is everything really okay, Ri?" I ask, knowing that it isn't.

He shrugs. "I guess. I mean, it sucks about my horse. But, I'm fine."

I set my soda down and face him. "I know you better than that, and I know that you and Joel haven't been hanging out again. What gives?"

"Do I need to tell you? Because I'm thinking you already know what gives."

I nod and look down at my plate. "I sort of do. I know about the kiss."

"Right. Great."

"Riley, you know me well enough by now to know that I am not one to judge."

"You know my plan and my reasons. I can't have any of it threatened by Joel and his feelings."

"So, you just give up the friendship?" I ask.

"It's complicated. Can we not talk about it?"

"I get that, but I think this is something you need to work out."

"I can't do that. Not right now. Maybe after graduation I will be free and clear to act like the person I really am. I want to be able to make decisions without having to worry about getting a terrible reaction from my family that might affect my future or, God forbid, my being with Santos. But for now, Joel needs to keep his distance."

I don't comment. I figure maybe this is one of those things that is better left alone for now. I want to ask him about what Joel is hiding because Joel had indicated that Riley had some of that information. "Want to walk the course with me?" I ask.

"I would, but I need to be around for the vet. Besides, it's probably something you should do with Christian first."

"Yeah. He told me to walk it, then we'll have a group walk, then an individual walk with him, and then he suggests we go out and do it again by ourselves," I reply.

"He's got a method, that's for sure. At least with horses. I still have no idea what he thinks he's doing with Kayla Fairmont. I really think the right thing to do is tell Holden."

"I know. I think that it is the right thing, but I'm scared and it feels intrusive."

He starts laughing. "Listen to you. You ask everyone else questions. You intrude on everyone else's stuff, but in this situation you won't do the right thing because you're afraid that it will change your life . . . maybe ruin your chances . . . take away your scholarship."

I eye him because I can't believe what I am hearing. And because, even though it's painful, I have to admit that he's right.

I stare at him. "Yeah. You're probably not totally wrong, Riley. Maybe I am being selfish on this front. But see, this is my one chance, so I guess that makes me human. I guess you and I are kind of alike in that way. You know if anyone finds out about you that it will turn your world upside down, so that fear guides your decisions. It's kind of the same way for me. If Holden learns about Kayla and Christian from me, it could change my life—and for that matter, yours as well. It doesn't make it right. I get that, but what you are doing isn't right, either." I stand up and start to walk away. He's hit a piece of me that hurts.

"Vivvie, I'm sorry. I'm just being defensive. Come back here."

"It's fine. I'm going to walk the course." I keep walking, fighting back tears. I ask myself why I want to cry right now. I know the answer. It's because Riley is right about being honest with Holden. And, it's making me question what kind of person I really am.

I really, really wish it wasn't all so complicated.

CHAPTER *forty-eight*

I try to forget my problems for a minute as I begin my first ever walk on the course where the famous Rolex has taken place for over thirty years. This is the place where the World Equestrian Games happened just a few years ago, and where so many powerful, courageous horses and their riders have performed. I am pretty awed. I just wish I didn't have so many other things going on inside my head.

As I walk up to each jump and count strides, I think about all the possible options for my approach, my position, and Harmony's position. I look at each angle. I take into account the technicalities and the difficulties. Three-day eventing isn't just about getting on the horse and riding it over some jumps or in a dressage arena. It takes skill and study. It takes composure and rational thinking. There is so much that goes into each section of this sport, which is probably one of the reasons that I love it so much. It is challenging. It challenges Harmony and me both physically and mentally, and the bond between the horse and rider is hugely significant. There needs to be trust in the truest form when sailing over solid obstacles.

I spend almost two and a half hours out on course, thinking it through and studying it. I come to the last jump and see that the vet box is being set up. This is the real deal. When the horses come off course, the riders will head to the vet box where buckets of water and ice will be used to start cooling off the horses. Their temperatures, pulse, and respiration will be taken. We have ten minutes to get them back to normal. Temps can run up as high as 107, and the average temperature on a horse is between 99 and 101, so it's super important for obvious reasons to get them back to normal as quickly as possible. All the horses here are prime athletes and in prime condition. They should be, anyway.

I hear my name and turn around to see Joel. I wave and walk over to him. "You walk the course?" I ask.

"Just started. You?"

"I did."

"Doing this right means a lot more today than it did last night," he says. "It has always been a big deal to me, but Melody and I have to come out on top."

"What do you mean?"

"My dad. I talked to him and get this: the jerk tells me that I can only bring Melody back with me to school if I win this weekend."

"What?"

"Yeah." He shakes his head. "Come on, you know how these events go. There is never a guarantee even if you are the best. And, I am not the best."

"Don't shortchange yourself. You are good and Melody is good. I just think that is horrible of your father."

"That's my dad for you. See, he knows this will be pretty close to impossible for me."

"Have you spoken with your mom?"

"Yeah. She's trying to do everything she can to make sure that he can't take Melody from me, but it looks like he has the upper hand since he bought the horse when they were separating. I don't know what to do. I can't lose her."

"You won't. Focus on the win. That's what you have to do right now."

"Yeah. Right," he replies.

"Rock star attitude." I try to make light of it, get him to smile, but it's not working. I know the magnitude of what his father is suggesting. Just putting that kind of pressure on someone could make them blow the whole thing. "Maybe you should talk to Kayla and Holden."

"What could they do?"

"I don't know." I do have something brewing in my head. It's sort of on the wrong side of things, but if Joel does not win the event, this idea might be a last-ditch effort to help him keep his horse. "You know the saying that every horse is for sale, for a price?"

"Sure. I've heard that."

"What if someone came in and made an offer that your dad couldn't refuse?"

"Well, how would that do me any good? Then, I would lose her for sure."

"Maybe not. Not if the person who bought her was someone you were close to."

"Do you have money stored away somewhere that you haven't told me about, Vivvie?"

"No. But the Fairmonts have money."

"I can't ask them. I can't," he replies.

"I understand."

"I guess I'd better focus on the win," he says.

My heart goes out to him. His face looks so determined and, at the same time, the worry in his eyes isn't lost on me. I am seriously afraid for him.

"Want to walk the course again?" Joel asks.

"No. I'll do it tomorrow after my dressage test. I have a lesson with Kayla in about an hour. We are going to run through the test again."

"Ah. I had mine a bit ago with Holden. I heard about Riley and Santos. Can you tell him that I'm sorry since he isn't exactly speaking to me?"

"You got it."

I walk back to the barns thinking that I have to find a way to help Joel keep Melody.

CHAPTER *forty-nine*

"Let's do that half pass at the canter one more time,
Vivienne."

Harmony and I come around and make the turn
at letter A. As we head down the center line, I maintain forward
impulsion as I begin the half pass with her, which is a movement
in which the horse moves forward and sideways at the same time.
Harmony's doing it exactly right as her head leads slightly in the
direction of the movement. I'm asking her to maintain the bend
to the right by keeping my inside rein quiet. I support her neck by
using my outside rein to prevent her head from being over turned
to the inside. I place my inside seat bone more heavily on the saddle, to help maintain balance. My outside leg goes behind the girth
and the half halt actions of the outside rein, and helps Harmony
move in the half pass.

We do this move with fluidity and precision, and when I come
back around, Kayla tells me to halt her down the center line.

Harmony comes to a perfect halt. Kayla claps. "You do everything like you did today, you will have a great test tomorrow."

"Thank you." I let Harmony walk on a long rein.

Kayla comes into the arena and walks alongside of us. "You feeling good?"

"Yes. Kind of nervous," I reply.

"If you weren't nervous, you wouldn't care, and you wouldn't be good at what you do."

"I have to talk to you," I say. I can't believe that I am doing this, but I have to.

"Sure. You can always talk to me."

"It's about Joel." I tell her what is going on with him as far as Melody is concerned and what his dad has told him.

"That's awful. Really terrible."

"We have to do something," I say. "I mean, no one is ever guaranteed a win at an event. You know that."

"You're right. I don't know what I can do, though, Vivienne. I can try and talk to Mr. Parker, but that is really a family matter."

"You have to offer to buy Melody. And, then give her to Joel."

She laughs at this. "I can appreciate you being such a good friend, but that isn't the right answer. I can't just go and buy the horse and give it to Joel."

"Why can't you? You can afford to."

"That's quite an assumption." She is staring up at me. Harmony has stopped walking. Kayla is shading her eyes with her hand.

"But you can and you have to."

"Vivienne, you're being a little bit irrational."

"I know about you and Christian," I spit out.

"What?" She drops her hand.

"I know that you're having an affair. I've seen you two together and someone else saw you kissing. Someone who I have begged not to tell anyone about it."

She sighs and doesn't say anything for a minute. "You're a good kid. You're a fantastic rider and student, so I am having a hard time right now because it sounds like you're trying to blackmail me. Are you honestly suggesting that I make an offer to buy Joel's horse to prevent you from telling people what you think you know about Christian and me?"

I don't respond.

"I'm disappointed in you, but I'm going to tell you the truth. Maybe once you hear me out, you'll put all your ridiculous thoughts of blackmail aside. The facts are that Christian and I are together and we are in love. Holden and I have never been in love. We are friends and business partners. I met him after he came here from Canada and needed a green card to stay in the US. I liked him enough to help him gain citizenship by marrying him. He helped me with my riding career, and also in starting the academy. We became very comfortable in our life together. But after Serena was killed last year, I got to know Christian as I helped him through his grief, and although we didn't mean to, we fell in love with each other. It just happened. Holden understands this, which is why he's fine with us getting a divorce but continuing on as partners and friends. The school will remain as it is. It's just other things that will change."

I am speechless.

"I can really appreciate you wanting to help Joel out," she says.

"You are a good friend, but don't screw up your future," she says. "I'll see you in the morning."

I want to ask her if she plans to kick me out of school. I want to know why she and Holden lived the way they have for so long. But I can't do any of that. In fact, I'm getting the feeling I should never open my mouth again. All I can do is hope that I haven't completely messed up my future at Fairmont.

CHAPTER *fifty*

W hat is it?" Tristan asks. "You're so quiet tonight. Is it more than just your nerves?"

I gaze out at the peaceful koi pond. Tristan and I decided to bring sandwiches here and eat a dinner along its banks since there isn't a party tonight. Of course there isn't, because tomorrow is when the competition all begins.

"Kind of. Not really. " Before I can start crying, I tell him everything—about Joel, Christian, and Kayla . . . and what she said to me.

"Hey, it's going to be okay. You were trying to do something good and Kayla knows that."

"It's not like me, though. I was willing to blackmail Kayla Fairmont!"

"For a good reason."

"That doesn't make it right."

He puts an arm around me and pulls me in close. "What you did makes me love you even more. You are human." He smiles at me.

"What did you say?"

"That you're human, and sometimes we do what we have to do to protect people who we love."

"No. That's not quite what you said," I say. "You said that what I said to Kayla made you love me even more."

"Oh, that. Okay. Yes, Vivienne . . . guess what? I love you."

Heat rises to my cheeks. "Oh."

"And?"

"I think I love you, too," I say.

"Think?"

"I mean, I do. I love you."

He tickles me around my waist. "Good. Now that we have that out of the way, let's eat our dinner. Tomorrow is big."

"Yes it is." I grow quiet again though because I really need him to be honest with me. "We just said we loved each other and that means the world to me, but . . ."

"Uh-oh. But what?"

"I need to know what you're keeping from me. About your family."

He sighs heavily. "I can't."

"I'm worried about you. I can help you, and I'm worried that Lydia is holding this over your head, and that it can really be bad for you. I have this feeling . . ." I can't tell him that his horse has also given me information. I am also curious as to what Lydia implied about him just keeping his secret because he can.

He shakes his head. "I'll tell you what. . . . I'll make you a deal.

Let's get through this week and think about doing the best that we can out here so we can both wind up together at Liberty Farms this summer, and when we get back to Fairmont next week, I promise that I will tell you everything. Okay?"

"I think it'll have to be okay."

We finish dinner and walk back to the house. Once again he leaves me at my door with me wanting him to come inside the room, but God knows if we got caught it would surely seal my fate at Fairmont, which I think is in limbo as it is anyway. If I were Kayla, I wouldn't be thinking too highly of me right now. On top of feeling my nerves race in regards to the competition, I'm having anxiety about whether or not I'll even have a school to go back to. I'm also coming to grips with the idea that Tristan isn't going to tell me what's going on in his life until we are back at school. As I think about all of this, a terrible thought occurs to me: if I am asked to leave Fairmont, I will lose Harmony because she belongs to the school. As this thought sinks in, I run to the bathroom and throw up my dinner.

I'm sitting on the toilet leaning my head back against the wall when I hear angry voices coming from next door. Joel is in the room next to mine. I can't make out who he is talking to. It's a girl. Is it Lydia?

I crack open my door and wait to see who comes out of his room. I am pretty shocked when after a few minutes I see Emily storm out.

I don't even try to follow the *none of my business* rule—it just doesn't come to me naturally. I leave my room and go after Emily. I know that her room is in another wing of the house. I spot her up ahead and call out her name. "Emily, wait up."

She turns around and it looks like she's been crying. "What?" she says, sounding irritated.

"Is everything okay? I didn't mean to, but I heard you and Joel, and it didn't sound all happy."

She opens her bedroom door and doesn't respond. Finally, she looks at me and says, "Come in."

I walk into her room, which is as beautiful as mine but with just a slightly different décor. The room is light and airy, painted white with a dark wood canopy bed and a red lounge chair by the window. And, as to be expected, there are framed photos of famous event horses on the walls. I notice a bottle of over-the-counter sleeping pills on her nightstand and there are a couple of prescription vials as well. "Are you okay?" I ask and point to the vials.

She laughs in a sarcastic way. "No. I am not okay. I'm on antidepressants and antianxiety drugs."

My eyes widen.

"That's right. I have severe anxiety issues, believe it or not, and I have to take meds for it."

"Oh." That is all I can come up with because this is a bit of a shock. Sure, I know that Emily has issues. That much has been obvious to me, but I didn't know the extent of her problems. I have to wonder if the Fairmonts are aware of this, because I don't know what the rules are on riding horses at this level while taking the types of medications that she's clearly on.

"Right. Oh. Hey, so, did you know that Joel is gay?"

Once again—caught off guard. "Did he tell you that?"

"No. He didn't. I received a text message from an unknown number that said he is. I didn't believe it at first. I thought it was a joke because, first off, it came from someone who was claiming to be a friend. But then I started thinking about it. I see how all over each other you and Tristan are, and it sure isn't that way for me and Joel. He doesn't even seem to want to kiss me. He barely wants to hold my hand. It kind of made sense to me then that it might be true. I went and asked him, and he didn't exactly come out and say that he is gay, but he didn't deny it, either. He just looked at me and didn't say anything."

"I'm sorry, Emily."

She wipes tears from her face. "Did you know, Vivienne?"

"I don't want to get involved in this," I say.

"Great. Who else knows?"

I shake my head. "I wish I could help you. I should probably be getting back, and you should try and let this stuff go because tomorrow is a big day."

"Oh yeah, just let it go that Joel has been leading me on all this time and no one was willing to tell me the truth. Screw you, Vivienne."

"I'm sorry." I leave Emily's room upset with Joel—and angry with myself for knowing the part I played in causing her pain. Especially since, from the looks of it, she seems to have enough pain inside of her already.

CHAPTER *fifty-one*

reathe out there, kid. Just ride it like we talked about on the walk," Christian says. "You being the path finder is a big responsibility out there. You and Harmony are our strongest rider-and-horse combination, so remember that the job for you is to go clear, even if you get some time penalties. You come back and report how the course rides to me, and I'll share the information with everyone out after you. Remember everything we talked about when we walked the course together."

I try and take his advice and breathe. Today is a major day. Yesterday was dressage, but today is the best, the optimum, the most exciting day of all. It is cross-country day, and we are all at the barn before seven. The lines to get into the horse park were really long, and I have gone over the course yet again. I feel as ready as Harmony and I can possibly be. I am the eighth rider out, and my time to go is 8:58. Horses are being sent out on the course in four-minute intervals. The weather is a little sticky, and there is a drizzle every so often. It did rain last night, so I know there may be some slick spots to watch for out there.

I woke up with the fierce determination that my focus would remain solely on Harmony for the rest of our time here. The drama and antics of everyone around me is eating me alive, but I shouldn't be letting it distract me. I signed up to ride and win, and that is my plan.

And so far, my plan has paid off! Our dressage score was a 31.2, which is really fantastic. I am in second place at the moment, and Joel is in first. I guess he is finding his focus as well. I haven't spoken to him about Emily, and I haven't spoken to Emily any further, either.

"Okay." All I want right now is a moment by myself with Harmony. I am extra nervous to be chosen as the team's path finder.

"Why don't we go over and warm up?" Christian says.

I agree, and Kayla adds, "You've got this. I'll be in the vet box."

"Thank you." I appreciate that she's not being weird with me after the way I practically tried to blackmail her.

We head over to the warm-up area with Christian. I do a short hack on Harmony, and then Christian has me start sending her over the jumps. The clock ticks down, and it isn't long before Christian is letting me know it's time for us to go to the start box. I lean over Harmony's neck and whisper, "You ready? This is our moment, sweet girl. This is it."

The starter gives us a two-minute warning. I work to clear my thoughts so the only thing left in my mind is me and Harmony. I imagine for a moment what I want her gallop to feel like, how my body will react to set her up for the jumps, and quickly tick off the jumps in my mind.

"One minute," the starter says, breaking through my thoughts. My body has tensed and now Harmony knows what is coming. I have to let her break to a jog to keep her from rearing up. I circle her around the box, cutting in through the opening and out the side to keep her moving in a forward direction.

I check both of my watches to make sure they are cleared and ready to start. I concentrate on my breathing, willing myself to stay calm and collected as the adrenaline starts to pump through my body.

"Fifteen seconds," the starter calls.

I time my final circle around the box to bring me to a standstill just inside the side opening as he begins to count down from ten. I start my backup watch. Harmony is alert and suddenly stands stock-still, her head raised and ears pricked forward intensely out the opening.

"Five, four . . ."

I push the button to start my watch and glance down to make sure it is counting the seconds—three, two, one.

"You're off. Have a good ride," I hear the starter call as I nudge Harmony in the sides and she explodes out of the box.

"Easy, girl." I steady her with my voice and take a strong hold on the reins.

I need to settle her into a rhythm for these first couple of fences and not let her get too flat. I keep her to a steady pace and stretch up to the first ramp, emblazoned with the Young Equestrians Championships logo. As we fly over it, I let myself relish just for a moment that I am really here doing this!

Back to concentrating. We have a long gallop to the next fence, a fallen log, and Harmony wants to go much faster than I will let her. My instructions as the path finder for our team were to start out five to ten seconds behind the minute markers until the halfway point. Depending on how much horse I have left, I could use the second half of the course to take advantage of the down-sloping terrain and make up some time.

I see my stride to the log from at least eight out, and my stomach flips with pleasure. I lower my seat to the saddle and feel Harmony's strong uphill strides take us up to the log and over right out of stride.

The number-three jump is a big cabin with a bit of a drop landing, so as I approach I sit up taller and add a little leg to make sure Harmony stays strong to the base. She hits it just right, a little on the deep side, and as we fly over, I slip my reins to give her the freedom to use her neck in the air.

The first water combination comes up quick. Just one more table to set us up before the turn. My watch starts to beep. Perfect. I am about ten seconds behind my first minute. Plenty of time to make it up later. As Harmony's huge stride carries us to the table, I see a flyer coming. Shoot! That's exactly what Christian told me might happen. If I hit a flyer here, then Harmony will be too strung out for the big log drop into the water and might stop. There's nothing I can do to change it, though; she has locked onto the table and won't listen to my half halts. She leaves the ground from so far away, I feel like we will never come back down. As I land, I stand up and pull hard on the reins, moving the bit in her mouth.

Thankfully, she responds. It really clicks for me that I am actually here with her and we are doing this together! As Harmony slows her speed, I am able to sit deep in the saddle and really put my leg on to get her hind end underneath her and gather up her impulsion.

I know I need to really come at this strong, as sometimes she hesitates a bit at the first water. I round the turn and feel her powerful hindquarters pounding the ground. Her ears prick at the log and I know she is measuring it up.

I feel her tense up, there is a flash through my mind, and for a brief second I see that vision of murky gray that she has shown me in the past. Great. Just great. She wants to talk now, but I have no idea what she wants to tell me. Plus, this is weird. Usually we don't communicate like that when I'm in the saddle.

"Focus, girl!"

I feel her lose impulsion as she peeks at the water. I reach back with one hand and slap her lightly on the haunches with my stick. She responds to my touch and leaps off the ground, trusting me completely and flying over the log and down the 4'6" drop into the water. I remember to stay tall with my body so I don't get pulled forward, because I have to focus on the turn to the bank. Nerves are flowing through me because I have this bad feeling something is awry with Harmony, but I have no time to figure it out right now. We have to press on.

My reins still long from the drop, I widen my arms so I can guide her through the turn and work with my legs to keep her strides even and balanced and she gallops through the water, one, two, three, four, five, six. I count to myself and squeeze on six to bounce up the bank and over the brush on the way out. Yes! We're through! Maybe I am wrong and there isn't anything off with my horse. Maybe it's just that we're both feeling the anxiety of where we are and what we are doing in this moment.

I give Harmony a huge pat and I hear the cheers from the crowd as I gallop on through the roped lane. There is a long gallop here before the next jump, and Harmony has finally stopped pulling my arms out. I can hear the sounds of her strong and regular breathing and feel the air rushing by my face, making tears stream from my eyes in the wind. Our movements are in sync, my arms following her head and neck and my legs and hips rising and falling with each stride bounding off the ground. I feel as if we are flying.

I can see the trainer up ahead and I stand up slightly in the stirrups, raising my hands so Harmony knows a jump is coming. She adjusts her balance immediately without me having to touch the reins and we sail over it without losing any time. Just the angled brushes and the two-minute mark before I get to the coffin combination. I know the first two riders on course had problems there, so Christian's last-minute advice was to take the option on the right side. It was only one stride longer than the short way, and he felt the extra stride would give me time to get Harmony's shoulder straight and prevent a run out at the corner. I needed to get home with a clear round to start our team out right. Even if that meant getting a few time penalties and losing my individual medal position.

Before the turn, I slow up so that Harmony knows something serious is coming. She is down to business now and comes back to me way easier than at the water. I pulse with my legs, gathering her up underneath me and controlling her speed with my stretched back. I keep a strong stride to the first element of the coffin, an airy hanging log, and get ready to lean back for the sloping ground on the other side. Two short strides and she leaps the ditch, stumbling a bit as she lands. I react quickly, helping her get her head back up with my reins and find the curved line I need to ride to the corner. I see my focal point on the other side of the corner, a dead tree stump just up on the hill beyond the ropes, and ride with all of my body and mind to that point.

Ride the line, not the stride, I hear in my head. But I can't stop the ticking of strides I feel underneath me; one, two, three . . . and then suddenly my stomach is in my throat, as my horse drops out from underneath me, slipping on the grass in the turn and almost going down. *Noooo,* I scream out inside my head. *No!*

I don't take my eyes off my line, but kick hard with my right leg and open my left rein to show her the way. She picks herself up, and for a moment I think we are running past the corner, when in an instant, she shifts her balance and throws her shoulders up and over, making it between the flags. My right stirrup grazes the flag, knocking it down, but I know we made it clear.

Just one breather fence, the table before the next big combination. I focus on Harmony's gallop, making sure she is finding her footing easily. The sound of her hooves is muffled by the emerald-green turf, and I feel her strides coming easily as the damp grass gives her just the right amount of rebound. A few drops of rain hit my cheeks and the cool wetness feels refreshing.

The big drop looms ahead and I see another flyer coming. Not wanting to make the same mistake I did before the water, I check her back with two strong half halts and add in another stride before we jump the drop. The extra stride helps give her jump more scope and we soar into the air. I feel her back rounding up underneath my seat and we come down, Harmony staying light and balanced on her feet.

I know I made the right choice as I stay out for the curving seven strides and hit the first corner exactly on the line we had walked.

The next jump is crazy. The ditch and wall are so massive that we hadn't even stopped long to look at it on the course walk. Christian had said, "Just keep walking; don't look down in the ditch or dwell on its size; this question is all about the bravery of the rider. Focus on the top of the brush, not the ditch, for your takeoff spot and try to bring your horse right to the base of the ditch. You need to hit this jump with lots of impulsion on a bit of a building stride, just like a triple bar."

Joel and I had disobeyed him and gone back by ourselves later to psych each other out by standing down in the ditch, the wall looming two feet over our heads. We laughed about it at the time, but now I was sorry we had. My heart was thumping so hard in my chest. I had never jumped anything so big or intimidating in my life.

"Ten seconds of boldness," I tell myself. I remembered Brian Sabo telling us those words during a cross-country clinic that my mom had sent me to a year ago, before I had been accepted at Fairmont. It was the last clinic I'd taken Dean to.

I don't exactly close my eyes, but I stare beyond the top of the brush and pull from deep within myself a bravery I didn't even know I had. Harmony senses my renewed commitment and quickens her pace in response.

Suddenly, it's as if I am mounted on Pegasus, and I start driving her every stride toward the immense obstacle. The brush comes into sharp focus, and I feel I couldn't possibly be any closer to the ditch without falling in it. She shifts her weight back, pushing us up and off the ground and soaring over the wall, without even touching the brush on top.

OH MY GOD!

As we touch ground again, I lean forward, urging her on. Thankful that I finally am letting her out, Harmony gives a fresh burst of speed. I have about ten seconds down at the three-minute mark, and this is a good galloping stretch where I can pick up a few seconds before the sunken road.

The wine barrels were cleverly placed just before a turn to slow up horse-and-rider pairs and to help them get organized for the sunken road. After that bold jump at the ditch wall and the long gallop, I really need to get that short, bouncy "coffin canter" again. The distance in the sunken road only walked in thirty-four feet, so I know it's going to be snug. I don't quite get the balance I want on my first half halt, so I send Harmony forward again, and this time when I ask her to come back, it's just right. I count the strides to the rails, making myself keep the rhythm without speeding up. She drops her head and neck as she begins to land and I feel her hind legs coming down hard on the rails.

The sunken road catches her by surprise and she drops from the air too soon. Slightly stunned by the hard rub, she hesitates and I coax her on with a cluck. Quickly regaining her composure in one stride, she lowers herself easily down the bank and takes the two collected strides across.

I sit up and add as much leg as I can muster to help her jump up the second bank. I still have to get turned to the skinny, so I turn with both reins, close my outside leg, and pump with my whole body to close the distance in the three strides. We are still farther away than I would like, but Harmony leaves the ground anyway, and once again that gray, almost black image flashes through my mind. "Stop that!" I yell.

I get to the back seat, slipping my reins to avoid catching her in the mouth. Well, it isn't pretty, but as I know, sometimes in cross-country riding you've just got to "get her done!"

The next three fences fly by, flowing right out of stride.

As we reach the top of the hill, Harmony takes a big, deep breath and waits for my direction. I add leg to tell her we have a jump ahead of us, and her ears turn and focus on the giant log ahead. A big leap over and we land halfway down the hill on the other side, turning and refocusing to go back up the bounce bank steps on the other side. She covers the distance easily, gathers up, and bounds up the steps and the two strides out over the cabin. I hear the cheers again and reach out to give Harmony a huge pat on the neck. She has to be the best cross-country horse ever! She made that obstacle feel like nothing!

Now the ground has some downhill slope, and Christian had said I could let her gallop a bit on this stretch if I needed to make up time. That minute flies by with only the double brush and the hammock in my way. By the time I hit six minutes, I am right on my minute mark, with plenty of horse left.

The Head of the Lake. The famous water complex that I had seen on TV so many times during Rolex competitions. I see the crowds of people lining the ropes, and my stomach flips once at the thought of all of them watching me. Pushing those thoughts aside, I review what we had talked about in the course walk. I start to go through all the steps, see my stride, and push for the log. Harmony responds so quickly and with such force that I find myself flying into the one stride with way more power than I need. She jumps in so big that she hits the water with as much force as if we were leaping off a two-story building! I fall forward onto her neck and drop my rein.

I'll never get organized in time for the fish, but luckily we had walked the option line. I sit up, pulling hard on my left rein, as I yell "option" so the fence judge knows my plan. This way will cost me time, but I will at least still be clear. I circle back through the water, jumping the black flag option going the other way and finding my line to the duck. On any other day, the fish and duck might actually appear as intricate art carvings out of wooden logs, and they are, but today, to Harmony and me, they are a part of the challenges we are facing on course.

Shoot! I check my watch as we gallop away from the lake and see that we are down by fifteen seconds. A costly mistake.

The picture frame is next, and Harmony ducks her head and neck slightly as we sail through it. There is a long gallop stretch to the next oxer, and I take a chance and keep up my speed. Ears pricked, gallop strong and uphill, we meet it slightly long, but well within her abilities. If I can keep up this pace, I just might make it. My watch goes off signifying seven minutes. Two minutes from home!

At the bottom of the hill are the wine barrels and then the final combination on course, the chevrons on the mounds. The way Harmony is eating up the ground, I don't want to slow down, but I know I have to get the strides right between the chevrons. I jump the first one and sit up and say, "Whoa." Harmony immediately listens, shortening up her stride and meeting the second on a perfect four strides. Yes!

Two jumps left and a minute to get to the finish line. Harmony is tiring slightly but when I urge her on with a cluck, she responds with another surge of energy. We have never done a course this long before. In my head are Christian's words: "Riding a tired horse isn't the same as riding a fresh one. You've got to help them out a bit more. Help hold them together."

The time is going to be close. I keep up my speed, urging her on every stride with my legs and my voice. "Keep going, girl; I know we can do this." We fly down the hill and approach the table. I don't think I can gather her together to ride to the base, so I keep up the pace and move up the last three strides. Maybe a touch risky, but I just sense it's the right thing to do.

One jump left. I glance at my watch. Twenty seconds to go. I can't back off on my speed one bit. Christian had told us to ride the last fence with as much conviction as the first—"no last-fence-itis," he called it. I muster every bit of skill I have ever learned. I use my legs, my balance, my core. I keep my pace up, count my rhythm in my head, and thankfully, see the perfect distance. One, two, three, four, and over!

I lean forward, urging us on the final strides to the finish line. My watch shows us right on the optimum time, and my head explodes with sheer happiness! I drop my reins and throw my arms around Harmony's neck. Tears of joy stream down my cheeks as she pulls herself easily up to a jog.

She holds her head and neck high, like she is proud of herself, too. My pit crew comes running over to grab her. I unclip my air vest as I slide my right leg over and land lightly alongside her. The vets are already at her head, beginning to take her pulse and respiration. Another one comes up behind me, ready to take her temp.

The crew strips off her saddle as the vets do what they need to do. Harmony's nostrils flare pink and she is breathing hard. The crew goes to work grabbing cold sponges from an icy water bucket and they begin sponging her down.

My horse starts to breathe easier after a few minutes and by the time her final respirations, pulse, and temperature are taken she is where she needs to be in recovery.

I spot Christian running over to me. He gives me two high fives and then clasps my hands in his. He looks as emotional as I feel. He then gives me a quick hug. "Nice ride, kid!"

"Thanks." I've caught my breath, too, and I give him the low-down on the course so he can go back and report to the other team members.

"Really great, Vivienne," he says again. "I've got to see Tristan out now. I'm so proud of you."

I smile and wipe away tears of ecstasy as my crew hands me Harmony's lead rope. I kiss her nose and pat her on her neck. "I love you," I tell her. After a ride like that—after riding this horse on a course like this one, well, I know one thing: my life has just changed forever.

CHAPTER *fifty-two*

I take Harmony back to the barn, and even though I want to be out watching the rest of the team go, I owe it to her to be the one to take care of her. I could hand her off to the groom, but decide against it. This horse has just given me everything she has.

Back in the cross-ties, the first thing I do is get her a half-dozen cookies. Then, I prepare the icing machine by packing it with ice, placing the freezing wraps around her front legs, and turning the machine on. Cold immediately begins pumping through the hoses attached to the wraps. She shifts her weight slightly as this happens and I say, "It's okay. Stand still, sweet girl." I then pack a set of rear leg ice boots with crushed ice and wrap her back legs, since the ice machine can only function on two legs at a time.

I also get from the tack room an infrared machine designed for healing and recovery. I run the wand connected to the machine over her neck and back. She is standing there so kindly with her eyes half closed. She's exhausted, and I probably am, too, but it hasn't caught up with me yet.

I sit down in one of the folding chairs outside the tack room after treating her, and wait for her icing to be finished so that I can poultice and wrap her. Today was tough, and I want her as ready and recovered as possible for tomorrow's stadium round.

I close my eyes and finally breathe a sigh of relief that we made it through the cross-country phase. I am startled out of my reverie by someone saying my name. "Vivienne, isn't it?"

I open my eyes to see Chris Haverly standing over me. "Yes. Hello."

"Nice ride. Looks like you just sealed your fate in joining us at Liberty Farms this summer. That is, unless you bomb tomorrow."

"Thanks. You ride at Liberty Farms?"

"I do. I ride jumpers. Used to ride with your friend Joel all the time," he replies.

"Joel is your friend, too, right?"

"You know how friendships are. One day you're the best of . . . The next day . . . well, things change. Don't get me wrong. Joel is a great guy, but since he's moved out west, we've fallen out of contact, really."

The timer goes off on the ice machine and I stand up. "That's too bad."

"It is what it is."

"Right." This guy is so unnerving, and I have no idea why he is even here talking to me.

"Shouldn't you be out watching the rest of your team go?" he asks.

"I wanted to take care of my horse."

"Commendable. Very. Your teammate—Emily, I think her name is—should be finished soon, I think."

"I think you're right. I hope she does well."

I frown slightly. Why does he even know Emily?

"Okay," he says. "Well, I might try and catch her. I have something for her. Again, great ride. Have a nice day."

"You, too." I watch him walk away and get a bad feeling. My team members can be off, too, but not like that guy. He's just plain-out weird. And that instinct I have about him gets even stronger as I glance down the barn aisle while carrying the portable ice machine and look into the tack room to see that Chris Haverly is walking with Joel's future stepmonster, Tiffany. Paisley's weird boyfriend, James, from the dinner the other night, is with them. I have to wonder why Chris Haverly really came in here to talk to me, and I have to wonder what he wants with Emily.

CHAPTER *fifty-three*

"How happy are you right now?" Tristan asks as I lean into him.

"Pretty happy."

"Pretty happy?"

"Of course I am happy." I laugh. "I'm sorry you guys had a stop out there today."

"Happens. We didn't come in last and there is always next year. We always have a good stadium round, so who knows," he says referring to the last event, which is show jumping. "Wish we could have done better for the team, though. But, I am really happy for you ... and Joel. I'm surprised that Joel is right there with you, but after what you told me that his dad said, well, it's a good thing. Promise me, though, that you will compete to win. Don't throw this because of Joel."

We are at the coffee hut on the grounds at the horse park. Today is the third and final day of competition. Joel and I are nearly tied in the standings. I am barely in first place. One rail, one tiny mistake, could knock me out of position. Tristan and Sebastian had a stop out on cross-country yesterday, and the resulting time faults pushed them down to twentieth. Lydia actually had a great go and is now in tenth, and believe it or not, Emily, who is clearly avoiding everyone, is in sixth. Looks like she came to try and win, too. I hope it is for herself, though, and not for her mother.

I am troubled this morning that if I win, Joel will lose his horse. All I have ever wanted is to win a competition at this level, so yes, I am torn about how to feel. Completely torn. I look away from Tristan, because I don't know what I'll do when it comes down to it.

"Vivvie, promise me you will go out into that stadium arena to win this," Tristan says, repeating himself.

"I will."

"Good." He takes our coffees off the counter and hands me mine. "We'd better get back to the barns. Christian wants us to meet him there to go over and walk the course."

"We'd better." As we walk back to the barns, I blurt out, "I was also thinking that tonight we could sneak out after the party, and . . ."

He stops again and looks deep into my eyes. "And?"

I nod.

"You sure?"

"Yes."

"Maybe we, well, you, should think about this a little longer," he replies.

"I have thought about it, and it's what I want," I say. And, I really have been thinking about it, even though I keep swearing to myself that I am not going to. I know I'm supposed to be thinking about nothing but my goals, but I'm finding it impossible. I'm starting to think I am going a little nutty because I realize that I am becoming a big set of walking contradictions, but the facts are that I think about Tristan a lot of the time. And, he did tell me that he loves me, and he did promise to tell me what is going on in his life—so yes, I've thought about it. And I think I'm ready.

"Let's get through the day first, and take it one step at a time."

"You want to, don't you?" I ask. "I mean, you do want to be with me, right?"

"Of course I do. There's nothing more that I want. I just want you to be sure, and I know what today means for you. I think we should get through it and go from there." He kisses my lips and then says, "Trust me, there is nothing more that I want than you."

We make it to the barns and I spot Joel. He looks like he's been in tears for some reason, and I tell Tristan that I am going to take a minute and talk to him.

"You okay?" I ask.

"Sure. Nerves, but I'm fine," Joel replies.

"Have you been crying?"

"No, Vivienne. Stop being such a worrywart. It doesn't do anyone any good. Go out there today to win it, too. I'll know if you don't."

I look past the barn row and see Chris Haverly turning the corner, walking away from the barns. I wonder if he's just been down here talking to Joel. Every time that guy is around, Joel seems to be really upset. And, I think that Riley has some idea why Chris Haverly upsets Joel. But there I go again, thinking too much and too hard about other people's problems and troubles when I should be clearing my head for the day's events.

I pat Joel on the shoulder but feel like there is nothing for me to say. Joel has kind of made it clear that he wants some space from me, so I am going to let him have it. I don't say much else to anyone on the team as we meet Christian at the Rolex Stadium and walk the course with him.

Like yesterday, the time goes by rather quickly, and before long I am putting on my jacket, helmet, and gloves. I haven't see Kayla anywhere yet today and I wonder why. Christian comes by and gives me a leg up. "Rider up," he says. "I am proud of you, Vivienne. Why don't you head to the warm-up and let's get this done."

I do as I'm told. As we leave the barn, I see Austen talking with Lydia and it looks tense and somewhat heated. *Ignore! Ignore! Ignore!* I forcefully remind myself that this is no time for others' issues. Even if they feel like they involve me.

Standing in first place, I am last in the order of go. All the pressure is on me as I get to the ring. There are now only eight in my division left to jump the stadium round. The rails have been coming down all over the place on this very tough Richard Jeffries–designed course. I watched a few go and it hasn't helped to quell my nerves much. Christian told me, though, not to spend too much time watching the last-place riders. They weren't on their game the day before and that is why they are sitting in the lowest places.

When we walked the course, I was a bit intimidated. I felt so small down in that big ring looking up at the huge covered stadium. The footing is perfect, the same felt-and-fiber blend that had been put down for the World Equestrian Games. Here I was; I would be jumping on the same ground as my heroes Will Simpson, Beezie Madden, Mary King, and Gina Miles.

Painted in rich, beautiful colors, the jumps are the same ones used for the Rolex event, and each one is designed after a famous Kentucky farm. The course is in signature Jeffries style—very technical with lots of related distances and bending lines.

On a good day, with a fresh horse, we would have to be on our game to jump a clear round on a course this challenging—let alone on a tired horse that had just galloped three miles yesterday and over thirty-six obstacles!

Thankfully, Harmony seems to be ready for the challenge. I'm glad I treated her with kid gloves after yesterday, because now she does feel comfortable as she stretches out in the trot. I change her bend back and forth and ride her deep and low. Her canter is loose and rhythmic. I can't believe how great she feels after that grueling course yesterday. Two more riders leave the warm-up to jump their rounds, and Christian motions for me to jump the cross rail. As I canter my approach, I see it coming up a bit long, but maintain a steady, strong canter. Harmony punches the takeoff, flying into the air in an exuberant leap, and lands, shaking her head. Imagery flashes in my mind—pink, heart, and wings. I pat her on the neck. "You like that, huh? A little proud of yourself right about now?"

Christian chuckles and motions for me to head to the vertical, giving me the hand signal to bring her in a little deeper this next time. Each jump is better than the next, and after a couple jumps over the oxer at maximum height, Christian signals for me to come over. "Let's just try to get a rub over a vertical, and then you are ready to head in."

The stadium at the horse park is huge. It seats over ten thousand. The arena is large. I hear my name over the loudspeaker:

"Vivienne Taylor coming in the ring, standing in first place riding Harmonious Movement." My nerves set in, but luckily so does my focus. Joel, being in second, has just gone before me and had a clean round. It has been one of only three clear rounds so far today. The time is hard to make, too, and I don't even have room for one time penalty without losing my placing. Joel just took a very risky inside turn to the triple combination and it paid off. He left all the rails off and shaved off several precious seconds. I weigh my options in my mind. The competition is mine to win or lose. If I take my time and go the long way to get around to the triple, I will surely have time faults. Joel will be guaranteed the win and get to keep his horse. It wouldn't look like I was trying to throw it. No one could blame me for taking extra time in the turn to set up a clean ride and go through the triple.

It could totally backfire on me, though. It's always possible that even with the extra time I might still have a rail down somewhere on the course and then I would drop down several places and be out of the ribbons completely. My emotions are all over the place. It would be so hard to see Joel lose his horse. He loves that horse and would be totally crushed to see his new stepfamily take her away from him. But there is a fire burning deep within me. I have prepared my whole life to be here in this moment. I have dreamed of it and worked every day—and so has my mom. She has sacrificed so much for me to be here, too. My mind races through the last couple of years, and in an instant, my resolve is clear. I owe this to myself. And to Harmony. We are here and we earned it.

I square my shoulders, take a deep breath, and canter into the ring. I canter right past the liverpool, so that Harmony can get a quick look at the spooky blue water underneath it, and halt in front of the judges' stand. I can't see the judges, they are so high up in the tower, but I salute anyway and hear the buzzer almost immediately. I glance over to see the giant times start to count down from forty-five and am a bit startled to see an image of myself and Harmony on the Jumbotron in the corner.

I shake myself out of it and focus on the task at hand. It is up to me now. I have studied the course, gone over the lines and distances in my mind over and over until I could practically ride the course in my sleep. I have visualized what every stride needs to feel like, and now all I have to do is execute. I use up almost all of my forty-five seconds, weaving among a couple of the scarier obstacles. One of the great things about Harmony is that she is very careful in the stadium, but sometimes her spook causes me to flatten her stride too much and take down a rail behind. The first line is two oxers set on a bending seven strides. Just enough time to panic, but I keep my impulsion up with my leg and keep an even count in my head to force myself to wait it out. She clears the second with so much room to spare that I have a soaring feeling.

A hard right turn to a four stride of airy verticals on a tight distance. Long gallop now to the big oxer over the liverpool. Harmony peeks down and gives a stutter step, my stomach lurches, but then we are up and over and I can hear the crowd gasp. She lands clear and I immediately start counting the ten strides to get me to the double combination. Oxer in, land, rebalance, one-two, close my leg, up and over the vertical. Land, add leg, keep a steady five to the oxer. We land clear from that, and the crowd applauds in appreciation. Rollback turn and now we have the bending line. It rides in either an outside six or direct five. The short turn might make us lose impulsion and then the six would be the right choice, but Harmony is responding to me with such enthusiasm that I keep coming in the turn and see a forward stride to the first oxer. She jumps it boldly, so I instantly react and decide to go for the five.

Now I have to decide, Am I going inside or outside to the triple? After the forward line I just rode, going outside would make sense, but before my mind can decide, my body reacts. I am collecting Harmony, increasing my impulsion as I shorten her stride to turn. She whips around inside the cleverly placed arena decoration, and I am delighted to see a perfect distance to the triple. We can't miss now!

Keep it together, Viv, I tell myself. Harmony's rhythmic stride feels like a part of me. We are completely in sync as we cover the final three strides to the triple. Up and over the first, I can feel her flip her back end up easily clearing the vertical, one stride, and she coils and springs over the huge oxer in the middle. I hold my breath while we're airborne and give a gasp at the landing. One, two, I count it out and we are up and over the vertical on the way out, Harmony straining to push her way out of the deep distance.

I'm sure it is loud, but the crowd noise seems distant. I am all focus now. One jump left. A bending eight strides to the final vertical. It's an airy plank sitting on very flat cups. I had seen many riders, excited to be at the last jump, flatten and leave a stride out here, knocking the plank to the ground and taking four faults with it.

We sail over that last and final jump and my hand immediately goes to her neck, patting her in praise. "Good girl! Good girl!" I say out loud. The applause rings through the stadium. We trot out and I spot Joel. I turn back to look at the time again on the timer, and I see that we beat his time by two seconds. We've won!

My stomach sinks. Kayla comes up beside us. "Great! That was great!"

"Joel," I say, looking down at her.

She smiles up at me. "It's okay, Vivienne. I'm sorry I wasn't here to tell you earlier, but I was making a deal with Mr. Parker. I bought Melody for Joel."

I jump off Harmony and throw my arms around her. "Thank you! Thank you!" Tears are streaming down my face. "Does he know?"

"I just told him," she says.

Joel walks over to me and hugs me. "I'm happy you came to win. Good going."

"You're not mad at me?" I ask.

"No. I know what you did. I know what you asked Kayla to do, and all I can say is that I am truly happy. I don't ever have to worry again about Melody being taken away from me. Maybe your snooping so much does have a benefit." He laughs.

"Maybe it does."

CHAPTER *fifty-four*

I've taken more time getting ready than usual. It's going to be a big night. This was a big day. It was a huge, wonderful week and I am feeling so, so good!

The celebration takes place tonight again at the stallion shed. Just like the night when we first arrived, the space looks beautiful filled with flowers and candles, and the food is delicious. Tristan keeps touching my leg. He's handed me a card and told me to wait to read it when he gets up. I'm anxious to do so.

Austen is not sitting with Lydia tonight, and in an interesting turn I spot her seated across the way with, of all people, Chris Haverly. He looks animated as he's talking with the group at his table. Candlelight catches the shining gold of his watch. Hmmm. Maybe Chris Haverly and Lydia would be a perfect couple. They both seem to like expensive things.

I wish Riley was here, so I could be a catty girl for a minute and point out the obnoxiousness coming from Haverly's table. He wasn't feeling well earlier, so he wanted to rest up and try to feel better before flying back. I think he is pretty bummed out about Santos, and we've been a little distant since our argument. I feel bad about it and need to make amends with him. In another odd turn of events, I see Joel sitting with Emily and they seem to be talking. That is a good thing.

As we finish dinner, Emily comes over to me and says, "Can I talk to you?"

"Sure." I excuse myself.

We walk outside of the arena. The night air is crisp. A horse whinnies in the distance. The smell of dew on the grass is fresh and heady.

"I'm sorry I got upset with you last night. I was shaken up," Emily says.

"It's okay. It really is."

"Great ride today," she adds.

"Thanks. You, too." Emily had wound up fifth. The team would be taking third place.

"Surprise, surprise. Maybe my mother will finally be proud. Doubtful but maybe."

There is something in her voice that bothers me. There is a high-pitched quality to it—almost nervous. Granted, she has admitted having anxiety issues. "Hey, uh, that guy Chris Haverly came by the barn earlier and wanted to talk to you."

"He did? I don't know why. I don't even know that guy."

"I don't know, either," she says. "He's weird."

I cross my arms. "Anyway, I am happy you worked things out with Joel."

"Yep. We sure have. Ready to get back?"

"Sure," I say. I can appreciate the apology, and I am curious as to what has happened between Joel and Emily this evening, but not so curious that I want to ask right now. All I really want is to enjoy this moment. The win. After all the work it took to get here, I'm ready to linger here for a bit.

When we walk back into the arena I can't help but notice Lydia get up and go sit down with Austen. She looks like she's trying to get him to talk to her. Joel appears to be gone, and Emily sits down by herself at the table looking oddly like someone who has a secret to hide—one she is not happy about. I keep trying to ignore everyone else and their drama, but I have a sinking feeling I'm about to get sucked in.

Still, when the music starts, Tristan and I get up and dance. After a slow dance, he whispers in my ear, "Go read the card. I'll see you in a minute." He smiles at me.

I open the card:

Vivienne,

I love you, and I don't think there is anything more that I can say. I am the happiest guy in the world to know that you love me, too, and that you want to be with me. Meet me out by the koi pond. I have a special place for us to go.

Love, Tristan.

I put the card back in the envelope and decide I really will be able to forget about everyone else this time. I tell Kayla that I am tired and going back to the house to go to bed.

"Okay. See you in the morning," she says.

As I make it out of the arena, Austen stops me. "I have to talk to you, Vivvie. I know things are strained between us but we need to talk. This is important."

"Can we do it tomorrow? I have to go," I say.

"It's about Tristan."

"What?"

"Lydia told me something that you should know."

"Oh please. I really don't have time for this."

"Vivvie, Lydia fed oleander to Harmony last semester. It's why she colicked, and Tristan knew about it."

"What?"

"I'm sorry. Lydia and I had some beers last night and she told me. I wanted to wait to tell you tomorrow and let you just be happy tonight, but I thought you should know. I didn't know if I would see you before we all leave tomorrow."

I feel my heart go cold and my palms clammy. "I don't believe this." I look past him and see Lydia. She looks for once in her life forlorn or possibly ashamed. I walk past Austen and up to her. "Is it true? Did you do that to Harmony?" I am fighting back tears.

She nods and looks down. "I'm sorry. I really am."

"And Tristan? He knew?"

"He had good reason not to tell you. He really did. Let me explain."

I turn and run back to the house and up the stairs to my room. I run past Joel's room and see his door cracked. I need someone to talk to. I am so confused.

I knock lightly on Joel's door. There is no answer. My perfect day has been ruined. How could Tristan have kept this from me? Why?

I am completely spun. None of this can be true! Tears, and anger, and confusion blur my vision, as I open the door and call out for Joel. There is still no answer. He doesn't seem to be in his room. But, then I see . . .

At first my mind doesn't register what I am seeing. It's Joel, but I can only see his feet. He's half hidden by the bed because he is on the other side of it—on the floor.

I go over to him and I kneel down.

"Joel, wake up," I say. His eyes are closed, but something about his sleeping face looks strange and off base to me.

I put my hand on his forehead and fear begins bubbling up inside me as I say his name repeatedly. Panicked, I place my fingers on the side of his neck and then on his wrist. I begin to cry hysterically as it registers that Joel is not sleeping at all. Joel is dead.

CHAPTER *fifty-five*

I feel a jacket being wrapped around me. I know I am shivering but it isn't from the cold. My body feels like Jell-O as I sit in the downstairs library and watch my friend being taken out of the front door of Cardinal Estate in a body bag. I know people are here and I can make out their faces, but there is a blurry edge around each one of them. The team is here and we are waiting for Holden to speak with us. There are police and I think emergency personnel or people from the coroner's office doing their job. I really don't know, because I feel like I am in some kind of surreal haze.

Tristan is sitting next to me on one side and Riley is on the other. Emily and Lydia are both crying, and I can't explain what I am feeling or doing because, in this moment, I do not feel like me at all. I am not even sure the ground is beneath my feet.

Holden walks into the room. He looks as stunned as we all do.

"We have had a terrible blow, gang. I don't know how to say this other than to say it. According to the police, Joel took his own life."

"That's a lie," I say. I repeat myself, louder this time. "That's a lie!"

Tristan takes my hand and I pull it away.

"I'm sorry, I know that's not easy to hear. But they found a note and an empty bottle of sleeping pills in his room," Holden says.

I hear myself say over and over, "I don't believe it. I don't believe it."

The room is quiet as Holden looks directly at me. "None of us do, sweetie. But sometimes people are just sad and they don't see a way out."

"You're wrong. Joel would not have committed suicide." I feel very sure of myself as I stand up and say it to everyone in the room. "Someone killed him."

Holden wraps his arms around me. "Vivienne, the police say that he did it, and they know all the facts. Besides, who would have wanted to kill Joel?"

I can think of a few people, off the top of my head, but I don't say any names out loud. I don't say anything more about it. The next words I do say are, "He was getting to take Melody home. He did not do this to himself." The tears start pouring down my face again.

I see Christopher Haverly's face in my mind and remember Harmony showing me the intense conversation that Haverly had with Joel last week. I know that Joel had secrets, and maybe he did hide some of his feelings. But I don't believe that he killed himself. I just can't believe it.

CHAPTER *fifty-six*

I fly home with Harmony, just as I flew in, but my emotions are so different from only a week and a half ago. I've gone from sheer excitement to what I can only quantify as sheer dread. And, as self-centered as it sounds right now, I realize that there is no way I can ever enjoy what Harmony and I have just accomplished. Not ever.

My friend is dead, and supposedly by his own hand, which I know isn't true. As I sit in front of Harmony on the flight home while she takes intermittent bites of hay from her hay bag, I am dazed and stare straight ahead. I know that Joel was murdered, but I feel helpless. Who will believe me?

I think about that last day with Joel. I think about standing on the podium next to him when I was handed the blue ribbon and trophy and he was handed the second-place award. We'd looked at each other and smiled. He was so happy. He'd admitted afterward to me that he never in a million years ever expected to come in second.

I find myself crying and am grateful that there isn't a groom seated next to me. Harmony stops eating and looks at me. I stand and lean my head into her shoulder, closing my eyes and trying to keep it all together.

I sigh heavily, and I know she is trying to comfort me, but like a child who tries to comfort a parent who is sad, it is a daunting task. I know what it was like when my dad left. There wasn't any amount of hugs or anything that I could say back then that would take away the pain that my mom felt. And, right now, I know all Harmony can really do for me is be the precious gift that she is.

I sit back down in the chair, a heaviness weighing on my shoulders and chest. I close my eyes again, and recall this past week, knowing in my heart that someone at the event knows what really happened to Joel.

There is Chris Haverly, for starters, and as I think about his strange behavior and aggressive interactions with Joel, I also recall something else. . . . I am reminded of what Melody showed me back at Fairmont not all that long ago—the needle, the watch! Could Chris Haverly have drugged Melody? There was definitely some serious animosity between Joel and Chris, and I know Joel was afraid of that guy. That train of thought leads me to Riley.

I hate to even go there, but Riley knows things about Joel, and neither one of them wanted to talk about it. Riley, Joel, and Chris all rode at Liberty Farms together. Could Chris know that Joel and Riley are both gay . . . ? I swallow hard. Now, it's just Riley who is gay. Joel is dead.

I wipe away more tears.

There are secrets from Liberty Farms. That much I am sure of.

What about Tiffany, Paisley, and her weird boyfriend, James? What did Joel mean when he'd said to James during that awful dinner that he needed to remember the stuff he knew about him? I try to remember the details, but I'm so tired that I can't think clearly right now.

I wonder when and if I will ever think clearly again.

CHAPTER *fifty-seven*

We have been back at school for a week, and today a memorial is taking place for Joel. I've been in the same haze I left Lexington in, and although both Riley and Tristan have tried to talk to me, I've not responded to their calls or texts. I ignore their knocks on the door, and I only go and see Harmony when I know no one else is at the barn.

Kayla, Holden, and Christian came to see me after we returned. They told me to take a week off, and that Harmony should have one as well. The week in Lexington was physically exhausting for the horses as well as for us.

The three of them have checked on me daily, and although I will never understand their strange arrangement, I know they are all good people and they do care. I've also talked with my mom every day. She wants me to come home because she is worried about me, but I have assured her that I am fine. But if I am honest, I really don't know that I am fine.

Counselors have been made available on campus, but the last thing I want to do is talk to anyone. Part of that is because I know the truth is that Joel was killed, and I know no one will believe me.

It's time to get dressed, so I pull a black dress over my head and brush my hair. I don't care so much how I look. I just want to get this over with.

I spot Martina in the gym where the memorial is being held. She comes over to me and gives me a hug. "I can't believe it. I am so sorry you found him like that."

I nod and hold back the tears. I see both Tristan and Riley looking somber, and even Lydia looks saddened. Emily looks almost zombie-like, and something about it troubles me.

Tristan looks directly at me, and I know that we have to talk. Outside of what has happened with Joel, I am so hurt by what he kept from me for months—what he knew about what Lydia had done to my horse. He looks down at my wrist and I'm sure he's noticed that I'm no longer wearing the bracelet he gave me.

The memorial is nice, with classical music and all the instructors saying heartfelt things about Joel. There is a video of him with Melody and him hanging out with friends . . . him as a baby . . . him just being a kid . . . and I am once again overcome by my grief. I try to hold it back, but I can't. I finally just sit there on the bench in the gym and sob, as Martina wraps her arms around me.

Several minutes go by, and I feel another set of arms go around me—strong arms. I look up and see Tristan.

When the service is over, he takes my hand and we walk in silence out to the pond. We sit down on one of the benches and neither one of us speaks for several minutes.

"I know this has been really hard. For all of us—losing Joel has been tough. I don't know what to say here, Vivvie, but I miss you so much. I know Lydia told you that I was involved in the situation with Harmony last semester. Please listen to me. I need to explain."

I look out at the ducks on the pond. I can't look at him. I am shaking on the inside and feel like I am going to throw up. I finally say, "Yeah. This has been really hard. Joel was a great kid and he was my friend. We lost someone decent. Someone good. And, the crazy thing is, I thought for quite a while that maybe he wasn't so great . . . that he had horrible ulterior motives like Riley suggested at first." My voice is low and the lump in my throat just sits there. "And, up until Lydia told me the truth, I spent all semester thinking about how lucky I am to be with a guy as great as you. . . ." I choke out a laugh, but it isn't one that sounds happy or amused. "How? How? How the hell can you explain? How in the world are you going to explain to me, Tristan, that you knew your psycho ex-girlfriend tried to kill my horse!"

"Trust me, I didn't want to keep it from you. I didn't. I had no choice."

"Choice? Choice! Um, yeah, actually, you did—and the right choice would have been telling me!"

"Vivienne, stop! If I had told you, Sebastian would have wound up dead! I could have wound up dead!" He screams this and there are tears in his eyes, and it stops me—cold.

"What? What did you say?"

He closes his eyes and whispers, "It's true. This is all about my father and what he's done, and Lydia knows. She knows."

I feel heat rising to my face, because I am so confused. None of this is making any sense to me. "I don't have a clue as to what you're talking about."

He wipes his face with the back of his hand. "If I tell you, Vivienne, it will only put you in danger."

I now lower my voice to a whisper. "If you don't tell me, then I will have no choice but to go to Kayla and Holden and tell them the truth."

"You can't do that. You can't."

I sigh. "You'd better start talking.

He takes my hand, and I yank it away. He nods. "Okay. You're not going to like it."

"From my point of view, it can't be any worse than what I've already learned."

"It can. It really can, and it is."

"No, Tristan. The facts are this: You knew that Lydia poisoned my horse, and Harmony could have died, and you kept what you knew from me! *How* could it get any worse?"

Over the next half hour, he talks, and his story unfolds, and I am horrified—truly horrified because what he's just told me is worse than what I ever could have imagined on my own. Much worse. He's been abused both mentally and physically. His father is a horrible man, and his mother has agoraphobia and refuses to ever leave the house. My heart softens some as I listen, and I feel a sense of affection for him that is warm and familiar. But I don't trust him enough yet to actually get close and hug him. I slowly try and understand.

I close my eyes. I'm chilled to the bone.

"Vivienne, say something. Anything. Please."

I open my eyes and look at him—again there are tears in his eyes and I choke up, too.

"Please say something," he repeats. "Can we please work this out? I love you. I really do love you."

I get up off the bench and say, "I love you, too, but I need to be alone. I have to think."

CHAPTER *fifty-eight*

School is coming to an end. Tristan and I are trying to work things out. I do love him, but I don't know if I can get past all of this. He wants badly to go back to where we were, and I want that, too, but can I get past it? I don't know.

Then, there is Riley. . . . God, so much has changed with my relationships here this semester that it's no wonder I feel lonely. Martina is still at home, and even though Ri and I have hung out and talked some, I think he is as shocked and upset as I am over Joel's death. There is this part of me, though, that also doubts whether his grief is entirely real. And I hate that.

Facts are, I think that Riley would go to almost any lengths to be certain his family doesn't find out he's gay until after he graduates. And, as much as I hate to think it, it has crossed my mind that I still don't know what other secrets besides being gay Riley had shared with Joel. . . . Could they have been important enough that Riley might have wanted to kill him? I know it's a horrible thought, but I can't deny the possibility. Right now, I don't trust anyone.

Emily has sunk into a visible depression as well, but she is another one I have questions about. She was hurt by Joel, yet I saw with my own eyes during our last night in Lexington how she changed her tune toward him. There's something weird to me about the fact that she was his pal again less than twenty-four hours after she learned the truth about him being gay and seeming so angry. She's got issues. I mean, she just does. She takes meds for anxiety and whatever else. There's her mom, and the pressure she's under. I wonder what part Emily played in the events of Joel's last night alive.

Yeah—my mind has been swirling every single day since Joel's death.

The only place I know to go and to maybe get some insight is to the horses.

I plan to stick around the barn after my lesson with Christian. Maybe one of the horses will tell me something.

By the time I tack Harmony up and head to the jump arena, Christian is already there.

"Hey, Vivienne, you doing okay?"

I shrug. "I guess. If anything, what happened to Joel has given me a new perspective."

"How so?"

"Remember the talk you had with me after Martina disappeared?"

"Yeah."

"How you said that life would get in the way, and if I really wanted to be successful at this then I would have to maintain a level of focus that wouldn't necessarily allow life to intrude?"

"It's a good speech, right?" He smiles gently.

"It is. I've decided that I don't want life to get in the way of my riding." I feel tears start springing into my eyes. Emotion wants to take hold of me so often these days.

Christian looks up at me. He sighs and purses his lips together. "What I said isn't completely correct. The thing is, Vivienne, life does sometimes get in the way. It just does. I know how badly you want this. I know what this horse and this sport means to you, but after losing the fiancée I loved, I am telling you as your teacher, your coach, and as your friend, that sometimes you can't stop life from intruding. And that's okay. Just don't let it take over. Understand?"

I nod, but I am not sure that I do understand. If I really pay close attention to everything around me right now, I don't know how to keep from losing my focus.

"Good. Let's get you on the job here and warm her up, then send her over the cross rails. We'll build from that."

I do as I am told, and the lesson moves along very well, until the sun begins to go down. Christian has set a good little course for us. We are to first do the vertical to the oxer, then the gate, then do a rollback to the chevron.

Harmony does fine over the first three jumps, but as we do the rollback turn and head toward the chevron, she swerves out to the left.

"Go back and do it again," Christian says.

As we come back around, he instructs, "Left leg on, open that right rein a bit, and keep her straight. No, no, come at this straight, Vivienne."

I don't understand what Harmony is doing. We approach the jump, but she takes it two strides out and knocks the jump.

Christian sets it again. "One more time. Let's do this right. Focus. Keep her straight to the jump, look straight ahead. More leg and open that right rein up."

I do exactly as he says, but just as we take off, Harmony shows me her eye in my mind, and even though she's done this jump correctly finally, I get off her right away and take a look at her eye. There it is. Again. The small pen-point-size dot that I had seen a few months ago is back and it is larger. This must have been what was bothering her when we jumped out in Lexington.

Christian walks over. "What's wrong?"

I sigh. "Look. Look at her eye."

Christian peers at it. "Ah. Looks like a uveal cyst. It must be blocking her vision some. It can be taken care of."

"Great. My mom is a vet," I blurt out.

"I know."

"Any chance that the Fairmonts might let her take a look?"

"Worth a try."

"I'll ask."

He puts his arm around me and says, "It will be okay. We can get this fixed. She'll be fine."

"Thank you." It has been so long since I felt a fatherly-type figure comfort me that I don't know how to act, but I can admit that it is nice, even though the situation sucks. It does explain a lot, though. Clearly, this eye problem has been brewing for some time. Another problem—although I guess the silver lining is that it's something a vet can help her with.

I put Harmony up, and before calling my mom about Harmony, head to talk to a few of my favorite horses. I am just praying one of them has some information for me.

I try Melody first. But all I get is that damn blue color that then turns to turquoise. As I try hard to convey my own thoughts to her, I realize how sad she must be, and I decide to just allow her to be a horse and give her attention and affection. "It's okay, sweet girl. Your kid loved you a lot. He really did. I'm so sorry."

"Vivienne?"

I turn around to see Kayla standing there. "Oh, hi. I was, ahh, just talking to Melody."

She nods. "Did she say anything back?"

I have been asked this before, of course—Riley said the very same thing to me once. But he'd spoken in jest. There is something about the way Kayla's voice sounds that puts me on guard.

"Um, no," I say.

"I know," Kayla replies. "I know about you."

"What?"

"I know about your gift, Vivienne."

"I don't understand."

She takes a step closer and brushes her long blonde hair back behind her shoulders. "I talk to horses, too, and yes, *they* talk back. I knew there was someone here that was talking to them, and it took me some time to figure out who it was."

I shake my head.

"Don't deny it, sweetie."

I stare at her, and for the first time I am scared of Kayla Fairmont. I mean, I was kind of afraid when I thought she might kick me out of school after I practically tried to blackmail her into buying Melody for Joel. But this is a different kind of fear. I don't like the tone of her voice at all.

"You don't have to say anything. Here is the thing, though, about communicating with horses. You don't have enough skill and insight yet to really understand how to handle it. Your own thoughts, imaginings, and perceptions can get in the way. You have to be responsible about that. Otherwise, there can be serious problems in interpreting the communication. Sometimes, Vivienne, you need to allow horses to just be horses because, at the end of the day, they are not human."

It hits me in this moment that all of the color sequencing, all of the gray shading and murkiness—in short, all of the confusion that I have felt from these animals over this semester is because of Kayla. She has blocked them in some way.

"Okay," I say.

"Good. Let them be horses. They have jobs to do. They aren't humans, and it is not their responsibility to take care of us. Be smart about this. You have a big future in front of you. Good night."

"Good night."

I stand there for several minutes as she walks away, and I wonder now about everything she has said to me. What is right, and what is wrong? I have been talking to horses since I was a five. Why and how did Kayla Fairmont put a block between me and these animals? Is she being protective as she suggested, or is she being manipulative for some reason? Does Kayla have something to hide?

CHAPTER *fifty-nine*

The school year has come to an end with all of its up and downs and many unanswered questions.

The local vet has looked at Harmony's eye and confirmed the presence of a cyst. There hasn't been a decision yet to remove it, but I think there will be. The vet did say that she can go to Liberty Farms with me this summer and that the cyst won't grow rapidly. Apparently, I am a good enough rider to give her the confidence she needs to go over the jumps, so I'll wait it out with her until the Fairmonts decide what to do about the problem. I may not have paid for Harmony, but I know in my heart that she belongs to me. That is the truth.

I feel a lot weighing on me as I pack up my things to go home for two weeks before heading to Virginia—Harmony's eye, Kayla's knowledge of my gift and all that swirls around that, my confusion where Tristan and Riley are concerned—and topping it all off is the ever-present awareness that my friend is dead. Joel is gone and I miss him.

I wish more than anything in this world that I could forget all of this and just go and ride. But my conscience tells me that I would not be a decent human if I didn't follow my gut, which means that as soon as I get to Liberty Farms this summer, I'll start looking for answers about what really happened to Joel.

I am packing up my things when my cell rings. Tristan. I take the call. "Hello."

"I need to see you."

"Okay."

We agree to meet in the tack room in a half hour.

He is already there when I arrive. He looks like he has been crying. He stands up from the tack trunk when I walk in, and he puts his arms around me. I hug him back. "Vivienne, I love you and I can't lose you. Please, please forgive me. Can't we please go back to the way things were? I will never keep a secret from you again. I will never betray you again. I promise. I really do."

I look at him and then up at the ceiling in the tack room, and I believe him. I start to cry. "Yes. Fine. I don't want to be mad anymore. I don't want this to keep us apart, but if you ever lie to me again . . . if you ever keep . . . or do . . ."

He brings a finger to my lips. "I won't. I promise," he says and he seals it with a kiss.

CHAPTER *sixty*

Who knew the second semester at Fairmont would be more insane than the first? But it has been; I admit that much to myself in the moment I walk down the Jetway to board the airplane home. I'll only have two weeks to unwind there before I leave for Virginia, but I'm hoping that's enough time to get back to being me again.

I find my seat on the plane and pull out my cell phone. I need to talk to Tristan. I feel so much better about us, and I trust him again. It's one problem off my shoulders.

A text comes in as I'm about to make the call. It's from a blocked number. It reads: *Thought you might want to know.*

There is a photo. It's of Tristan and he is asleep in bed, but it isn't his bed. I study the photo for a minute and take in the nightstand next to the bed.

I swallow hard.

There's that saying, a picture is worth a thousand words—and for the first time I really understand how true it is. On the nightstand is a photo of a horse that I recognize: Lydia's horse, Geisha. Tristan is asleep in Lydia's bed.

I fight back tears. So everything he said before I left was a lie. One big, stupid lie, and if Tristan was protecting anything or anyone at all, it was Lydia and himself. Was he even being honest with me about his dad and mom? Was any part of what he said true? I feel so duped. What was last night even all about? How could I have fallen for all of that?

Thoughts run wildly through my mind. Thoughts of getting even, but that's not me. That's not right.

I close my eyes and wonder how in the world I am going to make it through the summer with them. Maybe I shouldn't go.

No. That isn't the answer. There are a few reasons why I need to go to Liberty Farms. The first is that I am resolved to find out the real truth behind Joel's death, and I think there are answers at Liberty Farms.

Second, going out to Virginia will bring me that much closer to achieving my goals. I know it. It would be stupid to pass up the opportunity just because I've been lied to by someone I thought cared for me. *Loved me.*

This thought makes me cry in earnest, and the poor woman who has just sat down next to me is shifting uncomfortably in her seat. I face the window.

I should have followed my one freaking rule. The one I've wanted to live by ever since I realized that humans can really hurt other humans—which I adopted, big surprise, when my dad left. I'll never forget my mom spending night after night trying to cover up the fact that she was in tears. My rule has been: focus on your goals. Get it done. Christian was right the first time he talked to me—never let life interfere.

I'm going back to that. Going back to my rules. No guys to interfere. None. Nope. Not allowed.

My cell phone dings again. I shake my head, not wanting to look at it, but morbid curiosity gets the best of me. What photo will I see now? Tristan and Lydia making out? Or worse?

I take a deep breath and look down. Whoa.

I read the text and reread it.

It's from Austen.

Hey, V, guess who is on as a working student at Liberty Farms this summer? I'll be seeing you soon.

"Crap," I mutter under my breath. "Just what I needed."

But I can't fool myself, because even as I'm saying those words, there is a tingle down my spine that goes straight to my toes. I wipe my tears away, and try to tell myself this feeling is the opposite of what is right. Austen Giles is my friend. That is it. Getting a text from him is not supposed to make me want to faint. And he is definitely not supposed to be going to Liberty Farms.

"Damn," I say—a little too loud.

The woman next to me glances over. She probably thinks I have Tourette's syndrome.

I shake my head and turn off my phone, knowing that if there is any guy in this world who might be able to get me to break my rules, then it's the one who just texted me.

GLOSSARY

air vest: An air vest is a safety vest used in the cross-country event. A strap hooks on to the saddle, and if the rider becomes disengaged in a fall, the vest acts much like an air bag, and inflates around the neck and spine of the rider immediately upon disengagement.

airy: The term "airy" before an eventing obstacle (such as "airy hanging log" or "airy plank") means that an obstacle is set above the ground with a clear, free space below it.

airy verticals: This particular jump possesses an open design, which makes it appear much higher compared to a normal vertical jump and thus more challenging to the horse.

bank jumps, bank steps: Bank jumps are steps up and down from one level to another, and can be single jumps or built as a "staircase" of multiple banks.

bay: The color of a horse. Bay horses' coats are a deep red to mahogany brown with black legs, mane, tail, and muzzle, called points.

bedded: Bedding for horses may be straw or wood shavings. Riders will bed the horse's stall frequently.

big cabin: a wooden fence on a cross-country course built to resemble a log cabin

bounce: A bounce, also called a no-stride, is a fence combination sometimes found on the cross-country course of eventing. It consists of two fences placed close together so the horse cannot take a full stride between them, but not so close that the horse would jump both fences at once. The horse "bounces" between the two jumps, landing with his hind legs before immediately taking off with his front legs.

building stride: moving forward and lengthening the horse's stride

chestnut: the color of a horse; chestnut is a reddish-brown color

chevrons on the mounds: Also called arrowheads, these fences are shaped like triangles, with the point facing toward the ground. They are generally very narrow, and usually only a few feet wide.

cleaning tack: cleaning the saddle and bridle

coffin canter: short, choppy strides to balance out to the coffin jump

coffin combination: Also called the rails-ditch-rails, the coffin is a combination fence where the horse jumps a set of rails, moves one or several strides downhill to a ditch, then goes back uphill to another jump.

course: Vivienne will have to maneuver two kinds of courses. One is a cross-country, with solid obstacles to jump. The other is a show jumping course, where the rider and horse have various obstacles to jump. Instructors may describe the course to the riders during a practice session, or the rider must learn it through walking it on the ground and studying it via diagram when competing.

cross-country: A popular phase of three-day eventing, cross-country is a timed event that requires the rider to walk the course previous to the ride and to memorize it. Horse and rider need to be in optimum physical shape as well as courageous and very trusting of each other. This phase consists of approximately twelve to twenty fences (at lower levels), or thirty to forty at the higher levels, placed on a long outdoor circuit. These fences consist of solid objects (logs, stone walls, etc.) as well as various obstacles such as water obstacles, ditches, drops and ditches, and various jumping combinations one might find in the countryside. Sometimes, particularly at higher levels, fences are designed that would not normally occur in nature. However, these are still constructed to be as solid as more natural obstacles. Safety regulations require that some obstacles be built with a "frangible pin system," allowing part or all of the jump to collapse if hit with enough impact. Speed is also a factor, with the rider required to cross the finish line within a certain time frame (optimum time). Crossing the finish line after the optimum time results in penalties for each second over. At lower levels, there is also a speed fault time, incurring penalties for horse-and-rider pairs completing the course too quickly. Going off course and refusal of jumps also result in penalties. After three refusals, or after missing a jump by going off course, the horse and rider will be eliminated.

cross-ties: A tie on each side that clips into the horse's halter to aid in grooming and tacking up.

dressage: Dressage consists of riding the horse through an exact sequence of movements in a square arena where letters are placed around the arena. The rider must memorize the test and perform different movements at the different letters. The test is evaluated by one or more judges who are looking for balance, rhythm, suppleness, and, most important, obedience of the horse and its harmony with the rider.

Each movement in the test is scored on a scale from zero to ten, with a score of ten being the highest possible mark and with the total maximum score for the test varying depending on the level of competition and the number of movements. Therefore, if one movement is poorly executed, it is still possible for the rider to achieve a good overall score if the remaining movements are very well executed.

Once the bell rings the rider is allowed forty-five seconds to enter the ring or is eliminated.

If all four feet of the horse exit the arena during the test, this results in elimination.

If the horse resists more than twenty seconds during the test, this results in elimination.

Many people refer to dressage as the ballet of horses. Good dressage is like watching a dancer. The horse and rider make the movements look easy, but they are far from it. Mastering dressage takes many years of study.

drop: A fence where the horse must jump over a log fence and land at a lower level from the one from which it took off. Drop fences require the rider to have a great deal of trust in the horse, because often the animal can't see the landing until it is about to jump.

eight out: the eighth rider to be sent out on course

eventing: Three-day eventing is the combined training sport that showcases dressage, stadium jumping, and cross-country.

fallen log: a log jump on a cross-country course

faults: penalties—time, knocked poles, refusals, etc.

fence: a jump

flat cups: The cups that hold the poles on the jumps can be more rounded, making it harder for the poles to be knocked down. A flat cup makes it easier for the pole to come down in show jumping.

flyer: taking off too early at a jump

forehand: refers to the front half of the horse's body

gate: a type of jump built to look like a gate

gelding: A male horse that has been castrated. A stallion tends to be difficult to handle and not good around other horses. Gelding male horses calms them and allows them to be used in the sport as working horses.

get spun: To fail to pass the vet inspection in the jog-out at a competition, resulting in elimination.

girth: Similar to a belt, the girth keeps the saddle from coming off. In English riding, girths are typically made from leather.

go clear: To have a clear jump round without knocking any jumps, or having any refusals or time penalties.

hack: to exercise lightly

half halt: A brief, almost invisible signal that tells the horse to use its hind end to balance itself and be prepared to pay attention. The rider must be sitting tall and balanced; the leg remains on the side of the horse and it is a simple closing of the fingers around the rein, usually the outside rein, which is closest to the arena on the outside. The half halt is a quick and subtle movement, but it is effective and one used frequently when riding correctly.

half pass: A lateral movement seen in dressage, in which the horse moves forward and sideways at the same time.

hands: Horses are measured in "hands." One hand is equal to four inches. A horse is measured from the ground to the top of the highest nonvariable point of the skeleton, called the withers.

haunches: a buttock and thigh considered together

Holsteiner: A breed of horse originating in the Schleswig-Holstein region of northern Germany. It is thought to be the oldest of warm-blood breeds, tracing back to the thirteenth century. Though the population is not large, Holsteiners are a dominant force of international show jumping and are found at the top levels of dressage, combined driving, show hunters, and eventing.

ice boots: Wraps that have pockets to place ice into. Ice is placed in the boots, which are then wrapped around the horse's legs in order to bring down any inflammation.

impulsion: Refers to the movement of a horse when it is going forward with controlled power. Impulsion helps a horse effectively utilize the power in its hindquarters. To achieve impulsion, a horse is not using speed but rather muscular control; the horse exhibits a relaxed spinal column, which allows its hindquarters to come well under its body and "engage" so that they can be used in the most effective manner to move the horse forward at any speed.

infrared machine: A machine that uses infrared light with a wand directed over parts of the horse's body for healing purposes.

Jeffries, Richard: a world-renowned jump course designer

jog-out: A jog-out is the first presentation of horse and rider going into an event. The rider jogs the horse out on a lead line.

the lead: Similar to a leash, the lead is hooked on to a horse's halter and is used to lead the animal out and around.

leg on: Riding a horse is about balance. Proper riding comes from riding with leg. When Vivienne's instructors tell her to "put her leg on," they are asking her to use the calf of the leg as an aid. The horse feels the pressure, and with Vivienne also using her core, and steady contact with the reins, the horse is able to balance itself. The horse can then use its hind end properly, and the hind end of a horse is its "motor." If a horse is always on the forehand because a rider doesn't know how to properly balance the horse, then the horse will lose muscle definition and not utilize her or his body properly, causing soreness and many other ailments. That is why learning proper balance and how to use one's body and various aids is so important to riding.

letter A: One of the letters on the outside of a dressage arena. At each letter a rider-and-horse team is expected to ride a different maneuver.

liverpool: a ditch or large tray of water under a vertical or an oxer

minute markers: Riders are given an optimum time for a cross-country ride. Riders know at their minute markers where they need to be in the ride. For example, at three minutes in they should have reached a particular obstacle. They wear a special watch that they look at while riding the course to check their progress, since cross-country is a timed event.

obstacles: fences/jumps

one star: Preliminary (USA) or Novice (Britain) level, used as an introductory level to the three-day event.

Rules:

• Riders must be at least fourteen years old, and horses at least six years of age.

• Cross-country has a maximum of thirty-two jumping efforts on a 4160–4680-meter course, ridden at 520 mpm (meters per minute), with a total course time of 8–9 minutes.

• Stadium has a maximum of thirteen efforts and 10–11 obstacles, ridden at 350 mpm, with a course length of 350–450 meters.

option line: At times the rider is given two options on a cross-country course with certain obstacles. The first option is usually more difficult, and the second is an easier ride but may cause time penalties. A rider may take the option for various reasons including a tiring horse, or if the rider doesn't feel she has set the horse up correctly to succeed with the first option.

order of go: the rider's turn to be on course

oxer: A type of horse jump with two rails that may be set even or uneven. The width between the poles may vary.

path finder: The path finder is the first rider to go out on the cross-country course. It is her objective to ride the course and be able to come back and relay to the instructor and other riders how it rides, for instance, whether it is slick in certain places, what they should be careful to watch for, etc. The path finder is typically the strongest rider/horse team.

poultice: Poultices are medicinal in that they are used to bring down inflammation. Clay poultices are applied to the leg and then wrapped with standing bandages to decrease any swelling and heat in the horse's legs.

rollback: A rollback is a stopping and turning movement all in one, in which the horse turns 180 degrees over a hind pivot foot. The movement helps to "supple" the horse by asking for a lifting action from the hindquarters, a softening of the body, and lateral crossing of the front legs all at the same time.

run out: when the horse refuses a jump

scope: a horse's amazing ability to jump

short hack: A basic warm-up of the horse where the rider will put the horse through the walk, trot, canter, and possibly warm-up over fences. It depends on what phase the hack is dedicated to.

show jumping: Show jumping is the third phase of the three-day event. Once again, the rider must memorize the course, which consists of twelve to twenty fences (jumps). This phase tests the technical jumping skills of the horse and rider, including suppleness, obedience, fitness, and athleticism. These jumps are usually painted with bright colors. Unlike cross-country jumps, the fences in show jumping can be knocked down. This phase is also timed, with penalties being given for every second over the required time. In addition to normal jumping skills, eventing show jumping tests the fitness and stamina of the horse and rider, generally being held after the cross-country phase in higher level and international events.

side passing: In the side pass, the horse moves sideways without stepping forward, a maneuver executed from a halt. It originated in the cavalry, to help correct the spacing of two horses that were side by side in a line.

spook: When a horse is frightened by something, he may spook at it. He may go sideways, halt with his ears forward, or prance around. A spook can consist of any anxious behavior the horse might display. It essentially means that the animal is afraid of what he is seeing or hearing, and he doesn't understand it.

stick: Also called a crop, it is a long handle with a leather flap at the end, and the rider uses it to encourage the horse to move forward.

stride: a single, coordinated movement of the four legs of a horse

sunken road: These are combination jumps involving banks and rails.

At the lower levels, it may consist of a bank down, with a few strides to a bank up. At the upper levels, the sunken road often is quite complicated, usually beginning with a set of rails, with either one stride or a bounce distance before the bank down, a stride in the "bottom" of the road before jumping the bank up, and another stride or bounce distance before the final set of rails. Sunken roads are very technical, especially at the upper levels, and require accurate riding.

table: A fence with height and width, with the top of the table being one piece of material. Tables are also usually built so that the back part is slightly higher than the front, or with a piece of wood at the back, so the horse can easily see that there is width to the obstacle and therefore judge it appropriately. Tables may be extremely wide, and generally test the horse's scope. They are intended to be jumped at a forward pace with a slightly long stride.

tack: The equipment used on the horse. This umbrella term for all equestrian-related equipment includes the saddle, bridles, halters, and saddle pads. When Vivienne "tacks up," it means she is putting on her saddle, bridle, etc. When she "untacks," she is removing the tack.

tack room: where tack is stored

Thoroughbred: A horse breed best known for its use in horse racing. Although the word *thoroughbred* is sometimes used to refer to any breed of purebred horse, it technically refers only to the

Thoroughbred breed. Thoroughbreds are considered "hot-blooded" horses, known for their agility, speed, and spirit.

three-day eventing: The sport that Vivienne and the students at Fairmont Academy participate in is called three-day eventing, an Olympic equestrian sport where a single horse-and-rider combination compete in the three disciplines of *dressage, cross-country*, and *show jumping*. Competitions may be run as a one-day event, where all three events are completed in one day (dressage, followed by show jumping and then cross-country) or as a three-day event, with dressage on the first day followed by cross-country the next day and then show jumping on the final day. Eventing is essentially an equestrian triathlon.

In the United States, eventing is broken down into the following levels, all of which are recognized by the United States Eventing Association (USEA) and are run in accordance with their rules. International events have specific categories and levels of competition and are conducted under the rules of the FEI (Fédération Equestre Internationale). CCI (Concours Complet International, or International Complete Contest) is one such category and defines a three-day event that is open to competitors from any foreign nation as well as the host nation.

CCI: International Three-day event (Concours Complet International)

CIC: International One-day event (Concours International Combiné)

CCIO: International Team Competitions (Concours Complet

International Officiel). Includes the Olympics, the World Championships, the Pan Am Games, and other continental championships

The levels of international events are identified by the number of stars next to the category; there are four levels in total. A CCI* is for horses that are just being introduced to international competition. A CCI** is geared for horses that have some experience of international competition. CCI*** is the Advanced level of competition.

The very highest level of competition is the CCI****, and with only six such competitions in the world (Badminton, Burghley, Rolex Kentucky, Adelaide, Luhmuhlen Horse Trials, and the Stars of Pau) it is the ultimate aim of many riders. The World Championships are also considered CCI****. Rolex offers a financial prize for any rider who can win three of the biggest competitions in succession. These are Badminton, Burghley, and Kentucky.

One-, two-, and three-star competitions are roughly comparable to the Novice, Intermediate, and Advanced levels of British domestic competition, respectively, and to the Preliminary, Intermediate, and Advanced levels of American domestic competition, respectively.

time faults: penalties for going over the time allotted

trainer: The trainer is responsible for daily care and education of the horse.

Trakehner: A light warmblood breed of horse originally developed at the East Prussian state stud farm in the town of Trakehnen from which the breed takes its name.

triple bar: a spread fence using three elements of graduating heights

triple bounce exercise: Bounces are jumps set close together so that the horse lands and takes off again without a stride in between. Therefore, a triple bounce would be three jumps set very close together that does not allow a stride in between them.

verticals: A jump that consists of poles or planks placed one directly above another with no spread, or width, to jump.

vet box: An area sectioned off so that when horses come off the cross-country course they are taken here to have their pulse, temperature, and respiration monitored. The rider and the rider's team have ten minutes to get the horse stabilized. They will use cold water and walk him or her out. It is vital to stabilize the horse within these ten minutes.

warmblood: A warmblood is not a breed of horse. A warmblood is a horse that is distinguished from many different kinds of horse breeds that share certain characteristics. The warmblood breeds were the result of breeding large coldblood draft horses of northern Europe such as Clydesdales and Percherons with hot-blooded, lighter and faster Arabian horses that warriors captured in the Middle East and Africa and brought back with them after their battles during the Middle Ages. The combination resulted in horses with smaller heads and bodies than large work or draft horses and with temperaments less excitable than hotbloods. Many Olympic horses are from the warmblood breeds.

wash rack: Where horses are bathed. There is typically a rack on either side of the horse to keep the animal from moving around too much. There are usually cross-ties that hook on to each side of the horse's halter. This makes it easy for riders to bathe their mounts.

water combination: These fences range in difficulty from simple water crossings at lower levels to combinations of drop fences into water, obstacles or "islands" within the water, and banks or obstacles out of the water at upper levels of competition.

ACKNOWLEDGMENTS

This is always the hardest part about writing a book. It's when I turn it in and let it go, and hope it reaches readers who will enjoy it as much as I have loved writing it and living in Vivvie's world.

It's also the hard part because it is inevitable that I will miss acknowledging someone who has helped in the process along the way. I will do my best to remember everyone!

First off, I want to thank my family: John, Alex, Anthony, Kaitlin, and my mom. My entire family is super supportive, but there are a bunch of them and it would take five pages alone to list them. I am positive they know who they are and how much they mean to me. I do have to point out one of them, though—my aunt Anita. She reads everything I write before it goes to print and she's been doing that now for twenty-two years.

I want to thank the editors who worked on this book. I started out with Alison Dasho, who is a lovely woman and very supportive. I haven't lost her completely (thank God) as she edits my thriller work over at Thomas & Mercer. I was a little nervous to switch from Alison to Kate Chynoweth, but that is no longer the case. An author simply could not ask for a better person to be on her team. Kate has a skilled eye and her suggestions are always "spot on." She took her time learning about the horse world and the sport of eventing and we worked beautifully together. I can't wait to start book three with her. Amy Hosford saw many authors through a digital transition that I think was a bit scary for all of us. She did it with grace and what appeared to be ease—although I am sure there were moments when she wanted to scream.

Thank you to Larry Kirshbaum for always asking me about the horses and my family. Erick Pullen handles the author relations and he does a great job. He is always there when needed.

Timoney (T$), you are seriously one cool chick. You get the job done, and I am so appreciative for all of the marketing and promotional efforts you put forth and into this series. It is a good feeling to have you on board!

Many thanks to Katrina Damkoehler and her design team, who are the magic behind the awesome covers. I LOVE my covers!

Thank you to the team at Girl Friday. You ladies know how to copyedit and get the work done. I am indebted to you for catching all my little mistakes.

Jessica Park and the other nineteen (you know who you are)—thank you for always listening, supporting, suggesting, and just being there. I love you, JP and the crew, you bunch of glittery unicorns, you!

As always, thanks to the amazing horsewomen in my life! Gina Miles is a rock star. That's all I can say without gushing further. She just is. There were scenes in this book that could not have been written without her! Tami Smith is another rock star who supports the work. Jessica Burch and her daughter, Molly, have also contributed to this book in ways they may not know, but I thank them and am happy to have found such great friends. I want to thank Neely Ashley for being like another daughter. I love her very much and thank her for The Woo (her old event horse, who now lives happily at my house). Debbi Rosen is another supporter and amazing event rider who I lean on from time to time. Love you, Deb. Also, my sister Jessica, who may not be an event rider but who is an amazing barrel racer, and she knows horses like she knows the back of her hand.

And, to the two most important horsewomen in my life. I have to give a huge shout-out to the woman who has taught me more about these amazing creatures in the past six years than I had known in the past . . . well, let's just say several decades. She opened the world of eventing to me, and she introduced me to all of the other horsewomen mentioned here—Terri Rocovich. I love you and I am grateful to you on so many levels. The other one is someone I refer to as Terri's kid, even though she is also my kid. My daughter, Kaitlin, rides under Terri's tutelage and has dreams and goals that I know she will achieve because she has desire, determination, and a passion for horses and the sport. Kaitlin is a major part of the inspiration for this series!

I have to acknowledge the horses I am privileged to have in my life. There are too many to name, but I will mention my special girl, Bronte. When the days are a little rough, I know I can head to the barn and she will be waiting and happy to see me. There isn't a better feeling in the world than knowing your horse is happy to see you.

ABOUT THE AUTHOR

Photo by Denise Thomas of Thomas Photography

michele scott lives in California with her family, which includes her husband, three kids, three dogs, a cat, and nine horses. With her days spent in the barn or at the keyboard, she has forged a flourishing career as a mystery writer who is also deeply involved in the world of horses and equestrian riding.